Murdered on a Wednesday

A Pride and Prejudice Mystery

Jaime Marie Lang

Chapter One
Lady Catherine was Dead

IT REALLY WAS A confusing morning for Elizabeth. Woken by her cousin's yelling and Charlotte proclaiming that he could not go into her room, she threw on her dressing gown and rushed to her door.

"What have you done?!" Her cousin, Mr. Collins, was being barred from her door by his wife, Charlotte. He had never been an attractive man, and his face, turning a deep, blotchy red, wasn't helping his situation.

Elizabeth had spent the last two weeks visiting Charlotte grimly, enduring her cousin's speeches, but this was a new level of annoyance. Though the sun had just barely peeked over the horizon, she would have normally been up soon to start her morning with a peaceful walk, enjoying nature. She would never choose to start her morning having to endure a nonsensical rant. "All I have accomplished today so far was being awoken from my sleep."

Elizabeth responding at all only spurred his anger higher. "You have done something! Lady Catherine is most seriously displeased. Lady Catherine summoned you and you will leave immediately. I will not keep her waiting."

Elizabeth had no intention of cowering before the fool or being sent to see Lady Catherine in what she currently wore. "Unless you want me to arrive in my nightclothes, I will take the time to put on something presentable and style my hair."

"I knew you were no good the moment you turned down my magnanimous offer." Mr. Collins shook his finger at Elizabeth over his wife's shoulder.

"Dear husband, Elizabeth can never get ready to see Lady Catherine if you do not leave and allow me to help her hurry. I know you are eager for her to get to Rosings with all possible haste." Charlotte finally spoke up, her voice soothing despite her husband's exasperation.

"Yes, I have every inclination to dress once you leave. With Charlotte here to help, I am sure things will proceed with all due haste." As much as she didn't want to, Elizabeth knew she would never have a moment's peace if she did not go to Rosings to face Lady Catherine. Why put off the inevitable?

"You have five minutes! If you are not ready by then, I will drag you to Lady Catherine as you are. I do not know what conniving action on your part has angered Lady Catherine, but I will not stand for it. Not in my house." Stomping away, Mr. Collins continued to complain and grumble as he paced in the hallway.

"Hurry, before he changes his mind." Charlotte rushed into her room, the door creaking softly as she closed it behind her. Her serenity vanished as she leaned up against the door, and her trepidation came to light.

Elizabeth quickly began stripping out of her nightclothes and dressing robe, trying not to trip while she moved to the odd closet with shelves. Choosing one of her more comfortable dresses, she began putting it on as Charlotte went to the dressing table to get her brush and pins. "If I am going to be yelled at, I will be comfortable. Do you know what any of this is about?"

"The scullery maid and the cook received the message very early this morning. They sent it up with the man of all work when he went to bring Mr. Collins his coffee." Charlotte worked on her friend's hair, putting it in the simplest of styles. It was all they had time for. "Lady Catherine wrote she was most seriously displeased by your actions. Apparently, you are deliberately trying to disrupt her plans that have been firmly established for some time."

Lady Catherine had always struck Elizabeth as a woman who liked to control every little thing, but this was more than that. Elizabeth had witnessed Lady Catherine's tendency to belittle those in the room, but even she seemed unlikely to demand an audience before dawn. What could have caused Lady Catherine to be so upset that she would have summoned her? Had she been upset that Elizabeth had found the ornamental maze and spent her day wondering there earlier in the week? Tilting her head, she checked the blue dress she wore. It was overly simple but was comfortable and gave a greater range of movement than what she normally wore to Rosings. Her hair was up in a very simple knot at the back of her neck, though some of her curls were attempting to escape already. "Do I look ready to face Lady Catherine?" Elizabeth took a step back from her friend, trying to check herself in the small mirror the room provided.

"You will do. She would comment negatively on anything you wore. Do you have any idea what had her in such a state?" Charlotte questioned her friend, biting at her lip nervously.

Elizabeth knew her friend was in an uncomfortable situation. Lady Catherine could make Charlotte's life more difficult than it already was if she attempted to shield Elizabeth from her wrath. She did not have the stubborn streak that Elizabeth herself often struggled with. "I truly do not know. I have had very little interaction with Miss Anne de Bourgh. As for her nephews who are visiting, I cannot imagine why there would be a problem there. You know what Mr. Darcy's opinion of me is—his stares alone speak of his disregard. How would I derail any plans there?"

"You know I have told you before that I think he does not look at you in any negative way. But we do not have the time to argue that point. I am afraid that my husband will not allow you to stay after this."

"Well, if it comes to that, I will return to London and stay with Jane at my uncle's. She has been fighting melancholy ever since Mr. Bingley abandoned Netherfield Park and Caroline sent that horrid letter." Reaching out, Elizabeth gave her friend's hand a squeeze. She knew Charlotte wished to do more, but this was a sacrifice she would make to keep the peace in her home.

"We best get into the hallway before Mr. Collins attempts to force his way into your room." Charlotte set her shoulders and turned to leave the room and face her husband's excited nature. Opening the door, she found him standing at the doorway, his arm raised to pound at it.

"Finally! You have dawdled long enough, cousin. It is time for you to hurry to Lady Catherine. I am certain she will set things to right." He did not even acknowledge his wife. Moving around her, he grabbed for Elizabeth's wrist, attempting to force her out of the room and his house.

"I will accompany you to see Lady Catherine, but you will not manhandle me." Slipping around him, Elizabeth proceeded down the hall and down the stairs. She made her way through the house and to the kitchen with her ability to move faster than his bumbling form. She smiled at the tremulous cook and scullery maid. They were both sweet, but afraid of Mr. Collins and Lady Catherine's power and retribution. She grabbed a couple of slices of buttered toast on the table as she moved through the room and out of the house.

When she reached the path to Rosings, she glanced behind, checking to see if Mr. Collins was still there. He was, but falling further behind with every step. His outraged expression spoke of his desire to drag her by the scruff of her neck all the way to Lady Catherine. He tried to keep up, but she left him behind, his breath loud and desperate, his feet too slow to catch her. Keeping her pace brisk, she took the time to eat the toast and enjoy the winding path through the garden.

What could Lady Catherine want with her? Was it possible that she was merely attempting to show her power for some unknown reason? Elizabeth wondered if Charlotte's hints that Mr. Darcy was interested in her could possibly have anything to do with this. But it was impossible. A complete and outright impossibility. Charlotte may see things clearly most of the time, but she was not infallible.

The easiest proof of that was the fact that she had willingly married Mr. Collins.

Realizing that her best friend was set on marrying her buffoon of a relative had been hard to take. She had not handled that with as much grace as she would have liked. Despite feeling uneasy about it, she went to visit Charlotte after she moved into her new home. Wanting to support her friend had meant putting up with Mr. Collins for the last month. Look where it led her—on the way to Rosings before the sun was fully up. She prepared herself for what was most likely to be a tirade of epic proportions. Resisting the urge to kick the gravel on the way down the path, Elizabeth instead contemplated the peace of nature and the glory of the sunrise.

As she approached the main entrance of Rosings, she noticed a footman waiting for her on the stairs. The question was, did she wait for her puffing red-faced cousin to catch up or face the lion's den alone? She supposed she should wait for him. It would not do to leave poor Charlotte a widow if she could help it. Taking a moment, she checked her appearance and made sure she did not have any crumbs or butter on her face. She slowly ascended the stairs to greet the footman waiting for her.

"Good morning, Gregory." Elizabeth had made a point of remembering the staff's names. She always thought that it was not right to treat the staff like nameless, faceless cogs.

Gregory smiled at the young lady climbing the stairs. "Morning, Miss Bennet. She is right upset this morning. I would advise you to stay clear of her cane." He paused as he took in the scene behind her. "Are you sure Mr. Collins will be all right? His color looks off."

"You conniving strumpet! Flirting will not...help you—" Collins stopped mid rant to gasp for breath, his hands on his knees.

"Mr. Collins, Lady Catherine is waiting for us," Elizabeth reminded him gently, knowing she could distract Mr. Collins easily if she brought up Lady Catherine.

Mr. Collins began making his way up the stairs. What had been a brisk walk for Elizabeth seemed to have undone her cousin. He wiped at his forehead, leaving a streak of moisture on his skin, and his cravat was soaked through with sweat. "I will not allow your improper actions to distract me from attending my patroness."

Gregory opened the oversized door with a wink at Elizabeth as he did so. Elizabeth began to go through the passage when Mr. Collins shoved her aside in his effort to get to Lady Catherine first. In a quick move, Gregory caught Elizabeth's elbow before she hit the wall.

Frowning at the uncouth man, Gregory looked at Elizabeth with concern. "Are you all right, Miss Bennet?"

"I will be well, Gregory, thank you." Elizabeth attempted to maintain her positive demeanor despite her increasingly unpleasant morning.

After an endless number of turns and ornate hallways, they arrived at what Elizabeth had been calling Lady Catherine's throne room. Someone had covered the room in gilt molding and draped purple fabric with ornate statues. At the end of the room, on a raised dais, sat Lady Catherine in the most ornate chair Elizabeth had ever seen.

"My Ladyship, I have come at your request, and I have brought my wife's guest. That you have uncovered her horrid actions shows how magnificent you are." Mr. Collins bowed so low that he nearly upended and landed on his face. Even after he stood, he stayed hunched over and he still fixed his gaze on the ground. As Elizabeth watched him from where she stood, she was eminently grateful that her father had not tried to force her to marry the servile man.

Lady Catherine sat on her throne, her expression thunderous. Her outfit reminded Elizabeth of the old painting of her grandmother back at Longbourn. It always seemed to Elizabeth that she was stuck in the previous century. "You may go, Collins, but I would advise you to consider how you run your household and who you allow into your home."

"Lady Catherine, I apologize for being swayed by my dreadful wife to allow this scapegrace into my home. Please." Mr. Collins practically collapsed on the floor in supplication, his forehead touching the ground in reverence at her dais. Elizabeth could not keep from rolling her eyes at his display. How did Charlotte stand being married to him? Elizabeth found it hard to be in the same room as him. The sound of his smarmy voice made her want to cover her ears. She couldn't help but feel a sense of disgust at his speech and his quip about his lowly wife made her want to kick him in the ankle.

"I have dismissed you. Be gone!" Lady Catherine sneered at her rector, her distaste for his display clear in her cruel mien.

Mr. Collins scurried from the room like a rat fleeing a sinking ship. Elizabeth hoped Charlotte could manage him when he returned to the parsonage. Turning her gaze to Lady Catherine, she let the silence grow. She would not kowtow to the supercilious woman like her distant relative did.

Lady Catherine harrumphed and stared down her nose at Elizabeth. "You can have no doubt as to why you are here."

"Despite being unaware of your displeasure with me, I have arrived as you requested," Elizabeth replied, holding her hands out to her sides, the picture of innocence. This simple gesture seemed to set Lady Catherine off. She came out of her chair, her rage apparent in her stance and how she tried to loom over Elizabeth.

"You, who are wholly ungrateful for the proposal I encouraged Collins to offer you, think to come into my domain and act as if you have done nothing wrong? I have seen nothing so outlandish in my life. Your parents should be ashamed of allowing you out of the schoolroom with such a despicable behavior." Her cane hit against the dais with a resounding crack and Elizabeth worried she might break the structure.

"I suppose I am ungrateful, as I do not regret turning down the offer at all. But as my matrimonial choice cannot be any of your concern, not being a blood relative, you are wholly unconnected to my decision. As for outlandishness, I do not see a lady turning down a proposal of marriage as beyond the bounds of the typical. Women do it every day. It is one of the few powers we have. It is certainly not despicable."

"None of my concern! The man you are dangling after is my blood relation. I have the authority to lead things in the manner that I deem appropriate. His path was determined at birth, and his destiny was clear from the cradle. What say you now?" Lady Catherine howled her rebuke so severely that spittle flew from her mouth. Elizabeth was glad that the distance between them kept her dry.

The tremor of the Lady's hand caught Elizabeth's attention momentarily before she felt the need to respond. "Only that I do not know of who you mean. I was under the impression that we were discussing Mr. Collins, but he is my blood relation, not yours. As for dangling after anyone, I say it is not in my manner, nor is there anyone here after which I would choose to dangle."

"Do you claim to be ignorant of the fact that my nephew believes he is in love with you?" In a move that startled Elizabeth, Lady Catherine attempted to shake her cane at her, only to drop it when her hand continued to shake.

Elizabeth found she could not focus on Lady Catherine's words because she noticed other, maybe more important, things. It soon became apparent that Lady Catherine was not at all well. Her mouth started to overflow with saliva, which was dripping down her chin and onto her clothes. Her complexion had an odd yellow tinge to it, and her eyes, though furious, were dull and sunken. "Are you well, Lady Catherine? Do sit back down. Can I help you?"

Lady Catherine grew confused at Elizabeth's concern. "I will not be distracted. My fool of a maid tried to convince me to stay abed, and I fired her for her impertinence. You will do no better in our interaction. I am determined to see this through, as my family is at stake. What say you of my nephew's love?"

"Nephew? I did not know that Colonel Fitzwilliam had any such feelings for me. He is a pleasant person to speak with at dinner, but I was under the impression that he needed an heiress. If I gave any impression that I wished otherwise, I apologize," she said sincerely, her concern for the woman growing. "Please sit down. I will speak with you civilly. There is no need for all this excitement." Elizabeth was sure there had never been a morning more bewildering and now she was told that Colonel Fitzwilliam was in love with her. How had she not known?

Lady Catherine began feeling behind her, her arm outstretched, blindly groping for her chair. "Do not be daft girl, I thought you intelligent. Darcy! We are talking about Darcy!"

"Mr. Darcy?" Elizabeth questioned incredulously, convinced she didn't hear Lady Catherine correctly. "He stares at me all the time and can barely string two civil words together at a time with me. Unless it is, of course, it was to argue with me." Her shock could not be more complete. Up was down, left was right, and Fitzwilliam Darcy of Pemberley was in love with her. Maybe tomorrow the sun would rise over the western horizon.

Lady Catherine slumped wearily into her chair, her head coming to rest on the tall, gilt-covered back. Eyes narrowing, she judged Elizabeth before attempting to wipe at her chin with her shaking hand. "And people wonder why I am constantly directing the people around me. He does not argue with you, he debates. My clumsy fool of a nephew has been trying to find ways to talk with you. He quite enjoys your agile mind, my dear. Do you never watch him when you argue? His lips twitch—he only does that when he is trying not to smile. I thought you claimed intelligence."

Elizabeth brought her hand to her chest, resting it over her wildly beating heart. Had she really been so blind? "I thought I did too, but if you are correct, I have been seriously mistaken, and for quite some time. He said 'She is tolerable, but not handsome enough to tempt me' the first time he saw me. After that I always believed, well, I believed differently."

"I said he was a fool, did I not? Have you ever read Shakespeare? 'He doth protest too much.' I am sure he was at a gathering of some sort, being encouraged to socialize. It is a skill he does not have, by the way." Her eyes fluttered closed as she spoke, as if it was an effort to hold them open.

Unable to stay where she was when the lady before her was obviously struggling, Elizabeth hopped up on the dais and went to her side. Taking her handkerchief out of her sleeve, she offered it to the Lady who then dabbed at her face, trying to get some of the drool. "And I suppose he does not stare at me because he dislikes and disapproves of me then."

A throaty chuckle burst from the woman, and she opened her eyes to stare at Elizabeth. It was the first genuine laugh Elizabeth had ever heard from Lady Catherine. "I cannot say I do not see what he sees in you. You are compassionate, vivacious, and smart, on occasion," she paused, and her laughter bubbled forth again as she rolled her eyes. "But he is for my daughter. I cannot let you interfere."

Elizabeth was truly concerned for the woman. "We can talk about this at a later time. Let me call for help, or is there a physician nearby? You do not seem well."

Lady Catherine waved her hand shakily in refusal, and Elizabeth noticed that the tremor was still increasing. "I am merely tired; it is probably this headache. It has been trying me since Wednesday, and it's unending, but I refuse to be stopped by mere pain. Life is full of pain, yet we must still do what is required and I must see to my Anne.

She is not comfortable with society, nor is she capable of running an estate. She must marry someone who will care for her, and my nephew Darcy is the best man I know."

"I understand wanting to protect someone, but I have seen no inclination that your daughter would be comfortable as a wife or be capable of running a household. You understand how difficult it is to do." Elizabeth reached out and then pulled her hand back. She knew that Lady Catherine was not one to enjoy the assistance of others.

"Marriage is the best protection a woman can have if she is married to a good man. Besides, my nephew is strong. He has been running his estate on his own since he was twenty-two. Darcy is his father's son. He was a good man, too. He can see to Rosings just as well as Pemberley."

Unwilling to do nothing while she suffered, Elizabeth moved closer and knelt at her feet, gently enclosing her trembling hand in her own. Her skin felt too thin to be real, as if simply wearing clothes would bruise her tender flesh. She was completely astounded when Lady Catherine gripped her hand tightly and then brought her other hand to clutch at her as well. "Why did you call for me in such a fury, Lady Catherine? It's as if you have known of his feelings for some time."

"His father did the same sorts of things when he fell in love with my sister. It was simple for me to recognize. One of the maids overheard him practicing a proposal last night, and it sent me into a bluster. I have always found comfort knowing that Darcy would protect my Anne. It has been my only assurance that she will be well when I am not here to protect her." Her speech gradually became more labored and ended in a wet gurgle.

Alarm was turning into real fear in Elizabeth's churning stomach. She had helped various sick tenants, but she was not an apothecary. The only similar experience she had to what was happening was sitting with Widow Tyler before she passed. In fact, it was the similarity that had her glad that she had only eaten toast. The fragility of her hand as well as the gurgle had her fearing for Lady Catherine's life. It was the only thing that kept Elizabeth from reacting to the fact that Darcy was intending to propose to her at some point. "Let me go for help. Something is horribly wrong."

"No, the headache is finally fading, and for some reason, I find I do not want to be alone." The fragile hand in her own clutched at her spasmodically.

Elizabeth felt it in her bones that this would not end well, but she could not leave the woman alone in case the worse should happen, no one deserved that. She tried to come up with something that might be reassuring for Lady Catherine to talk about. "I am glad that the pain is leaving you. Tell me of your Anne. I have not had the opportunity to spend much time with her during my visit."

"She was such a bright child with the loveliest cheerful laugh. That was before she got ill the first time. I have collected every tonic to boast of healthful benefits, every charm, and every trinket. I could not lose the one bright thing in my life. I..." Lady Catherine trailed off, unable to complete her thought because of the wet cough that strangled the breath out of her and left her gasping.

"Oh dear, maybe you would be more comfortable somewhere else—" Elizabeth stopped her suggestion when she saw Lady Catherine shaking her head.

"Too tired…later…" The gurgle was back, and Elizabeth struggled to breathe herself. She had never really liked Lady Catherine; she was rude and opinionated. However, she could not help but see the humanity in her at this moment. If nothing else, she was a mother who loved her daughter and wanted her to be protected. For that, Elizabeth found she could love her, especially as she feared she was taking her last gasping breaths.

"All right, we will stay here for now until someone comes, and you have enough strength to move." The moment dragged on forever and then Elizabeth could see when realization struck Lady Catherine. That she finally understood that she may never have the strength to move, and this could very well be the end of her struggle. "I am here, Lady Catherine, and I will not leave you."

Lady Catherine moved, putting forth an enormous effort to draw closer to Elizabeth. Looking into Elizabeth's eyes, she blinked and leaned further forward to rest her forehead against Elizabeth's own. She breathed for a moment, struggling for each gasp. Elizabeth waited, knowing that she was putting forth effort for something important to her.

"Anne?" Foam was forming at the corners of her mouth and dripping down her chin, along with her drool.

Elizabeth regarded it as unimportant for the moment and squeezed her hands in what she hoped was reassurance. "Yes, I promise I will make sure that Anne is happy and well."

"Darcy?"

"I'm choosing to give him a chance; maybe it will allow me to believe that he is the greatest of men. I will not go easy on him though—he called me only tolerable, after all." Elizabeth tried to smile. It was a watery version of her typical grin, as her eyes were overflowing.

Lady Catherine's attempt at a laugh morphed into another wet gurgle, but she smiled. It was a sad smile, full of loss. "Good girl," reaching up, she tried to clasp Elizabeth's cheek. She toppled forward and into Elizabeth's lap and she struggled to catch her in her arms as she shook. She could do nothing but hold her close and be there for her in her last moments.

And then she was still in her arms and the room grew quiet. The gurgling rasp was gone, no longer echoing around the garish room. Lady Catherine was dead. Elizabeth reached out a trembling hand to close her eyes and hide her tormented and empty gaze. A click from an opening door across the room brought Elizabeth's head up even as she clutched Lady Catherine to her chest. "Now someone comes," she whispered.

Chapter Two

Darcy is a Fool

DARCY AWOKE TO A mouth full of bitterness and assumed it must be what unspoken words and regret tasted like. Or maybe to be more accurate, words unspoken to the right person. Spending the night drinking whisky with his cousin and practicing his proposal to Miss Bennet had not helped him at all. He still felt like a ball full of nerves.

His cousin's inquiry about the progression of their courting only added to his anxiety. When he looked puzzled and asked if he should have been trying to court her in some special way, his cousin laughed until he fell out of his chair. In the end, his cousin suggested he try courting the lady first. Theodore suggested he start by complementing her and actually letting her know he liked her.

He was adamant that Darcy should never utter a single disparaging word about Elizabeth's family, connections, dowry, or figure. He pointed out fiercely that she had no ability to control those things and saying that he loved her despite those things was not the compliment he considered it to be. Darcy was glad that he had decided to talk to Theodore about his intent. He was realizing in the cold light of day that things could have gone badly had he attempted to propose in the manner he had originally been planning.

The door to his chamber opened and he heard his valet, Reeves, arranging things in his dressing chamber. He was a pleasant fellow and Darcy was glad he was at Rosings with him. He was always calm and collected, providing a sense of security and stability.

"Good morning, sir. How are you faring after your night spent in Colonel Fitzwilliams's company?" As Reeves spoke, his face lit up with a knowing smirk. Most likely he had been talking with Theodore's batman. He would know that his cousin had returned to his rooms slightly bosky and thoroughly entertained by Darcy's ineptitude with women.

Pinching the bridge of his nose, Darcy gauged his headache. "Well enough, besides a wish for some coffee. You knew I intended to propose to Miss Bennet. Why did you not tell me I should have tried courting her first?"

"That is not for me to say, sir. I did not know whether she had the power of a witch to read minds. It was always a possibility, though slight. She has certainly bewitched you." Reeves kept a straight face, even with his joke at his employer's expense. Darcy knew he considered himself a funny man.

He squinted at Reeves, and though they were just kidding, he also knew it would have been a devastating experience. Reeves had been his valet since shortly before his father had passed. He was closer to Reeves than was strictly proper, and he would have expected to have been at least warned that he was headed for disaster. "If Theodore is to be believed, she would have sent me on my way with nary a regret. You would have let me walk into that without knowing any better?"

Shaking his head at his master's foolishness as if to say, do I really have to explain that a girl wishes to be courted properly, Reeves explained, "You were determined, and I suggested you at least bring her flowers, if you recall. You simply have not been receptive to my hints. I blame it on the fact that women are always throwing themselves at your feet. It has given you a distorted view of the process."

Even avoiding most of London's social gatherings as he did had not protected him from the fawning ladies that made up every season. Had his years fending off increasingly forward advances and even compromise attempts jaded him to how a woman of worth might expect to be treated? As he reconsidered his actions, Darcy realized it was only right to court Miss Bennet. She deserved to know how highly he esteemed her. That, in fact, she was cherished. Had he really assumed merely giving her notice was enough? Was he genuinely that conceited? "I know I have always been avoidant of the women who trail after me, but I do not think that anyone has been throwing themselves at my feet. This could have ended in heartbreak if Theo had not stopped my wayward path. Next time I am that unreceptive to important hints, tell me you will send for Theodore and his whisky. Or maybe borrow a frying pan. It may be less injurious to my ego." Darcy may have realized that his course was flawed, but he was still unwilling to admit that he had been completely blind as well as foolish.

"You cannot suppose that Bingley chit is truly clumsy. It is a calculated effort to get you to help her up and possibly compromise you. I am always on guard, ready to prevent a compromise whenever she is in the same residence as you. As for Colonel Fitzwilliam, I will summon him as needed and hold the frying pan in reserve." Reeves spoke as he began straightening the room, clearing it of the abandoned clothes that Darcy had shed as he put himself to bed. When things were to his standard, he laid out Darcy's clothes. He was aware that Darcy preferred to dress himself while he went to fetch his morning coffee. "If everything is as you need it, I will retrieve your coffee and toast."

Darcy nodded and while Reeves left to get the amazing beverage, Darcy drew himself from the bed and readied himself for the day. The only thing that he would leave for his valet to do on his return was his cravat. He could never get the blasted things right.

He contemplated his interactions with Miss Elizabeth, no, Miss Bennet, once again. Since seeing her once more, he had been tripping over calling her Miss Elizabeth. Without her older sister in residence, she was Miss Bennet, and it had been slightly difficult for him to make the proper adjustment. He had fumbled a time or two when he first saw her, and his aunt had taken him to task at his lack of propriety. He would not have minded in the least, but her look of discomfort during his aunt's tirade made him amend his wording, however difficult.

Considering his conversations with her until now caused him to feel remorseful. He had assumed that because he had sought her out to accompany her on her walks, she would recognize the momentous significance he was placing on the action. However, thinking back, he realized that he rarely spoke when walking with her. When he did, it was to debate something which Theodore had pointed out that she could interpret any number of negative ways. Reeves was correct in implying that she would have to have mind-reading abilities to understand his motives.

How did one go about properly courting a woman of depth? He knew he would only have to nod in the direction of many women of the ton and they would begin planning how they wanted to redecorate his town house, but Elizabeth was not that kind of woman. That is what he liked about her. It was one of the many things that drew him to her.

The key thing that had clued Theodore into his blunder was when he asked what her favorite color was. Darcy did not know what it was. He saw her in a lot of blues and greens, but that could just be because she looked well in those colors. Darcy knew she had a sharp mind and a companionate heart. To her, a person's worth was not determined by their status, but by their humanity. He realized he was unaware of the secrets and stories that she kept close to her heart. Did she skin her knee as a little girl? She did not strike him as the sort to have sat quietly indoors learning to embroider. He realized he had countless unanswered questions and yearned to know the answers. What was her favorite flavor? Did she prefer biscuits or tarts? What was her favorite memory, and yes, what was her favorite color? He wanted to know so many things, but in his difficulty figuring out what to say, he had said nothing at all. Or argued about trivialities.

He rested his head in his hands and allowed himself to wallow in his stupidity. Yes, he, Fitzwilliam Darcy, was a fool. After long deliberation, he had to admit to himself that he was in love with a woman and decided that he should make her an offer of marriage.

He could almost picture them walking the grounds of Pemberley, content and fulfilled. What he had not done was take the time to consider her emotions on the subject, nor had he given her the respect and adoration she deserved. He had certainly put the carriage before the horse on this one.

His door crashing open had Darcy jerking in place and looking to see Reeves rushing in, obviously concerned. "You do not have time to wallow. Someone overheard you practicing your proposal and told Lady Catherine she was livid and had Miss Bennet summoned before dawn. She is with her now in her receiving room."

"Botheration. I must go help her. She will never accept my proposal at this rate." Flinging himself from the chair where he had sat, he rushed to the door.

"I commend your actions, sir, but maybe you should put your shoes on first and let me tie your cravat. I also have your coffee. You might need the fortification. Here, sit back down and drink your coffee. I will help you with your shoes."

A flurry of activity later, Darcy was rushing down a hallway, his mind concocting all kinds of scenarios. He was confident that Miss Bennet would not be easily intimidated by Lady Catherine's tirade, but he knew it would still have an emotional impact on her. There was, however, a chance that she would find the situation humorous. He loved how she could find humor in life, and how she did not bend to the will of others when she knew they were wrong. He loved so many things about her that he struggled to keep his mind on the topic. Castigating himself for once again letting his mind wonder, Darcy increased his pace. When he arrived at his destination, he pushed the door open without knocking and was immediately shocked by what lay before him.

There, sitting on the dais, was his Elizabeth with tears rolling down her cheeks and Lady Catherine in her arms. Rushing to her side, he tried to take in the situation's magnitude. There must be something horribly wrong with his aunt. "Miss Bennet, what can I do to help?"

Miss Bennet was looking down at his aunt in her arms. She embraced her with such compassion as if she was close to her and was filled with sorrow at her departure. "She is already gone. There is nothing to do, or there is nothing we can do to help her any longer," she whispered, obviously upset.

Darcy found it hard to wrap his mind around the fact that his aunt was gone. He reached out and cautiously touched her throat, feeling the stillness of her skin. Finding no pulse, he knew she was gone. He had not doubted Miss Bennet but had to confirm it for himself for some reason. Looking into Miss Bennet's eyes, he saw something he had never seen before: despair. "What can I do to help you? Do you want me to help you lay her down?"

"I suppose I cannot stay like this. If you could help me, I would be... Yes, thank you." She seemed to struggle as he had never seen before. Obviously, whatever had happened was truly horrible. Reaching out, he took his aunt gently from her and lay her next to her throne-like chair. She weighed so little. Her bright, colorful clothes, that were so outdated and ostentatious, made him think she was bigger than she actually was. Between that and her powerful presence, she had thoroughly deceived him. Turning back to Miss

Bennet, he saw her staring off, probably thinking about what had happened.

"Miss Bennet, I have so many questions and at the moment I cannot decide what I should say and what order. No, first, are you all right?"

Shaking her head, Miss Bennet clutched handfuls of the material of her dress. "I seem to be. I wanted to go for help, but she did not want me to leave her. This feeling is completely unexpected. She was not at all close to me, but I cannot help feel for her. For all her bluster, she was simply a woman at the end."

Darcy paced momentarily. His mind rushing over what must be done. He had to send for the physician, he supposed. Theodore must be told, letters needed to be written, a funeral arranged, but he could do none of that because of his need to be with Elizabeth and see to her sorrow. "My mind is preoccupied with thoughts of your wellbeing, even though there are pressing matters that require attention. I think I should get my cousin the colonel, but you could come with me."

"No, I think I should stay here. She did not want to be alone, and so I will stay." Elizabeth's voice faltered as she tried to speak, and then she broke down, tears streaming down her face. She wiped at her face ineffectually, before seeming to bring herself under control.

Darcy was grateful that he had a handkerchief to offer her. Holding it out to her, he realized she was not paying him any attention. Then he gave into the desire that he had had more than once. He reached out, the fabric of his handkerchief gentle on her skin as he tried to blot her tears. He was uncertain of what had transpired in that room, yet he knew he was mostly responsible. If they had not overheard him, his aunt would not have forced Elizabeth to come up to Rosings and she would not have had what must have been a very trying morning.

Looking up at him, she stared at him intently, as if trying to gauge his soul. "She was right. You love me, and I did not know." She leaned into his hand as if by a force beyond her control, but then straightened. "We have many things to discuss, but we must care for your aunt first. Truly, we must discuss your aunt as well. Get your cousin. I will be here when you return."

"I will return as quickly as I can." Forcing himself from his kneeling position, he stood and left the room despite how his heart was telling him to stay and comfort her. She was completely correct in stating that they must talk, though his heart was triumphant at the small sign of her acceptance of him. He hurried in search of his cousin. He would most likely be in the stables, checking on his horse. Hopefully he could catch him before he left for his morning ride. There was nothing that they could do for his aunt any longer, but he could not stand the thought of having to trail after his cousin, especially if it meant that it left Miss Bennet alone and in distress.

***

FINDING HIM AS HE had hoped in the stables was a godsend. Calling out as he approached, he got his attention. "Theodore, we have a problem!"

"I would have guessed you would not be quite this enthusiastic this morning after a night like last night. Have you come up with a plan of attack for courting your lady love?" Theodore laughed at his cousin's expense.

Shaking his head, Darcy tried to explain the situation they were finding themselves in. There was no way but to be blunt. "That can wait. Aunt Catherine has died."

Stepping back from his horse, Theodore fired off questions. "Where is she? What has happened? Is there anyone else at risk?"

Darcy gritted his teeth as he willed himself to stay and not rush back to Elizabeth. He had never seen her so vulnerable before. It was evident from the way she trembled that whatever had happened was truly dreadful. He took a deep breath, trying to steady himself before conveying everything to Theodore. "She is in her receiving room. Someone heard us talking last night and reported it to Lady Catherine. She summoned Miss Bennet before dawn. I found out from Reeves and went to mitigate the situation. When I arrived, I found Elizabeth holding Aunt Catherine in her arms. She was dead. We must go back." Darcy had assumed Theodore would follow him back to the house, but it seemed he had gone into soldier mode as he often did when there was a crisis.

"Jeffers! Summon the physician as fast as can be, man. Ezekiel, see to Samson. I was getting ready to take him out but can no longer do so," he shouted, calling to the stable hand and head groom. Then, having completed the task, he moved past Darcy and took off back to the house. "Could you tell what happened?"

"Frankly, I felt for a pulse and helped lay her out on the dais, but I did not look too closely. I did not feel it right looking her over somehow." Darcy tried to recall what he saw, but his focus had been on Elizabeth, not on the scene.

"Well, the physician should be here soon enough." Theodore added under his breath, as if frustrated that Darcy had not determined the need to look for signs of her demise.

"Why? What does it matter how? We know she is dead." Darcy fought his frustration as they made their way through the ornate garden path. They were both rushing, but not quite running.

"We need to find out why she died, Darcy. Otherwise, it could look very bad for your Miss Bennet." Theodore kept a brisk pace as they entered the building and wound through the halls. He also called out to the servants as they went, calling out orders. He asked for the icehouse to be checked and the housekeeper to be summoned to the receiving room, as well as a countless number of things that Darcy had not realized would be necessary.

"What? Miss Bennet would do nothing to harm anyone." He almost stopped, his mind balking at the thought of anyone questioning Miss Bennet's innocence.

"We may know that, but people talk and tongues wag. If you knew that Aunt Catherine had it out for her, there is no telling what people may say that Elizabeth did in a fit of spite." He shook his head at his cousin's naivete.

"I had never imagined that anyone would question what happened."

"Yes, but you do not enjoy spreading gossip. You look at things in a straightforward manner and have no desire to pull people down. People are not as wholly good as we would wish. Did you know bored soldiers can be the worst gossip mongers?" He shook his head as they turned the last corner. As they drew near the door, the unmistakable sounds of a quarrel reached their ears.

"You must have done something. You were already dangling after her nephew in such an unseemly manner. I would not put it past you to have poisoned her tea." He heard a female voice being raised on the other side of the door and suspected it was his cousin's new companion. He had never been fond of the woman, but his aunt had brooked no argument against her. Anne's previous companion, Mrs. Jenkins, had recently retired to live with her daughter in Bath. She had been a sweet woman who genuinely cared for his cousin, while Mrs. Stevenson was not.

"Do you see any tea in the room, Mrs. Stevenson? I could not have very well poisoned her tea this morning, as she never offered me any." And that was his Elizabeth responding. Darcy somehow made it around his cousin Theodore in his rush to get to her and threw open the door.

There in the middle of the room stood Mrs. Stevenson, obviously upset and castigating Elizabeth. His cousin Anne stood beside her companion, her expression slightly vacant, as it always was. Elizabeth stood at the dais, her face a picture of pained composure. Her face still had evidence of her tears fresh on her face, but her back was straight, and her eyes accepted no nonsense from the woman across from her. Darcy could not help feeling that she was marvelous.

Chapter Three
Poisoned?

WHEN THE DOOR OPENED, Elizabeth had assumed that it would be Mr. Darcy returning. It was not. In fact, it was Anne de Bourgh and her companion. Anne did not speak when she entered the room. She rarely spoke much at all, which Elizabeth had never thought much about until now. After the way Lady Catherine had talked, Elizabeth wondered if there was a specific reason she had worried about her daughter.

"What are you doing here? No one may enter this room unless Lady Catherine summoned them," came Mrs. Stevenson's less than civil greeting.

Anne's companion had never been friendly to Elizabeth, but she had also never been strident. It was a surprise, but Elizabeth took it in stride. It had been a morning of surprises, after all. Looking at Anne, she became concerned. She did not feel this was the setting to explain matters. "Lady Catherine summoned me early this morning. But she became unwell. Mr. Darcy is going for Colonel Fitzwilliam. They should be returning momentarily."

Mrs. Stevenson's eyes widened as they took in Lady Catherine's motionless figure on the dais before turning to Elizabeth. "What have you done?"

"Do you really believe I would do something to harm her? Rest assured that I have no intention of causing harm to anyone, least of all Lady Catherine." Elizabeth was growing tired of how badly her morning was progressing. She had not even had her coffee yet.

"You must have done something. You were already dangling after her nephew in such an unseemly manner. I would not put it past you to have poisoned her tea." She flushed, apparently upset that Elizabeth had countered her.

Elizabeth told herself that she must not roll her eyes at the contrary woman. "Do you see any tea in the room, Mrs. Stevenson? I could not have very well poisoned her tea this morning, as she never offered me any."

The door flew open, and Mr. Darcy and Colonel Theodore entered the room with a loud crash. With a look of alarm on his face, Darcy rushed to Elizabeth's side, and her tense muscles softened with relief. It was certainly another symptom of her odd morning. If someone had told her yesterday that she would soon be relieved to see Darcy enter the room, she would have laughed herself silly and yet today it was true. Even if she had not had the time to properly think about things, she somehow knew in her bones that he would be on her side and would never support Mrs. Stevenson's accusations.

Elizabeth knew she must look a mess. Her face was sticky from her tears, and she had not had enough time to really see to her appearance that morning. Yet Mr. Darcy was once again staring at her. Only now that she had been told that he loved her did she understand he was looking at her with admiration, not to find fault. As he examined her, his eyes were soft, not searching for any mistakes. He never set out to find flaws in her, and she could say with certainty that he had never done so.

She was only vaguely aware of the fact that the colonel had gone straight to his aunt, bypassing the conflict, and leaving the battle to Mr. Darcy.

"I have returned with Theodore, Miss Bennet. It appears as if you have been dealing with some unpleasantness in my stead." Though he spoke to her and gave her a slight smile, his gaze shifted to Mrs. Stevenson as he spoke. Standing next to her, shoulder to shoulder, he intentionally moved to present a united front. As if she was automatically in the right and Mrs. Stevenson, who lived there, was the interloper.

"Mr. Darcy, I am glad you and the colonel have come. I have been doing my utmost to manage the awful occurrence in your absence." The tone of voice that Mrs. Stevenson used instantly changed from brash to more subservient. Elizabeth recognized she would want to impress Mr. Darcy and not care for her at all, though she found such two-faced behavior distasteful.

Elizabeth felt his shoulder brush hers as Mr. Darcy straightened his posture. "We heard what you were trying to do through the door as we were arriving. I do not appreciate what you were implying." His tone of voice was imperious, and she could see the family trait he carried that had been strong in Lady Catherine as well.

Mrs. Stevenson kept most of her expression serene, but Elizabeth caught the flash of anger in her eyes. "I was only seeing to—"

"It is not your place to see to anything." Elizabeth heard the anger in Mr. Darcy's voice and shivered to know that it was in defense of her. Her father loved her dearly but rarely protected her from even her mother's wrath. That the man beside her was so willing to believe her innocent and take up her cause without a word from her in her own defense meant something significant. She would think on it later after they had dealt with all the things necessary for the day.

"Is Mother sleeping? Someone should tell her that you are supposed to sleep in bed," Anne spoke, reminding everyone that she was in the room. It concerned Elizabeth that a grown woman of twenty-seven was speaking like she was only seven.

Elizabeth glanced at Mr. Darcy as she walked over to Anne, drawing her away from her mother's prone figure. "We will take care of your mother, my dear. Have you had breakfast yet?"

"Not yet, and I was going to say good morning to Mama," Anne spoke, glancing behind her to where her mother lay, obviously confused by the morning's events.

Elizabeth drew the woman to her as she would a child, corralling her away from the sight. She did not need to see that, and she was sure this was not the venue to explain to her that her mother had passed. "Why not go have breakfast with Mrs. Stevenson. I am sure the cook made something delicious just for you."

Mrs. Stevenson approached, hands clenched and a glare firmly in place. Elizabeth knew that the woman might have intimidated someone, but she merely found her posturing inappropriate. "Really, Miss Bennet, I do not think—"

Once again, Mr. Darcy came to Elizabeth's side and from what she could tell of his posture, he was becoming increasingly frustrated. "You have made it evident that you do not think, Mrs. Stevenson. My cousin obviously needs to have her breakfast and not be here. As her companion, you should have seen to it before now."

The poor woman's mouth fell open, gaping like a fish for a moment before it snapped shut and her eyes turned hard, all pretense of subservience gone. "If that is what you wish, Miss de Bourgh, come this way. It is time you had your breakfast."

Anne showed no signs of being affected by the brisk tone and smiled blandly at her companion as she moved toward the door. "Do you think there will be marmalade for my toast?"

"Yes, there will be marmalade for your toast." Mrs. Stevenson's put-upon voice responded as they went through the door and shut it behind them.

"That woman is going to be a problem. She is most likely going to spread some very vicious rumors the moment she has the chance," the colonel finally spoke up once the woman was out of the room and most likely far enough away to not hear him. Standing from his crouched position next to the body, he came to where she stood with Mr. Darcy.

Mr. Darcy faced his cousin Colonel Fitzwilliam with a posture only slightly more relaxed than when facing Mrs. Stevenson. "Did you notice anything? It was obvious that you were looking for something specific."

Shaking his head, the colonel conveyed his bad news with a grim voice. "Yes, and it is not good. Her color is off and with the foam at her mouth, it looks like she could have been poisoned. I am glad we already called for a physician."

"Poisoned?" Mr. Darcy's voice grew faint and shaky, conveying his shock. Elizabeth fought the desire to reach over and offer him comfort for the struggle that he was obviously facing. She squashed the instinct and tried to focus on the disaster at hand and not on how Mr. Darcy and his cousins must be suffering. Even if she was not that close to Lady Catherine, it still affected her. She could only imagine what they must be feeling.

War had made Colonel Fitzwilliam all too familiar with death, far more so than Mr. Darcy or herself, and she was aware of this. The colonel spoke softly when he said, "I'm not suggesting a murder was involved, but this wasn't a natural death."

"I have no special knowledge, so I cannot say what exactly went wrong, but it was all very odd. This entire morning has been odd." Elizabeth responded while rubbing at her forehead. She wished she had a cup of coffee to at least fight her rising headache.

When the door opened again, the housekeeper stepped inside, her footsteps muffled by the thick carpets. Elizabeth was fond of the pleasant lady, who gave her a kind, yet faint smile before turning to the colonel. "You asked for me, Colonel?"

"Yes, Mrs. Graham. I know this is going to come as a shock, but Lady Catherine is...dead."

Clutching at her throat with her weathered hand, she responded. "Oh, great merciful Father. What happened?"

"That is one of the things we are attempting to discover. In the meantime, we cannot simply leave her here. She will need to be moved either to her chamber or to the icehouse if something delays the physician. Can you see to that?"

Her brisk nod reminded them all that she was the woman who ran the estate like a well-oiled army. She was always ready to serve guests or respond to an outbreak of summer colds, as if she had been expecting it all along. She could see to the careful consideration taken for someone's last wishes. "Of course, sir. Does the young miss know?"

"Not yet. She came in earlier but assumed she was sleeping. We will tell her later today, but she has gone to have breakfast for now. We need to keep a tight lid on this, Mrs. Graham. I fear there will be rumors because of the suddenness of her death. As of now, we know nothing of the cause and to say otherwise would only be speculation. I do not want anyone's reputation to be bothered by unfounded gossip," Colonel Fitzwilliam spoke with the voice of authority.

"I will attempt to control things, but you know how gossip is," she spoke with an annoyed sigh. Elizabeth assumed she would know who the gossipers were, but it was tough to keep people from speaking. Elizabeth had experienced trying to control gossiping back at Longbourn.

"Yes, I know very well." Nodding in agreement Elizabeth was mortified when her stomach growled so loudly that everyone turned to look at her. "I am sorry, I was summoned so early and with such urgency that my cousin forced me to arrive without having partaken a proper breakfast."

Elizabeth looked up when she felt Mr. Darcy's hand on her arm trying to get her attention. He leaned down to try and catch her eye. "I think that was my fault, Miss Bennet. I am so very sorry about that."

"Mrs. Graham, would you be able to arrange for breakfast to be sent up to my sitting room and taking care of Lady Catherine? We have a lot that needs to be discussed, and it needs to be done away from prying ears," Colonel Fitzwilliam spoke up, but Elizabeth was entranced by the warmth of Mr. Darcy's eyes. The intense concern she saw there had the power to draw her in. There was a golden halo around his pupils that glowed vibrantly against the brown of his eyes. She had never noticed it before.

"Then may I suggest you station Mr. Reeves at the open door, for Miss Bennet's sake? We do not need you to be adding to the gossip." The stern but maternal voice of Mrs. Graham allowed Elizabeth to look away. She looked over and saw that Mrs. Graham had an amused glimmer in her eyes. She had caught her. Elizabeth had always liked Mrs. Graham—she was a widow who never had any children of her own and was very maternal to everyone to make up for it. She also could keep her head in a crisis which would serve them well today.

Nodding his head, Darcy grinned ruefully. "Thank you for the advice, Mrs. Graham. I will speak with Reeves on our way up. Can you be sure to send plenty of coffee? I think we will need it."

"Yes, I will make sure. Though it might be a few minutes, I will make sure we brew some fresh. If you will excuse me, I have Beth waiting in the hall to take my instructions. I will stay with Lady Catherine until someone comes to move her. The physician should be here soon enough. I will have her moved to her bedchamber." With that, she went to the door and began talking in hushed tones with someone on the other side of the door.

Mr. Darcy faced Elizabeth. Whatever he saw there caused his forehead to wrinkle. He almost spoke, but instead he reached up to smooth an eyebrow, and she understood that his look spoke of concern. Something about her had disturbed him on some level. Taking a breath, he finally spoke. "I hope you do not mind coming with us to go over what has occurred?"

Elizabeth attempted to reassure him with a smile, but she knew that her spirits and energy were lagging. "Well, seeing that you will have coffee, I am more than happy to comply. Regardless, I feel you should know of your aunt's last moments."

When Mrs. Graham took a step towards Lady Catherine, Colonel Fitzwilliam quickly stepped in and blocked her path. "I know your instinct would be to clean her up a bit and to have her body prepared for burial. However, we need to leave her as she is as much as possible. The physician needs to see her as she is."

"It will be as you say. I will do no harm, only sit with her quite like. She was not the easiest woman in the world, but we got on well enough," she said, smiling sadly at Lady Catherine's still form. "Everyone deserves some compassion in the end." Moving over to the body, she sat down next to her, unconcerned with what it might do to her dress.

They left the room in silence, with the colonel in the lead. As Elizabeth had never been in the family wing, she was glad she had someone to follow. Rosings was a warren of hallways and turns and she had gotten turned around more than once on visits. After traversing a staircase and several long hallways, they reached a door that Mr. Darcy went through without knocking. Elizabeth could hear him speaking with someone in hushed tones.

Mr. Darcy came out of the room with someone in tow. He was slender and maybe ten years older than Darcy himself. Elizabeth did not know what it was about the man that made her think he was jolly, but she couldn't shake the notion. She was pulled away from her analysis by Mr. Darcy as he spoke.

"Miss Bennet, this is my valet, Reeves. If you are ever in need of me, he generally has the ability to find me." Reeves smiled warmly at Elizabeth.

"Mr. Reeves, you must have some time of it trying to keep up with Mr. Darcy," said Elizabeth.

"You really have no idea of it, ma'am. Though he gave me permission to take a frying pan to him only this morning. So that is something, at least." Though most of Reeves's face was deadpan, his eyes gave the clue of his joke and Elizabeth confirmed he was in fact jolly.

Once again, the group began moving down the hallway, but they stopped a few doors down. Mr. Darcy gestured as she preceded them into the room. It was a very masculine room, with lots of leather and polished wood. It suited the cousins well enough, she assumed.

"Please take a seat, Miss Bennet. I can only imagine how harrowing your morning has been." Mr. Darcy gestured widely, encouraging her to choose any of the chairs.

Looking around, Elizabeth spotted a plush chair next to a small table that appealed to her somehow. It was smaller, not as tall or imposing as some of the other chairs. Besides, she could put her breakfast and cup on the table as needed. Sitting down, she spoke up once she had straightened her skirt. "Where would you like me to begin?"

"My aunt summoned you quite early." Elizabeth was unsurprised when Colonel Fitzwilliam took the lead. It was not that Mr. Darcy was unintelligent, but the colonel would have more experience directing people in times of crises. It would be second nature to him.

"Yes, my cousin was quite put out when he received the message from his revered patroness. He at first wanted me to leave immediately but was convinced eventually that I should have five minutes to change out of my nightclothes. We came here straight away, and he bowed his head in shame while making his plea, leaving with disappointment when he was dismissed." Elizabeth rolled her eyes, thinking of the sight of her cousin's intense, illogical attitude.

"And so he left you alone in the receiving room with Lady Catherine?" Colonel Fitzwilliam prompted.

The memories flooded back, and Elizabeth found herself nodding her head as she recalled the moments that somehow had already felt like a lifetime ago. It felt a world away. She had her preconceptions irrevocably altered. Those about Mr. Darcy and his opinion of her had shifted, and her view of Lady Catherine had changed as well. It had changed her when Lady Catherine died. "Yes, at first I did not notice she was unwell. There was a lot of talk about my behavior and dangling after her nephew that distracted me from it."

Standing up from his chair, Mr. Darcy paced. Then, turning, he looked at her, upset. "I must apologize again for putting you in such an awkward position. It is entirely my fault that you had to go through the experience."

"Darcy, sit down. You can blame yourself to your heart's content after we discuss our aunt's untimely demise. I will give Miss Bennet free rein to rake you over the coals once her story is complete, and we have come up with a plan of attack."

Darcy went back to his seat, looking like a chastised child. Elizabeth fought her inclination to laugh at the cousins. This was not a side of them that she had seen before, and it reminded her of how she was with her sisters. Closing her eyes, she tried to remember what had happened and in what order. "I realized that something was very wrong when she tried to gesture with her cane. She dropped it and her hand was shaking."

Chapter Four

To Want to Punch a Rector

DARCY HAD A HARD time believing how the morning had preceded. So much had happened, and he was sitting here watching Miss Bennet sip at her coffee in obvious bliss, her eyes closed as she savored the hot brew. She still took it with cream and sugar, though less sugar than was common. He had watched her eyes widen in surprise as he made her the cup when it had arrived. She truly did not know how much he had watched her when she was staying at Netherfield.

Her hair was coming out of its hasty knot, and she looked worn. His desire to care for her was almost overwhelming. "Miss Bennet, I know you have had a dreadful morning. Mrs. Graham has sent up some of her ginger cake and hot rolls with butter. Please allow me to get you some of each."

His comment stirred her from her pondering, and she opened her eyes in response. "That would be delightful. I am partial to bread and cake of all sorts."

Picking up a plate to put together some nourishment for Miss Bennet, Darcy looked at his cousin and wondered what he was thinking. Miss Bennet had described a very disturbing scene of his aunt's last minutes. She had quickly disregarded his aunt's comments about him and all mention of her famous temper. He knew he would talk to her about it in more detail later, but for the moment, he was concerned about what was going through his cousin's head. Taking the plate to Miss Bennet, he sat in the chair near her before questioning his cousin. "Theodore, what are you pondering over there so seriously?"

"Aunt Catherine spoke of being ill since at least Wednesday. Miss Bennet saw she was shaking and her skin had a sickly color. She had a trail of drool and foam dripping from the corner of her mouth. It is more than likely that she was exposed to something that was harmful to her. The question was how? Or where was she exposed? And most important, was it intentional?" Theodore's hands were steepled as he concentrated, staring off into the distance.

"When do you suppose the physician will be here to see her?" Miss Bennet spoke up between bites of a well-buttered roll.

Darcy calculated how long it might take for the man to arrive. "It should not be so very long, unless he was away on something like a difficult birth."

Pausing to take another sip of her coffee, Miss Bennet hesitated, pondering something before she spoke up again. "Do you think I should stay here until he arrives, or should I go back to the parsonage? I am slightly worried about how Charlotte is managing Mr. Collins. He was rather upset when Lady Catherine dismissed him."

Theodore shook his head in response and spoke. "No, I think it would make sense for you to return to the parsonage. If more questions arise, you are close enough that it should be no trouble to come to you."

Darcy opened his mouth to say something, then closed it and looked out the door at Reeves's shoulder. He cleared his throat before trying again to speak, his words coming out in a rush. "Would you permit me to accompany you back to the parsonage? I can arrange for one of the maids to accompany us."

"Yes, I think that would be a good idea. I rather think that we need to speak of some things." Miss Bennet looked up from the remains of her breakfast. She sat fidgeting with the last of her roll, shredding it into tiny bits.

"Have you had your fill, Miss Bennet? There is more of everything."

"No, I have had enough. The ginger cake was splendid. I shall have to compliment Mrs. Cooper."

Darcy found himself reacting to her comment. He had been coming to Rosings his whole life and had never thought to inquire after people below stairs that he did not have direct contact with. Miss Bennet had visited once for only a couple of weeks and knew more than he did. "You know the cook?"

"Yes, she is a charming woman. Her daughter is a lady's maid in Bath." Her expression turned dark, and Darcy knew he had somehow misspoken. She stood, putting her plate on the table beside her chair and shook out her dress slightly. Miss Bennet's glance at the door told him that she was ready to return to the parsonage, and the shape of her shoulders told him he would be apologizing most of the way there.

Glancing at his cousin, Darcy raised his eyebrows in a plea for assistance, practically begging him to help salvage something. "Miss

Bennet, do you mind waiting in the hall with Reeves for a moment? Before he takes you on your way, I wanted to have a quick chat with my cousin, who tends to be a bit awkward," Theodore piped up.

"Not at all." With a brief smile at Theodore, she hastened from the room.

"You are a blithering idiot. While I know you were merely surprised that she knew the cook, it sounded like you thought the cook was beneath your notice. Miss Bennet is the type of woman who tries to notice everyone." Theodore lectured but kept his voice low so as to not let Miss Bennet overhear.

Head in his hands, Darcy ran his fingers through his hair, pulling at it in frustration before responding. "Yes, I know, I know. I did not mean it that way. I am a fool and what is worse, I have eaten here hundreds of times and I know nothing of the cook. It never occurred to me to inquire."

"Yes, but you know all of your staff at Pemberley and your house in town. You make it a point to see to everyone's needs, from the butler to the scullery maid. Show her that man. The man that you are when you are not nervous and accidentally insulting people." Theodore shook his head. Had the day not been so dire, Darcy knew he would be laughing at him.

Looking at his cousin's weary face, he remembered all the things that he had to arrange when his father died and felt guilty that he was leaving it to him. Darcy forced his mind to the bigger problem at hand. "Do you need me to see to anything? I know that our aunt's death will mean we must be at the duty of making arrangements for many things."

Theodore leaned back in his armchair and crossed his legs at the ankle. It was a posture Darcy was familiar with; he sat like that when he was coming up with a plan of attack. Normally, he lost the chess match when Theodore sat like that. "I am going to speak with the staff and set my batman on looking out for rumors. I might have him pay special interest to Mrs. Stevenson. There are also letters to write. I must let father know."

"Do you suspect Mrs. Stevenson of doing Aunt Catherine harm?" Worry creased Darcy's brow.

"I did not intend to imply it in the way you understood it. It is simply that I could not help but feel uneasy about her inconsistent behavior today. I feel she could get up to mischief is all. See to your lady love, and I will start on things here. Do not think you will avoid helping me with all the letters," Theodore said with a pointed look. "You know you have a better hand than me at writing. You will do your fair share. More than if I have any say."

"Yes, I will once I return." Darcy saluted Theodore, took a deep breath, and headed towards Miss Bennet, ready to face her ire.

***

"I KNOW I HAVE said it before, but I cannot but apologize for everything." Darcy held his hat in his hands, worrying the brim and most likely ruining it. They had made their way out of Rosings and to the path before he begun to speak.

Miss Bennet stared at him for a long time, as if weighing his heart and intentions. "You have apologized enough. I will accept your apology for all of your past errors against me going all the way back to your insult at the assembly in Meryton. But only if you try to do better. I cannot ask for perfection from anyone, but I can ask you to try." When Elizabeth moved to push her hair back from her face, Darcy's fingers twitched with the desire to do it himself.

Shaking his head as if to clear it, he tried to focus on what was important in her words and not on the way her hair continued to rest against the curve of her cheek. "The Meryton assembly? I did not think we spoke there."

Elizabeth's nose wrinkled at his comment. She looked him directly in the eye and said, "No, we did not speak, but you spoke of me, loud enough for myself and several of the town's best gossips to hear. '*She is tolerable, but not handsome enough to tempt me, and I am in no humor at present to give consequence to young ladies who are slighted by other men.*' You can imagine that I was rather put out to be spoken of so."

"I am so—"

Holding her hand up, she silenced Darcy with a hard look. "Not going to finish that sentence! Any more and you will begin to remind me of my blathering cousin. I have said you are forgiven. While we are discussing apologies, I too must apologize. Your comment struck a nerve, and I found myself constantly thinking about it and interpreting your actions in light of it. My words and feelings towards you have been unkind, and for that, I apologize."

As she apologized, he stood there, stunned and unable to respond. Although Elizabeth never hurt him, her concern showed her empathy and compassion towards him. He had believed himself in love, but seeing what he did not know about her left him feeling small and unequal to the woman that she was. It left him wanting to do better, to be better. "I never expected an apology from you for your behavior. Upon reflection, I understand your actions were reasonable, and my mistakes led you to those conclusions. If you want to hear me, say I forgive you, I do. Please know that I was not upset by your actions."

They walked on in silence for some time before they came across a pretty little clearing in the garden and, as if by unspoken agreement, they stopped to take in its serenity. Maybe they both needed the calmness of the leaves, resulting in the breeze and twittering of birds. After a morning of chaos, it was nice to just be.

"What did my aunt say to you, Miss Bennet? Before everything else, what did she say?" Scuffing the ground with his boot, Darcy tried to imagine all that could have been said by his aunt and could only feel embarrassed.

Elizabeth's eyes turned misty while contemplating the conversation with his aunt. As he suspected, what he half-guessed would happen, happened. She smiled. "She said a great many things that confused me until she clarified that at the root of her concerns was the fact that she was of the opinion that you loved me. Loved me so much, in fact, that you had been overheard practicing a proposal. She also called you a fool."

Darcy found himself smiling as well. "She always was one for strong opinions."

"She appeared very sure of your feelings. In fact, she compared your behavior to that of your father when he was courting your mother. Was she wrong to think you cared for me?" Darcy considered Miss Bennet's pensive appearance. She was uncertain in a way that reminded him of his sister. Elizabeth was looking off into the distance as if considering the scenery, but he was sure that, in reality, she was becoming lost in her thoughts. Despite her normally brave demeanor, he couldn't help but notice how uncertain she was when it came to understanding his emotions.

Darcy tucked the information about his parents away for later. Instead, he faced the now and the fact that Miss Bennet was asking him about his love for her. He wondered to himself about the possibility that she was not happy about his feelings. "She was not wrong. Does it offend you to hear it confirmed?"

Shaking her head, she continued, her expression bemused. "I am not offended, merely astonished. I thought you disliked me and found me wanting."

"I would never find you wanting, it was only—"

"Yes, it is the 'only' that I am concerned with. I know that my family is not perfect. Their actions are sometimes something even I disprove of but realize those are people I love." Elizabeth's soft voice had an edge of steel he had only ever heard from Theodore.

Pausing on the path, he considered her words. What would he do if someone criticized his family for their behavior? His cousin Anne was different in a way that he was unable to explain and yet he loved her like a little sister, despite her being older than himself. His cousin Titus, the viscount, had a reputation for being less than honorable due to his love for gambling and keeping mistresses. That his uncle the earl was as top lofty as could be could not be disputed.

Yet they were his family, and he would not hear them spoken against. Did their higher position in society mean that they should not be criticized? No, his heart told him. His father had always told him that having a title or property did not mean you could behave as you wanted, it meant that you should be better. If someone claimed his friendship but sneered at his family, he would cut them in the street. And he was doing that to Miss Bennet and her family. His father would be ashamed of him and his behavior.

Turning back to Miss Bennet's waiting face, he let his mask slip if only a little, allowing her to see the depth of his contrition. "You are correct. I can only say it is something that I will endeavor to work on. It was not something about myself that I recognized until now."

"I suppose as long as you are trying, you are moving in the right direction," Elizabeth said, not unkindly. As she progressed down the path, she looked over her shoulder to ensure he was following her.

"I must warn you of my propensity to struggle with social situations. I know I am often called proud, and I admit that I can be, but I am also uncertain, and I know that I say the wrong things more than I ought."

Miss Bennet appeared to take the information in and pondered it momentarily. "I will keep that in mind. What would you do if I called you out when your efforts were slipping?"

"I would bluster, but that would be my frustration with myself, not with you. If I am being truthful, I think I will need the reminders on occasion." Darcy watched Elizabeth walk in front of him. He had enjoyed the walks that he had had with Miss Bennet in the past, but despite the unease of the day and subject, he was realizing how much he loved actually talking with her. It was ever so much better than his earlier monosyllabic responses and quiet interludes.

"Then I will endeavor to keep you on your best behavior." Darcy could hear the laugh in her voice.

Deciding to be bold, Darcy spoke the question that had been with him since Theodore had laughed himself out of his chair. "What would you have said if I had proposed?"

Looking away, Elizabeth spoke solemnly, "It would not have been a favorable reply."

"That is what my cousin told me. How would you like to proceed from here?" He spoke not of the physical path that they were taking, but how their relationship would change. His feelings had not changed on that day, though he hoped hers might shift in a more favorable direction.

"Well, perhaps we will not be the adversaries I considered us to be at one time. Instead, we can be on friendly terms and see how things proceed from there?"

"That is fair enough, and a much better prospect than yesterday," Darcy spoke, his voice subdued.

Turning to him, she reminded him of all the ground he needed to make up and how much he had bungled things with the woman he cared for. "I still have several questions I want answered, Mr. Darcy, but I do not have the fortitude for them today. I only want to rest for a time."

Understanding her needs, Darcy nodded in agreement, silently promising to do everything in his power to see that her needs were met. "I have a proposal, not one with matrimony as the goal but of our mutual understanding of each other. I find myself full of questions for you as well. What say you to a daily trade of questions? We speak daily and exchange questions to endeavor to understand one another and see about developing a friendship."

"I find that prospect tolerable." Elizabeth did not manage to keep a straight face and actually laughed when Darcy's expression turned to shock.

Laughing as well, he found he needed some gaiety. Shaking his head, he sighed. "You will keep me on my toes, Miss Bennet. I suggest you rest and have some tea. Maybe let Mrs. Collins pamper you, and we will get our answers eventually. I would never want to push you after a morning like this."

Turning the last corner to the parsonage, Elizabeth abruptly stopped. He looked to where her gaze rested and fury filled his veins when he saw what had caused her to halt her progress. There, in front of the parsonage in the mud, were piles of clothes and possessions. He could only assume that it was all her things and someone had trampled them into the ground. That fool of a parson had thrown her things from the house, not even bothering to put them in her trunk.

Darcy had spent his fair share of time at Gentleman Jack's and learned to excel at fisticuffs but had never felt the need to use his skill outside of the ring before. He had never imagined wanting to punch a rector or that a rector could possibly anger him so, but Mr. Collins had found a way.

Chapter Five
Dealing with a Fool Man's Tantrum

Elizabeth stopped. She felt as if she had been holding on to everything with the hope of tea and maybe a nap to regain her equilibrium. Despite her hopes, she instinctively knew that it was not going to happen as she rounded the last curve. The tears dripping down her face went unnoticed as she went to gather her things from the mud. Falling to her knees, she tried to gather some of her belongings. Her lovely pink gown that Jane had painstakingly embroidered at the neck and cuffs lay splattered with mud and it was next to the book her father had given her of Aesop's Fables. Trying to wipe at the cover of the book with her sleeve, she found herself sobbing and cradling the book to her chest. The day had been too much. It was all too much.

Behind her, she eventually heard whispering between Mr. Darcy and the maid that had quietly followed them all the way from Rosings. The girl seemed to move off. Noticing Mr. Darcy's presence beside her, she dragged her gaze up into the weight of his own. Kneeling in the muck beside her, he waited for her to compose herself.

There was fury in his gaze. White hot rage brewing in the normally calm visage. It did not intimidate her. Seeing his anger somehow gave her strength. His anger was on her behalf and was directed towards her cousin. No one else would have done such a thing, but Mr. Collins. She lamented the fate of Longbourn at that moment. Any man who cast a relation out as he had done was undeserving of such an inheritance.

"Miss Bennet, what can I do? What do you need right now?" His words were soft despite his anger, or maybe because of it.

"I need to gather my things. Maybe some of it can be salvaged."

Nodding in acknowledgement, he moved to gather some of her books. His chocolate eyes, full of a bitter determination, met hers as he asked, "Do you wish for me to speak with your cousin?" It appeared as if he wished to speak to him with more than words and Elizabeth found herself surprised that she would be all right with that outcome. She had always been against using violence to solve problems, even if it was for her own benefit. Normally, she believed one should rise above the inclination to violence and settle their differences in discourse. Today had been too much, and her normal inclination for peace, for bravery, had washed away with her tears.

"Not now. I do not have the strength for it at the moment."

"Then let us get your things gathered. I have sent Mary to acquire a basket to put your belongings in."

Once Mary returned, things moved swiftly. She had not brought so very much with her to the parsonage. She knew she would be staying with s friends and had not sought to impress anyone with her wardrobe. Looking at her clothes, all dirty and mud covered, she realized she would impress even fewer people now with her practically ruined wardrobe. She despaired at ever getting it all clean.

"Do not fret so, Miss Bennet. The laundress is a right wiz at getting things clean. We will have you set to rights in no time," Mary spoke up in earnest. Her face illustrated her concern even though, like everyone, she was dirty from gathering Elizabeth's things from the ground.

"Thank you, Mary," Elizabeth spoke softly, feeling a knot in her throat at being treated so kindly after such a bad day.

A large hand filled her field of vision, and she looked up at Mr. Darcy. He reached out to help her, and she felt the mud squishing between her fingers as she tried to get up. "Come, Miss Bennet. I will see you settled safely at Rosings and if we have missed anything, I will gather it myself when I return to speak with your cousin." She could tell he was trying to be careful with her, as if she might shatter, or worse, maybe burst into another bout of tears. She was torn between feeling exposed and grateful that he understood her emotional state so well.

Taking his hand, she allowed him to help her to her feet. Taking a moment to glance around for anything vital she might have missed, Elizabeth spotted movement in the window. The woman who she had always called her friend stood there watching, eyes moist. She might have whispered that she was sorry, but Elizabeth was certainly too far to hear. Then the curtain closed, and Elizabeth felt as if it was a door closing on a very long friendship.

"Let us be gone from here." Elizabeth heard an emptiness in her voice, as if it was just a shell of her true self.

"Yes." Elizabeth suspected from Mr. Darcy's tone of voice that he might have seen Charlotte close the curtain as well. His ridged jaw line and clipped voice confirmed his opinion of the Collinses now. Though, to be fair, they were both quite out of her own charity. She would have to do a lot of praying about forgiveness in order to overcome this day.

The procession back to Rosings was mostly silent. Elizabeth had passed the point of endurance and Mr. Darcy obviously was able to sense it. He had offered her his arm, and she leaned on him, not out of mere formality but in genuine need of support. As Elizabeth made her way to Rosings, she couldn't help but feel as though time was passing faster than usual. She found herself arriving at Rosings sooner than she expected, and even the walk through the garden felt shorter. Once they made it to the building, she found herself guided to a chair near the housekeeper's office. She found little ability to concentrate on the whispered voices between Mrs. Graham and Mr. Darcy. Her mind was shrouded in a gray, heavy fog of emotions, making it hard to navigate through her thoughts.

"Oh, you poor dear, look at you. I have words I would wish to say about Mr. Collins, but I won't. I will tell you he might just be finding all his meals cold when he visits. You are a dear girl, Miss Bennet, and he is a fool who thinks more of himself than he should. I will say no more on the matter. What you need is some sweet tea and a hot bath." Mrs. Graham tsked over Elizabeth's state in a way that she found familiar. Maybe all maternal women clucked over their charges in the same way. Elizabeth wondered idly if there was a lesson you took at some point. Maybe there was a book?

Shaking her head to clear it of the lingering fog, Elizabeth fought to bring herself out of the emotional mire she was stuck in. Taking a deep breath, she looked up into Mrs. Graham's smiling eyes. "You are too kind, Mrs. Graham. I would love both."

Mrs. Graham clucked over her, smoothing her hair where it was coming more and more undone. "And so, you shall have it. I will get you set to rights in no time. What with your experience this morning and then dealing with that fool man's tantrum, you deserve a bit of pampering. Now you be about your business, Mr. Darcy. She will be well looked after. I know you will have a hundred things to see to caring for your aunt's passing."

Elizabeth looked up, startled to realize that Mr. Darcy had been standing there without her notice. The look on his face was more powerful than any of the times that she had caught him staring before. She was amazed at how wrong she had been in thinking he disliked her. When he looked at her, his expression conveyed a tenderness that was matched only by his profound concern. He had a restlessness about him that suggested he wanted to take action, and he appeared to be in search of something to do. "Mrs. Graham is right, Mr. Darcy. I am well in hand, and you have many things to see to. We can speak later. There is nothing you can do for me right now that a hot bath and some sweet tea will not fix."

Hearing her comment, he approached her and took her hand and, even though it was still rather dirty, he kissed the back of it and gave her a very solemn bow before turning to go. Elizabeth watched him walk away, feeling a fission of sensations run up her arm. Halfway down the hallway, he turned to look back over his shoulder, as if to check that she was still there and still well. His actions had a profound effect on her, causing her to feel startled and unsure.

Mrs. Graham smiled broadly at the display. "You have certainly made a conquest in him, my dear. Let's get you up. I hope you do not mind using the bathing room we have for the servants. You do not have a room yet and it would be quicker and the water hotter. Or do you wish to wait?"

"I think that quicker sounds fine to me. I feel filthy. Only I have nothing decent to change into. All of my other things were in the mud." Looking down at her dress, Elizabeth took in how much mud was on her dress in dismay.

Putting her arm around Elizabeth's shoulders, Mrs. Graham guided her through the labyrinth of corridors. "I will find something that you can wear by the time you are washed up. In fact, there is an entire trunk of clothes that were sent over for Anne from Lady Matlock a month or so ago. Lady Catherine found them to be, in her words, 'indecent' and refused to allow Anne to wear them. They are of the latest style from London, but Lady Catherine was very much in preference of the older styles, as you might have noticed. As they did not alter the dresses to fit Anne, they should do very well for you."

"Oh, I need nothing so very grand. I would not wish to overstep." Elizabeth did not feel the need to present herself in high fashion, especially in a house entering mourning.

"I found the dresses to be quite lovely and considered it a pity that they have stayed in the trunk unused." Mrs. Graham continued to lead her and stopped at an unassuming door. Entering, Elizabeth found a small, yet inviting room with a tub being filled by a young maid and a small table and chair in the corner that had a tea service waiting for her. Mrs. Graham was both kind and highly efficient.

"Well, I suppose it would hurt nothing. Maybe you could find something in more subdued colors in respect to Lady Catherine's passing." Sitting down at the table, Elizabeth let out a sigh of relief, grateful for the considerate treatment she was receiving from someone after experiencing the opposite from those she trusted.

Mrs. Graham poured her a cup of tea and added a liberal amount of sugar. "You get this down you before you do anything else. I have Hattie helping you. I am going to get you something to change into." With a warm smile and a swish of skirts, she left the room.

Elizabeth took a sip of tea and grimaced. She was not partial to very sweet things. Looking into the cup, she gathered her courage to drink down the rest. If Mrs. Graham was anything like Mrs. Hill, she would know by some mystical ability if she did not drink it.

"My momma always said sweat tea was good for bad times, but I never liked it any better than you do." A small voice came from across the room and Elizabeth looked up from her tea ponderings.

Now that Elizabeth was looking, she realized that the young maid was little more than a girl. She was all large gray eyes and freckles in an elfin face. Her maid uniform was well kempt, though damp with humidity from pouring the hot water into the tub. Smiling at the obviously hard-working young maid, she responded kindly. "I think your mother and my mother must have heard the same thing somewhere. She said that to me all the time as a child. Would you be Hattie?"

Nodding her head, Hattie performed a credible curtsy. "Yes, Miss, I am to help you with whatever you need."

"Well, I am Elizabeth. Thank you for helping me today. As soon as I am done with this sweet concoction, I would love to get out of these filthy clothes and get clean." Elizabeth attempted to drink down the rest of the tea with dignity but feared that she had failed when Hattie giggled behind her hand.

Going over to the tub, Hattie fiddled with the things around it. Reaching into a chest, she pulled out a large towel and a chunk of soap and put them on a low stool. "The water is nice and warm, and I can open up the screen to give you a speck of privacy. Did you want to wash your hair?"

Stepping out of her dirty dress, Elizabeth stood in her camise. The feeling of her hair on her shoulders reminded her that her hair was coming loose. "No, it is not dirty and would take forever to dry. I will need to make sure I put it up, but I appear to have lost some of my hairpins. Do you know of any extra that I could borrow?"

Reaching into her pocket, Hattie pulled out a handful of pins, a shy smile on her face. "My hair is all ways coming free of its pins, so I carry extra with me. They are not special like you are probably used to, but you can have 'em."

"Oh, you are so sweet to offer. I will get them back to you as soon as I am done." Reaching up, Elizabeth pulled the pins that remained in her hair loose and shook her head slightly. Her hair came tumbling down in a cascade of exuberant curls. Twisting it up and securing it with the borrowed pins, she made sure her hair would be dry after she bathed the morning's grime away.

"Your hair is so beautiful, miss. My hair never looks like that when I pin it up, no matter how hard I try." Her wheat-colored hair was definitely more straight than curly. Elizabeth understood from helping her sisters that it could be difficult to get to stay up.

"Thank you, but curly hair can be its own handful too, you know. It is a disaster to brush," Elizabeth spoke while helping the girl to open the screen. When Elizabeth was finally concealed, she wasted no time undressing before sinking into the hot water. She could feel her muscles beginning to relax with each inch she sank.

"You just stay there and soak. I'm not sure what happened, but judging by the state of your poor dress, your morning has been quite rough," Hattie said quietly from the other side of the screen. "I will see to your dress while you relax. Mrs. Graham said that she would be back with something for you to wear in a bit."

As Elizabeth sank into the deep, inviting tub, she couldn't help but feel grateful for the unexpected indulgence. Sliding down far enough to submerge most of herself and lean her head against the back of the rim, she contemplated the morning. She had forced herself to act when she had to, but now that she had the time, she really needed to allow herself to think properly about the events that had taken place. So much had transpired and being the woman that she was, she wanted to sort it out in an orderly fashion.

Lady Catherine had died. That was something significant that would most likely impact the rest of her stay at Rosings. The Lady's last minutes had surprised her. You never knew what motivated a person and Elizabeth had assumed incorrectly about Lady Catherine. She had believed that Lady Catherine was full of herself and her position, and maybe she had been, but she had also loved her daughter a great deal. It looked like most of her concern was on providing for her daughter. Elizabeth decided that despite her faults, she could no longer judge the woman harshly. In the end, she had simply been a mother who worried for her daughter and tried to do what she could for her.

Then there was Miss Anne de Bourgh, who on further contemplation was not quite as she should be. Elizabeth could not put her finger on what it was, but something was concerning. Lady Catherine had said that as a girl she had been happy and healthy until there was an illness. What had gone wrong to have her so altered? Elizabeth could appreciate Lady Catherine's desperation to protect her daughter, however forcing her to marry Mr. Darcy would have been cruel to both of them.

Lastly, Elizabeth considered Mr. Darcy. If she was honest with herself, she had to admit that he was quite handsome. Before he had opened his mouth and insulted her, she had heard more than one voice stating that he was a fine figure of a man. She quite preferred his dark visage to Mr. Bingley's lighter one. Shaking her head and sloshing the water slightly, Elizabeth forced her mind beyond the physical and to the genuine matter at hand. Apparently, he was in love with her.

She had never once guessed as much, though she had more than one person suggest as much. Did the fact that knowing his feelings change her own feelings? That was a possibility. Knowing that he was not looking to find fault with her had completely changed the way she reacted to him and his comments. If she viewed him as having a genuine affection for her, she could reinterpret his comments in a more positive light. She had often assumed that he was speaking to her mockingly, but if you took his true feelings into account, that would not have been the case. He could have been trying to compliment her, albeit in a very clumsy fashion.

But how did she wish to proceed? She still suspected that he had separated her sister from Mr. Bingley. There was also his ill treatment of Mr. Wickham. How could that be explained away? She had many questions now that she realized she had not been sketching his character as accurately as she had assumed. Remembering his request, Elizabeth smiled. He obviously had questions as well. She would have to wait and see and form new, more accurate judgments. Had she not always found it more accurate to read a book, even if it was hard to understand, than to read a summary by someone else? The analogy did not quite match, but Elizabeth found it adequate to her pondering.

The sound of the door opening caused Elizabeth to freeze. Maybe it was Mrs. Graham, but maybe it wasn't, and she was certainly not in the best position laying naked in a tub.

"Hattie, you slovenly girl, sitting here when there is work to be done." Elizabeth recognized Mrs. Stevenson's voice and frowned.

"No, miss, I—"

"No, nothing! News of Miss Bennet's arrival at Rosings has reached my ears. Apparently, she will stay here for some duration. I want to avoid giving her the impression that she is better than others, and Miss Anne de Bourgh shares this sentiment. I want you to put her in the green room on the west wing."

"That room is for visiting ladies' maids, not ladies like Miss Bennet," came a timid reply.

"It is Miss de Bourgh's wish. With her mother gone, she is the mistress of this household. Do you want to go against her? I know you have nowhere else to go if we turn you out without reference. Besides, that woman may very well have killed Lady Catherine, she deserves no better. You will do as I say, or you will be out on the streets."

"Yes, miss." Hattie's response was even more subdued this time and Elizabeth could feel her eyes narrow. That was no way to treat the staff. Her opinion of the woman was plummeting.

The door slammed and Elizabeth decided it was time for her to get herself clean and out of the tub. If there was going to be a confrontation, she wanted to do it with clothes on. Quickly scrubbing herself, Elizabeth called out to Hattie. "Hattie, are you all right? Mrs. Stevenson was rather rude. Is she always like that?"

"Yes, she is a right nasty one. I know we should not put you in that room, but like she said, I have no means of going against her. I am sorry."

Elizabeth was put out at Mrs. Stevenson for her cruel treatment of the girl. She knew that her choice of room was some kind of retribution for earlier. It was certainly not Hattie's fault. "Never you mind, I can sleep there as well as I could sleep anywhere, I would guess. I do not want you to feel uneasy about it. She said you have nowhere to go. What about your family? You are very young to be very far from them."

"They all died from a fever this winter. I was the only one left, but Uncle Gregory works here as a footman, and he asked Mrs. Graham to take me on as a chambermaid. He looks out for me." Her voice was strained, and Elizabeth shook her head in sympathy at the circumstance of the sweet girl.

"I am so sorry that you lost your family, Hattie. You have my condolences."

"Thank you, miss, they were a wonderful family. Momma and Da loved each other so very much. I think neither of them would have been happy to be without the other." Elizabeth could not see the girl but could picture a wobbly smile from the tone of voice.

Carefully getting out of the tub, Elizabeth grabbed the towel and dried off. Wrapping it around herself, she picked her camise up from the stool and inspected it. It was mostly clean, and Elizabeth felt it was better than nothing. After dressing, she came out from behind the screen. She spotted Hattie sitting at the table with her soiled dress in hand, trying to blot the mud off.

"Thank you for working on my dress, Hattie." Elizabeth reached over and poured herself another cup of tea from the still warm pot.

Shaking her head, Hattie smiled at her. "It isn't nothing. I help in the laundry sometimes."

They spoke for some minutes, talking about anything and everything that came to mind while Elizabeth sipped at the tea. She enjoyed the normalness of talking and drinking tea, and found she was fond of the cheerful girl, and they got on well. She did not react at all to Mrs. Stevenson's claim that Elizabeth had murdered Lady Catherine. Hattie's only response when Elizabeth had asked about it was to say that Mrs. Stevenson was a viper who enjoyed talking nonsense, and Elizabeth should not pay her any mind.

Once again, the door opened, only this time Mrs. Graham entered the room, her arms full of dresses. Seeing Elizabeth clean and dry with a steaming cup of tea in hand brought an enormous smile to her face. "There now, I am sure you feel much better after a hot bath and some tea. I have brought you a dress, but I am wondering if you would prefer the dressing gown I brought as well. Maybe you would like a brief nap before dinner tonight?"

"A nap sounds splendid. I am never this tired, even after one of my long walks in the country." Taking the dressing gown, Elizabeth slipped it on over her chemise and tied it at the waist. A light peach. It was as lovely as Mrs. Graham had claimed.

Nodding her head, Mrs. Graham smiled at Elizabeth in approval. The peach color brought the color out in her cheeks. "It hits one like that sometimes, after a shock. Here, take this gown for later and I brought you some clean slippers."

"Mrs. Graham, Mrs. Stevenson demanded that I put her in the green room in the west wing. She said that it was Miss de Bourgh's wish," Hattie spoke up from her spot behind Elizabeth.

"Then we are going to have to follow her request. I am so sorry about this, Miss Bennet. I had planned on having you put in the peacock room near the family wing, but I guess we will have to follow Mrs. Stevenson's dictates for now." Shaking her head, Mrs. Graham folded the rest of the clothes in her arms into a neat bundle and placed it on the chair Elizabeth had just vacated. "Let me see Miss Bennet's dress, Hattie. It looks like you have done well, but it still needs to be laundered. I will take this and see about having the rest of your belongings cleaned and sent to your room. Hattie, please take Miss Bennet to the green room and check it over to see if she needs anything while staying here."

"Yes, Mrs. Graham." Hattie leaned over to gather the clothes on the chair and moved over to the door.

Going to the door, Elizabeth followed her out, eager to take a moment to lie down. She tried to take note of the various turns of their winding path but found her powers of observation waning along with her energy. Eventually, Elizabeth made it to the room and in the bed that called to her. Closing her eyes, she let herself rest.

Chapter Six
Resisting the Urge to Bludgeon Mr. Collins

Darcy's steps reverberated down the hall as he stomped his way to where his cousin was. The intensity of his anger resonated throughout his entire body, from his head to his fingertips. The feeling was foreign to him and left him uneasy. He couldn't help but draw parallels between this and when he discovered Wickham's plan to elope with his sister, but this felt even more personal.

The door to his cousin's sitting room flew open with a loud bang as he barged in. "Give me something to do, Theodore, before I go bludgeon Miss Bennet's preposterous cousin."

Startled, Theodore looked up and surveyed his cousin's disgruntled and disheveled state. "Good God, man, what happened on the way to the parsonage?"

"We made it to the parsonage only to find that her cousin had thrown all of Miss Bennet's possessions outside into the mud. The look on her face, Theo, was almost more than I could bear. She cried." Darcy paced around the room, prowling like a caged panther, unable to chase his prey.

Theodore turned from his spot at the desk to watch Darcy roam. "That little worm needs to be stomped. Why are you hesitating?"

"Though I will confront him eventually, I feel like I could seriously hurt him right now and I want to be more in control of myself before I face him." Darcy did not want to risk permanently hurting the man. He knew Miss Bennet would not approve of it, even with how badly he had treated her.

"Well, the physician is yet to arrive. I have written to my father and sent it off. He should be here soon enough. We need to plan for the funeral, but I feel that buffoon of a rector should not receive that honor." Theodore fiddled with a stack of papers on the desk.

"No, certainly not." Darcy was adamant. If he had to listen to that man going on and on about his aunt, he might march right up to the pulpit and sock him in the jaw.

Putting the paper in his hands down, Theodore pointed out a few possibilities to his cousin. "You could write a letter to the bishop asking for someone to do the funeral. Although he holds the position for life, it can be revoked if they deem him unfit. Maybe we can impress upon him that he needs to improve his behavior." Theodore paused, taking in Darcy's appearance once more. "I might suggest you go on a long hard ride on your horse, but you might just ride over to the parsonage. Before anything else, Darcy, I suggest changing out of those clothes. Losing to a well-dressed man feels particularly impressive, unlike losing to someone who looks like they just crawled through the mud."

***

Darcy was uncertain if the change of clothes and time spent writing the letter to the bishop had done much good. He had even written to Georgiana telling her of their Aunt Catherine's death. In addition, he confided in her of his intentions to court Miss Bennet. He hoped they would become good friends. Miss Bennet's strength would be good for his sister. All of his efforts to distract himself, even thinking about the dreams he had for the future, did not settle his heart.

He kept seeing Miss Bennet's tears. The anger he felt towards her cousin for bringing her to such a low point was immeasurable. His heart swelled with an intensity that he had never known, and he realized that his past notion of love was merely superficial. Initially, he was enamored with the idea of her. He saw that now. The more he questioned himself and learned about her, the more he saw the incredible depth of her character and the stronger his love became. As if what he considered to be love was a flimsy thing with no more substance than a bit of lace.

***

Riding Castan had helped somewhat more than writing the letters. He took the letters to be posted before returning to the parsonage. Taking a deep breath, he dismounted his horse.

"Wish me luck, Castan," Darcy gave him a scratch behind the ears when the giant grey beast leaned in and butted him in the chest as playful as a puppy. He was a sweet natured and obedient horse and would stay outside waiting patiently until Darcy returned, without issue. Going to the house, he knocked loudly, eager to have his say.

A smallish maid answered the door. "Yes, sir?"

"I am here to see Mr. Collins." He had his card ready to present, but it was obvious that the timid creature recognized him. Her quick, deep curtsy made Darcy wonder what Mr. Collins demanded of his wife and staff.

"Yes, Mr. Darcy. He is speaking with Mrs. Collins right now, and he is in a right bad mood. I am not sure he will be accepting callers." She stood with one arm wrapped around her middle, as if protecting herself. Biting her lip, she gazed over her shoulder into the house.

"Well, then I will simply not ask. Do not worry, I will handle him myself." Stepping past the maid, he heard yelling and followed it to what he assumed was the man's study. He stood, listening for a moment in order to gauge what he was walking in to.

"How will I ever be able to explain having allowed that hussy in my home? I will never know. I should have followed my own judgment in the matter, but I allowed you to sway me with your wiles. What a useless wife you are. You have yet to fall with child and the first guest you have invited into my home is a disgrace. I will tell you now, you will beg Lady Catherine on your knees for forgiveness. Suggesting that we bring that woman into our home is unpardonable. You will pray to God for forgiveness on the matter. Allowing her to prey on the honorable Lady Catherine's nephew while under my roof? She is no better than a common trollop!" Mr. Collin's voice projected well beyond the door. Darcy was certain the entire household could hear his triad of insults. Hearing Miss Bennet spoken of in such a derogatory manner was too much for his patience.

Upon entering the room silently, he observed Mrs. Collins sitting in a cowed position while her husband angrily paced. She noticed his entrance and looked up, startled. Her pale expression was one of shame, and Darcy was careful to note a swollen and split lip. He gave her a quick bow. She was not to blame in this scenario. There was little a woman could do against her husband and he knew it.

"Mrs. Collins, would you kindly give me a moment to speak with your husband alone?" Though he spoke to Mrs. Collins, his attention was towards her wayward and disgraceful husband.

"Yes, Mr. Darcy. Would you like me to send in tea or refreshments?" Obviously, she was attempting to be the perfect hostess to appease her husband.

"No, that will not be necessary, thank you." Though Darcy had dismissed her, she looked to her husband as if to ask permission to leave. Darcy noticed the dismissive flick of Mr. Collins's hand, finally allowing her to leave the room.

Darcy settled into the chair in front of the desk with a slouch, something he rarely did. All his years running Pemberley had served him well. The way you presented yourself to others spoke as much of what you thought of someone as your words did. He had learned long ago not to look too eager in some situations. In others, slouching made people underestimate him. In this instance, the slouch was to show his disdain for the man who felt that he controlled the situation. He also knew waiting to speak would make the fool uneasy.

Collins's pacing, which had been an example of why rotund men should not pace, eventually stopped and he settled into his chair. Unable to wait, he blurted out his concerns. "I would like to apologize for the forwardness of my houseguest. You will be pleased to know that she is no longer a guest in this home. Not even her possessions remain."

"Oh? I take it you mean Miss Bennet. Where is she now?" Darcy questioned. "I assume that as her cousin, you ensured that she was safely escorted to her nearest relatives with a maid to accompany her. They are in London, I believe."

"We are cousins in only the barest sense of the word. It is a relationship that you would have to go three generations back to find." Collins tried to brush the connection away as if it were no more matter than a speck of lint.

"That may be true, however is it not by that connection that you have the hope of inheriting her ancestral home of Longbourn?"

"Yes," came his petulant reply.

"The question remains, where is Miss Bennet?" While he knew she was securely settled at Rosings, Darcy wanted the man to admit his folly before experiencing his ire.

Collins sat straighter in his chair as if he was proud of his actions. "I do not know, and neither do I care. She acted in an ungrateful and inappropriate fashion, and I have had her things thrown in the lane."

"So you do not know where she has gone? Her father entrusted her to you, giving you the duty to protect her, but you failed to fulfill your responsibility. Are you a man of God or not? Your actions this day are decidedly unchristian. You are acting more like the Priest or the Levite than the Good Samaritan, that is for sure."

"Good Samaritan? I do not know who you mean?" The weak man's irascible reply proved just how inadequate he was as a spiritual leader.

"Then I suggest you read the gospel according to Luke. Your behavior has been completely unacceptable and goes against all moral standards." Pinching the bridge of his nose, Darcy wondered just what you had to learn to become ordained.

Ignoring the prompt to read the Bible, Mr. Collins instead attempted to point out the correctness of his actions. "Lady Catherine said I should get my household in order, and so I have. There can never be any repercussions in following her orders. She is the daughter of an Earl. She oversees Rosings. Even the Queen would do well to ask her advice." Shaking his head, Mr. Collins took on the tone of one attempting to chastise a wayward child. "You would do well to listen to her dictates. As her nephew, you should respect them as well. Your interest in such a nobody does you no favors, Mr. Darcy. It is all for the best that Cousin Elizabeth is gone, as she is nothing but a grasping trollop."

Darcy stood so fast that his chair careened to the floor behind him. In a blink, he was around the desk and looming over the fool. The man's reaction was so severe that it would have been comical if Darcy had not been so angry. He was all flailing arms, wide eyes, and wordless pleas not to hit him.

"I am a gentleman. I do not hit people without a substantial amount of provocation. You seem to lack an understanding of the level of standards I have set for myself. However, I am not sure you understand the gravity of your errors." Darcy grabbed at the fraying edges of his control. Taking a breath, he pushed it through pursed lips, trying to take the edge off his aggression towards the imbecile.

"Why are you so upset? She is a no one, from nowhere. You are above her in every way and she is nothing but an avaricious harpy. She is unfit even to be a governess, teaching children. She will make her way in the world on her back—" finally pausing to look up into Darcy's eyes, Mr. Collins quivered in dread at the fury he saw there. Darcy's sudden change in demeanor was like a portent of divine punishment and fury. In trying to evade the presumed retribution, Mr. Collins's reaction was to crouch and cover his head to avoid being hit. Only he was so engrossed in his fear that he forgot he was sitting at his desk and struck his face hard against it.

Darcy heard the crunch of Mr. Collins's nose breaking on impact before the man crumpled to the floor, holding his bleeding face. The absurd man began moaning piteously. Darcy's glare shifted to a more contemplative expression. He had never been one to derive pleasure from another's pain, but he couldn't ignore the satisfaction that came with watching the man writhe on the floor. He would have liked to think that he would not have hit the sniveling worm, but he was uncertain. He had rarely experienced such a rage as had had in that moment. That anyone would think that about Elizabeth, let alone her cousin and a man of the cloth.

"You will listen and listen hard. I cannot underscore enough how much your behavior today has angered me." Darcy's frigid voice caused Mr. Collins to shiver involuntarily. He realized too late that ignoring Mr. Darcy was a mistake, and his allegiance to Lady Catherine may not provide him with enough defense. "Miss Bennet is at Rosings and will stay there at my invitation because you have proven to be a disgrace of a man. You are never to speak poorly of her again. If I hear otherwise, I will endeavor to teach you the error of your ways. Do you understand?"

"But Lady Catherine!" Mr. Collins's broken nose made it difficult for him to speak clearly, and his exclamation sounded more like 'ba yadie kafrine'. Darcy's expression made him grow silent and wince in pain as he pressed a dirty handkerchief against his broken nose.

"Lady Catherine is dead." Darcy was blunt. He recognized that he had little ability to cushion the blow, though he had little care to do so with such a sorry excuse for a man.

Mr. Collins's attempt to get off the floor was halted by his shock at the news. "That cannot be true! I must see to her!"

"You must do nothing but stay here and apologize to your wife for your appalling behavior. I saw her face. A man who takes his frustrations out on someone smaller than he is no man at all."

"But!" Shaking his head, Mr. Collins sent the blood from his broken nose flying around him.

"But nothing! You are no longer welcome at Rosings. Before you go blaming this on anyone else, it is all your own doing. I am in contact with the bishop. He will arrange the funeral for my aunt. I will also make him aware of your very unchristian behavior. If I am not mistaken, he will be investigating the care you provide for this parish. If I were you, I would work on providing better care for your parish and your wife before you lose your position."

"You cannot keep me from my lady!" Jumping up, Mr. Collins grabbed for Mr. Darcy's arm only to realize that the cut of his jacket hid just how well muscled he was. Stepping back, he begged. "Just what am I supposed to do?"

"Be a better man. Be a better husband. And for God's sake, read at least the gospels. You should be seeing to the spirituality of the people here."

Leaving the room, Darcy searched out Mrs. Collins and found her in the sitting room she appeared to have claimed as her own. She had a stack of letters in her hands and was crying over them.

Darcy rarely roamed through other people's households, but he found he had done just that. If he wanted to be the person Miss Bennet deserved, then he should check on her closet friend. "Mrs. Collins, I do not mean to disturb you, but I wanted to see if you are all right staying here with that man."

Charlotte's eyes widened as she studied Darcy, her mouth dropping into a surprised 'o.' She seemed taken off guard by his concern, but after pausing momentarily, Charlotte nodded and replied, "A cup of hot tea and a good cry is all I need to feel better." She traced the signature on the letter with a shaking finger. "I wanted to be married so badly that I went against Elizabeth's advice, thinking that I could manage him. I never suspected his obsession would take him this far."

"I have warned him that he must take better care of you. The bishop is someone I'm acquainted with, and I've warned him of the possibility of losing his position if he doesn't change his behavior." Darcy watched her eyes widen as she brought her hand up to hide her split lip. Ignoring the desire to growl, he continued. "I know you must be worried about Miss Bennet. I have brought her back to Rosings for the time being, until we can figure out what to do next. Also, I must inform you that Lady Catherine has died. She passed away this morning."

Mrs. Collins narrowed her eyes, trying to read his expression. "You love my friend, don't you? I suspect all of this is because you love her dearly."

Darcy found it intriguing that she fixated on his feelings towards her friend, rather than the passing of Lady Catherine. It certainly showed where her loyalties lay. "Yes, I love her most ardently, and the more I know her, the more I find to love."

"Take care of her, then. He has forbidden me from even saying her name, never mind trying to speak with her. Would you tell her I am sorry and that she was right?" she asked before shaking her head and looking down at the letters in her lap.

"I will let her know." Darcy bowed and was turning to leave, but Mrs. Collins stopped him.

"Mr. Darcy, wait before you go. I managed to save some of my friend's things from her room without my husband's notice. Please take them to her."

"Of course, and should you have any concerns here, I am leaving word that you can come to Rosings at any time. Your husband, however, is no longer invited." He waited while she went over to a cabinet and took out what appeared to be a ragbag and rummaged around in it. She must have worried her husband would find and destroy it all. Taking the package from her, Darcy looked at it. It looked as if it was a bundle of letters and mementos—a small, dried flower and some jewelry, all wrapped in a shawl.

Bowing once again, he left the house and went back to his horse, Castan, who was still waiting patiently for his master's return. With the package for Miss Bennet safely cradled against his chest, he mounted his horse and set off for Rosings. He knew Elizabeth was resting and so would return her items when she came down to tea or maybe dinner. He had checked with Mrs. Graham prior to leaving for the parish who informed him that Miss Bennet was resting for now. She needed all the rest she could get after that morning, and he was glad for it.

It was a simple matter to get back to Rosings. It felt as if he had barely started to think on matters when he was already at the stable and handing his horse over to the groom. He was heading inside when he saw the physician approaching and changing his direction, he went to greet the man.

Observing him from a distance, he noted the physician had changed little since the last time Darcy had seen him. Despite being in his late thirties, he was doing well for himself, having been a physician for over a decade. His athleticism and skill as a rider were apparent. He must be going out to see patients all the time. "Good day, Mr. Clinton."

"Mr. Darcy, I knew you visited around Easter, but I was unsure if you would be in residence. I hear condolences are in order. I am so very sorry."

"Yes, thank you. It has come as quite a shock to all parties." Darcy turned and gestured him up the stairs and into the building.

"So there were no signs?"

"If there were, it was not anything we considered significant at the time. We have her in her room, but she passed in her receiving parlor. I presume you will want to see her body. It was so unexpected that I believe there will be a number of questions that need answered."

"Yes, I would like to take some time examining her so that I can see if I can get you those questions answered." He spoke in a distracted air, as if his mind was already on solving a puzzle.

"I believe we are having tea around four. I would be glad for you to join us to discuss matters." Darcy wondered if that would be enough time for the doctor to reach any conclusions. What exactly did a physician do to determine the possible cause of death?

"Yes, that should work."

"I would say splendid, but it is really not that quite appropriate." Looking around, Darcy spotted Gregory standing near the entrance. "Gregory, would you be so kind as to take the good physician to Lady Catherine's chambers and see that he has anything that he may need?"

"Of course, sir. If you will follow me, Mr. Clinton, right this way."

Darcy watched as they trailed up the stairs and towards Lady Catherine's domain. He headed towards his own rooms, the small package still in hand. He hoped that Miss Bennet would be at tea, and he could return her items to her.

***

Darcy had asked for a more substantial tea that afternoon, concluding it was logical to prepare a good amount of food since they had Miss Bennet, who required nourishment after her shock, and a busy physician who would appreciate it. Looking the food over, Darcy noticed one of his favorites on display—lemon cake. He would definitely have to get some.

"Darcy, this spread is impressive. Did you specifically request the lemon cake special or was it from Mrs. Graham treating you?" Theodore came into the room a smile on his face seeing all the food.

"I have not asked for the cake. I think she just likes me." It felt good to banter with his cousin after the long day he had had.

"I hear the physician is here and is looking our aunt over." Grabbing a plate, Theodore began compiling a selection of delectable morsels.

"Yes, he went up to her room some time ago. I believe he said he should have some information by now and hoped to come discuss it with us at tea. I know it may not be the most appropriate time, but I feel we should at least feed him for his efforts."

The physician had arrived while they were speaking and commented on their discussion. "That is very kind of you. If there's one thing I cannot resist, it's food. I never know when I will be called away, so I always eat when I have the opportunity."

"Good to see you, Clinton," Theodore greeted the doctor. "Come take a seat, or better yet, take a plate."

"I believe I will." Going to the food, Clinton looked it over and began selecting from what was available.

"I hope I am not arriving late. I must admit that I slept more than I thought I would," Elizabeth spoke from the entrance. As soon as he stood up, Darcy's gaze met hers and lingered. Her complexion was still somewhat pallid, which was unsurprising given the multiple shocks she was recovering from. Her dress was one he knew he had never seen her in, and he loved how it looked on her. He could see the way the fabric flowed around her as she moved, and it took his breath away. It was a pale lavender, he assumed, in respect to the family's loss. Its cut and style were the latest from London. It accentuated everything in the most becoming way and he almost wanted to beg her to only wear dresses like it for always.

Nervously smoothing the dress, Elizabeth worried her lip with her teeth. "I know it's a new dress. Nothing of my own has been salvaged yet and so Mrs. Graham said I should wear this. Lady Matlock had sent it for Miss de Bourgh, but Lady Catherine forbade her from wearing it."

Darcy realized he had unsettled her with his staring and quickly spoke up. "I find it quite becoming on you. I believe that Mrs. Graham is right. You should have access to the whole trunk of clothes. There is no point for such lovely clothes to be left in a chest."

They all settled around the chairs and tables, Darcy making sure to sit near Miss Bennet. Civil chatting about bland subjects began while they ate, but there was a heaviness in the air that grew stronger the longer they avoided the subject they all knew they should be discussing.

Theodore surveyed the room and observed that most people had finished their meals. Putting down his teacup, he addressed the physician. "Mr. Clinton, what did you find in your examination of my aunt?"

"I have no definitive way to tell. There are really no tests that I can perform, and I have to go by observation alone. From what I have observed, I can only come to one conclusion—she was poisoned." The physician's voice was grim and strained. Upon hearing the physician's words, Darcy's attention snapped to Theodore, his eyes filled with concern. Their suspicions were confirmed.

Chapter Seven
Why Did You Murder My Mother?

ELIZABETH'S TEACUP CLATTERED AS she set it down. "What evidence did you observe that lead you to that conclusion?"

"Her color was off, which implies an imbalance in her organs, possibly her liver. She would have shown jaundice earlier if it were a disease and I had seen her last month. There was no sign of it then. Also, there was foam and excess sputum. Signs that pointed to a violent and unnatural end. Who was with her when she passed?"

Elizabeth swallowed at the memory of Lady Catherine's unnatural end only that morning. "I was, and you are correct. It appeared to be very unnatural. Something felt wrong, but I am not an expert in death."

With an attentive posture, the physician leaned forward in his chair, ready to absorb every detail she had to share. "What did you notice? Was she coughing? Complaining of anything?"

"She began drooling a lot and at first did not notice it. She also appeared to have an odd color about her, but she had been fine when I attended a dinner on Tuesday. So that was a recent development. She complained of a persistent headache that she had had for days," Elizabeth continued, trying to help the physician figure out what had happened to Lady Catherine. It all made her shudder, remembering the trauma of her death and the powerful need she had to look out for her daughter.

The physician's fingers taped repeatedly on the arm of his chair. One after the other, in turn. Elizabeth watched them for some time while they sat in silence, waiting for him to finish cogitating. "I believe when she died this morning with Miss Bennet in the room, it was some form of poisoning."

Leaning forward in his chair, Darcy exclaimed, "I hope you are not claiming that Miss Bennet had anything to do with the situation."

Holding his hands up in defense, Mr. Clinton shook his head and clarified. "No, I am sorry if that came out wrong. Let me see if I can explain better." He took a deep breath before continuing. "So presumably she was fine on Tuesday at dinner, but by Thursday or even Wednesday evening she was experiencing a headache. She may very well have been poisoned on Wednesday, but it took her until Saturday to die."

"Do you believe, Mr. Clinton, that it was intentional? Is there a way of knowing what it was that poisoned her?" Theodore spoke from where he sat, with his hands steepled before him.

"Well, there are, of course, different poisons. Hemlock, for example, has been in use a very long time. Socrates is said to have died by it. But the symptoms do not match." Darcy watched as the physician pondered for a moment. "There are cases where it is accidental. I have heard of something being wrong in milk, for example, that kills people in the Americas. Unfortunately, I am not in possession of the necessary information to answer. I would suggest speaking with her staff and seeing if there was anything unusual going on in her behavior or if there was something new being served. Perhaps something exotic?" The physician's expression betrayed his desire for a deeper understanding of the world. There was really no way to determine what the poison was, even with the more recent advances in medicine.

Nodding his head, Theodore stood. "We will begin investigating. I would not have someone who deliberately murdered my aunt go free. Then again, if it was accidental, I do not wish the accident to be repeated. Did you wish to return home? I know you have some distance to travel. I do not want to keep you, unless you wish to stay the night?"

The physician stood and grabbed the bag that Elizabeth had not noticed. "Thank you for the kind offer. However, I do feel my own bed calling me. I think I could get home in a decent amount of time."

The typical farewells followed, and a footman was asked to escort him to his horse. The trio sat in silence for a time, all three lost in their own presumably dark musings. As Elizabeth pondered the potential for poisoning, she couldn't shake the feeling of dread that someone with ill intentions could be lurking nearby. Then again, it had been pointed out that it could be entirely accidental. She did not know which was worse.

"Theodore, are you thinking that our aunt was murdered?" Darcy drawled from where he sat.

"I do believe that is an actual possibility. You must admit that our aunt was a brisk woman, if you are being kind and a termagant, if you are being honest. She could very well have angered the wrong person with one of her tirades. Look how she treated Miss Bennet. Any person, even a good person, can be pushed past their point of endurance."

Sitting up straight, Darcy exclaimed, "You cannot be supposing Miss Bennet had anything to do with it."

Elizabeth noticed how quickly he was jumping to her defense yet again. Looking at him, she marveled at his easy defense of her. Here was a man who last fall could not string many words in a row when speaking to her. He had never outright defended her to the likes of Miss Bingley, but now, without hesitation, he was implying with conviction that she was innocent of murder.

Rolling his eyes at his cousin, the colonel huffed in apparent frustration at his cousin's jumping to conclusions. "No, Darcy, I do believe Miss Bennet entirely innocent. She was not here on Wednesday, and it appears that someone poisoned Aunt Catherine Wednesday."

Elizabeth watched Theodore explain matters, impressed that he was able to put two and two together. At least one of the people who had faith in her was able to see through the emotions and think logically. She looked at Darcy with a sigh and wondered whether his tendency to jump to conclusions could actually become endearing. "Mr. Darcy, if we are going to find out how your aunt died and possibly who killed her, we will need to keep cool heads. Also, as much as I enjoy being defended, you really must stop jumping to the conclusion that people are blaming me," Elizabeth smiled, seeing Mr. Darcy's look of embarrassed befuddlement. "Otherwise, we will get nowhere with our investigation. Knowing that you believe my innocence is enough."

Where Elizabeth smiled, his cousin outright laughed. "Brava, Miss Bennet. I have not seen that look on his face since he was fourteen and we were at Eton."

Darcy gave them a begrudging smile before speaking. "If we are going to investigate this with cool heads, where do we start? Theodore, have you ever investigated similar deaths in the military? Do you have any suggestions?"

"I suggest we start at the beginning. We find out what she did on Wednesday, where she went and who she talked to."

"Miss Bennet, why did you murder my mother?" Anne's comment caught everyone off guard.

Darcy jumped from his chair at his cousin's accusation, the colonel right behind him. "Anne! What are you saying? Who told you that Miss Bennet murdered your mother?"

"I hate black. I do not want to wear black, and Mrs. Stevenson said I must, because Miss Bennet murdered my mother."

Elizabeth saw the lack of understanding and bewilderment on the woman's face. Clearly, despite her cruel accusation, Anne de Bourgh was a confused and upset child, regardless of her adult body. She studied her closely, seeing things she hadn't before. Her cheeks were oddly rosy, but besides that, she was rather pale and wan. She was not a healthy woman. Which was something she had been told, but this was not the megrims that her mother always complained of. This was something else. "Anne, dear, come over here. Will you sit with me?"

Anne hesitated for a moment before making her way to the settee next to Elizabeth. Elizabeth could tell she was upset as she scuffed her foot on the floor, refusing to make eye contact. She could not believe that Mrs. Stevenson would say something so inflammatory to Anne. Anne had a clouded expression and a furrowed brow, as if not comprehending her mother's death. The woman's lack of compassion towards Anne went against the expectations of her role as a companion.

Holding her breath and blowing it out slowly in order to keep from showing her anger to Anne, Elizabeth continued in a calm and controlled voice. "Did Mrs. Stevenson tell you about what happened to your mother?"

"She said that you murdered her." Anne picked at a ribbon on her dress and Elizabeth realized it was a very old-fashioned dress, very similar to the kind that her mother wore. She also noted that Anne seemed to lack any evidence of womanly curves at all.

"Yes, besides that. Did she explain anything else?" Elizabeth could sense Mr. Darcy and the colonel exchanging confused and angry glances but kept her focus on Anne.

Shaking her head, Anne finally looked up at Elizabeth, her brown eyes large and confused in her pale face. "No, she just told me I must change and said she was going to go manage household matters."

Reaching out, Elizabeth took Anne's hand in her own. "Anne, do you know that your mother died?"

"Died? I thought she was sick. Does murdered mean died like my father?"

"Yes, sweetheart, murdered means died, but we do not know for sure that your mother was murdered. She died and we are trying to figure out what happened."

Anne clutched at Elizabeth's hand tightly, her voice coming out in a whisper. "So, she will not get better?"

"No, she cannot get better." Elizabeth did not know what was wrong with Mrs. Stevenson. She obviously had explained nothing to the poor girl.

"But what did you do to her?" Anne's confusion increased as she started to understand more about the situation.

"I did nothing to your mother to hurt her. But I was there when she died. Did you know she loved you very much? She was very worried about you, and all she wanted was to make sure that you were taken care of." Elizabeth could easily remember the desperation Lady Catherine had, how badly she worried for her daughter. The memory of her promise to ensure that she was well taken care of lingered in Elizabeth's mind. She was determined to make sure that Anne received the best care possible.

Startled, Anne looked at Elizabeth in wonder, as if the idea that her mother had been worried about her was something new to her. "Really? Mother and I always had breakfast and tea together and sometimes dinner. I enjoyed spending time with Mother."

"I am sure that you did."

Looking at Elizabeth, her brows drawn together, she questioned further, "Why do you want me to wear black? I hate black."

Elizabeth contemplated everything for a moment before coming up with some sort of response. Anne de Burgh was more like a child than her age would suggest. How did you explain mourning customs to a child? "People who had someone they loved die wear black to show their love for the person who they can no longer be with. I am sure, though, that your mother would want you to be comfortable. What do you think of another dark color? What about navy?"

"So black means that I miss mother?" She looked off into the distance. It was possible she trying to process all that the conversation revealed, though Elizabeth really could not be certain.

Nodding, Elizabeth smiled at her conclusion. "In a way, yes."

"Then I will wear it, because I do miss her." Standing up, Anne moved to the door. "I am going to my room now. I am sleepy. Goodbye."

Watching her go, Elizabeth wondered at Anne's life. She obviously would need even more support than your typical grieving unmarried daughter. Despite Lady Catherine's desire to marry her daughter to Mr. Darcy for protection, Elizabeth knew there had to be a better way. She turned her gaze back to the gentlemen watching her.

"Wonderful job there, Miss Bennet. You handled that admirably," the colonel commended her from where he had resumed his seat.

"Lady Catherine mentioned an illness that changed her daughter. I am seeing what she meant. Is she always this..." Elizabeth grasped for a word that would not be insulting but had difficulty finding one.

As Elizabeth struggled to find the right words to describe Darcy's cousin, Darcy interjected to help her out. "I think the word childlike will do. Yes, most of the time, she is quite childish. She is also often shy; she refuses to be around most strangers. The fact that she responded so well to you is something quite significant. Beyond that, her health is not the best, and she is often ill.”

Resting her chin in her hand, Elizabeth felt her muscles in her face tighten and her lips draw together in a hard line. She knew her emotions would always be more on display; she did not have her sister Jane’s skill with projecting tranquility. “I find that I cannot like Mrs. Stevenson. I do not know her well, but I am not impressed with her treatment of Anne at all.”

Darcy spoke up in agreement, his eyes trained on Elizabeth, apparently trying to watch her covertly. “Nor I. I simply cannot understand why she would tell Anne that you murdered her mother. What good would that do?”

“Rumor has a way of twisting the truth, Darcy. I am not sure what her endgame is, but I suspect it’s not good. I think she has some ulterior motive that she is not revealing,” the colonel responded.

“When Lady Catherine died, I promised I would see to Anne. Now that her mother is dead, how is she to be provided for? What happens to Rosings? Anne is in no shape to manage the estate. I know there is most likely a competent steward, but the household needs to be managed.” Elizabeth looked at them both, though her gaze lingered on Mr. Darcy.

“I think we need to reach out to Lady Catherine’s barrister. I think Anne is the last de Burgh, so I do not think there is an issue with an entail or anything else to be concerned with there, but you are right to be concerned. The steward is a good man, but he needs of oversight,” Darcy spoke aloud, his voice reflective.

"I know the household is at sixes and sevens and without information from the barrister, we cannot do much. I am worried about these rumors and think that something will need to be done," the colonel said, offering a smooth bow to Miss Bennet before exiting the room off in search of the woman in question.

"Miss Bennet, you have been very helpful today. I wanted to thank you for what you did both for my aunt this morning and, more recently, my cousin Anne. I never know quite how to interact with her. Besides that, she seems to do better with women." Running his hand through his thick chestnut hair, Mr. Darcy looked up at the ceiling.

Elizabeth appreciated the way Mr. Darcy so obviously wished that he could help, even if he did not appear to know how. "I have four sisters and so I have more experience with young girls. Which, sadly, is what I think we need to treat her as. I know that you have a sister, but you were probably at Eaton or Harrow when she was younger."

Sitting forward in his chair and looking at her almost desperately, Mr. Darcy spoke up. "That is true. My sister was still quite young when I was sent off to Eaton. Miss Bennet, I know that I probably should not ask, but we are already in an unusual situation. Would you be interested in working together to find out what happened to my aunt? I have always appreciated your keen mind and I feel that you will see things in a way that I do not. A different perspective from my own or even Theodore's could be very important at this juncture."

Elizabeth had pondered her morning as she was dressing after her nap, and the idea that it was possible Lady Catherine's death was not an accident was one she could not shake. It did not sit well with her.

"I would very much like to find out what exactly happened to your aunt. If someone did that to her on purpose, we can do no less than seek justice on her behalf."

"Thank you, Miss Bennet."

"It will be my pleasure to help you with this. Besides, if we are working together," she started with a small smile, "we will have more time to exchange questions."

"Yes, we said we would do that. Who gets to go first?"

"I think it's only fair that you go first. It is your idea, after all," she said.

Leaning back in his chair, Mr. Darcy crossed his legs and smiled at nothing at all for a moment before speaking. "I think my first question for you is, what is your favorite color?"

"That is not as simple as one might think."

"You are not a simple woman. I can expect no less, but my question remains the same."

Elizabeth's smile widened as she gazed at Darcy, realizing that there was much more to him than she had originally thought. Many men saw woman as simple empty-headed children, only concerned with fashion and lace and in need of direction. She found it pleasant that Mr. Darcy acknowledged her multifaceted nature. Closing her eyes to avoid the distraction of Mr. Darcy's penetrating gaze, Elizabeth tried to figure out how to explain her favorite color. She had always found it difficult to explain what she felt about colors. Jane would say she liked blue and be done with it. Mary would sermonize about not distracting oneself from the glories of God. Elizabeth, on the other hand, found the subject complicated. "I like the color blue, but not on me. If I was to pick out a fabric for a dress, I always prefer greens. But I think one of my favorite sights is a brilliant blue sky."

"But I see you wear blue often." Head tilted, Mr. Darcy pressed his lips in a hard line, clearly trying to fight a smile.

Nodding her head, Elizabeth smiled at his confusion. "I often get dresses from my sister Jane and her blue eyes and blonde hair look quite nice in a blue dress, so when I get her hand-me-downs, they are often blue."

"Fair enough. Now it is your turn. What is your question?"

Elizabeth knew that her question would not be an easy one like his, but she found she had to know. Learning more about Mr. Darcy was making her more confused. He was a good man who tried to do good where he could. It conflicted what she had been told about his past behavior. "I want to know about Wickham. Why does he say that you have destroyed his life?"

Chapter Eight
Perfidy and Deprivation

WHY DID THAT MAN constantly attempt to destroy his hopes for happiness? Wickham was not even in the room, but Darcy still felt as if he was lurking somewhere, laughing at his struggles. Darcy attempted to gather himself for a response. At least Miss Bennet had not been accusatory.

"Mr. Wickham says a great many things about why he has not succeeded in life. I presume he spoke to you of my refusing him of the living I have control of. Our relationship is long and complicated, and it has grown increasingly acrimonious." Stopping to rub at his forehead, Darcy tried to come up with a way to convince Miss Bennet that he was not the man Wickham had most likely painted him to be.

Elizabeth spoke up softly, as if noting his hesitation and wanting to fill the void. "He spoke of the living. At first, I assumed your proud demeanor pushed you to refuse to aid your childhood friend out of spite. However, I am starting to know you better, and that explanation no longer fits."

"I am relieved that you would feel that way. The story is tough for me to share, but I will share it with you if you are willing to listen."

"I will," Miss Bennet said, settling into her chair as if waiting to be told a story.

"Wickham was one of the few boys on Pemberley land my age while I was growing up. His father was my father's steward. He was a kind, hardworking man and was actually one of my father's closest friends. Sadly, the son did not take after the father. We played together as boys, but I soon noticed some odd behaviors that I could not like. Pranks that ended in injury, for example, and accidents that I could not be certain were accidents. My father was fond of Wickham's jolly manners where I have always struggled in the company of others. My shy demeanor prevented me from being the boy my father wanted for a son. When I told my father that I suspected Wickham's behavior, he would tell me that I was merely jealous of how well he got on with everyone. He encouraged me to be like Wickham. Eventually, I learned to keep my distance and my own counsel. Knowing that my father would hear nothing against his godson, things quickly became concerning. I learned of damaged property that was waved off as high spirits and ruined daughters that were waved off as scorned girls disappointed that he did not choose them." Darcy stopped, remembering the last argument he had had with his father. It had been about Wickham's latest misdeeds. A young village girl was with child, and Darcy's father refused to hear anything against Wickham. "Father sent Wickham to Eaton and Cambridge with me, where I observed his fall into gambling and even more disreputable behavior. When father died, I was only twenty-two and amongst taking over Pemberley and the satellite properties, I had to deal with Wickham. He wanted his inheritance from my father. His own father had passed some time before and he had already gone through all that his father had saved in a lifetime. Despite his eager anticipation, the Scottish property he hoped to inherit did not go to him. Father had left him one thousand pounds and the rights to the living. He was furious. He stated he need money immediately. I believe there were several debts to unsavory people that had come due. He told me he had no desire to serve God and wished instead to take up law. He requested the money that the living would give instead. In the end, he received a one-thousand-pounds inheritance and three thousand pounds from the living he refused on top of the two thousand pounds that he had received from his father."

Placing her hand on her chest, Miss Bennet became visibly overwhelmed by the magnitude of Whickham's behavior. "He received that much and yet he claims to have nothing to his name. I would never have suspected he was such a liar."

"I doubt he has any money. He is always playing cards, but he is not exactly skilled at the game. I believe he went through his funds within two years."

Shaking her head in disbelief, Miss Bennet appeared to be upset. "I cannot fathom such falsehood from someone with such engaging manners. I apologize for believing him, Mr. Darcy. But why did you not call him out for his lies?"

Darcy's jaw throbbed, a reminder to relax his clenched teeth. He had to take a deep breath and clear his mind before he could finally say what he needed to. It wasn't that he doubted Elizabeth's integrity; rather, there were other concerns at play. He just kept seeing Georgiana's face, seeing that anguish, and it broke him all over again. The weight of his failure to shield her from heartbreak was crushing, leaving him feeling angry and helpless. "That is due to what happened this last summer, and that is where the story is truly painful. It has to do with my younger sister, Georgiana," Darcy sighed, taking a moment to collect his thoughts in an attempt to keep his anger at bay. "At fifteen, my sister was a shy girl who did poorly at the school for genteel girls. She requested to leave the school, so I found her a companion and after a time, the companion suggested she stay at Ramsgate for her health. The physician suggested that sea air might help with her terrible cough, so she took a trip to the coast. Knowing that I had important business to attend to in London, I sent them ahead of me. I did not know that Wickham had seduced her companion, and it was all a plot to gain control of her dowry of thirty thousand pounds. I arrived early to the pair of them, trying to convince Georgiana to elope with him. He even claimed that it had been our dear father's wish to see him elevated into our sphere and he had suggested the marriage before his death."

Leaning forward in her chair, Miss Bennet's eyes were alight with fury and the desire for justice. "He could not be satisfied with his perfidy. He had to push ever farther into deprivation. Please tell me the poor girl is well."

Darcy's brow furrowed as he considered her most recent series of letters. They no longer gave such a forlorn feeling as they had at first, but Darcy was uncertain if she had truly recovered. "I can only say that she is better than she was. The entire experience was trying for her. Her previously small amount of confidence when dealing with people has seemed to vanish overnight. I found a better companion that appears to be helping her recover her spirits."

"To think that I fell for his charm. I thought, at one time, that I was a keen studier of character. Now I do not know what to believe. You are not the knave that I believed you were and the man I thought all goodness was, in reality, a blackguard." Elizabeth's frustration was palpable as she sat in her chair. She shifted in her seat, as if unable to find a comfortable position. "I have had several eye-opening realizations today," she added quietly.

Leaning forward in his chair, Darcy was eager to alleviate Elizabeth's distress. "He is an experienced deceiver. You are not the first to fall for his convincing tales. My own father believed him until he died. At least you have chosen to believe me when given the facts."

Elizabeth lifted her gaze to look him in the eye, reassuring him of her faith in him. Reaching out, she made to touch his arm. She only briefly hesitated before following through and squeezing his forearm. "I understand why you hesitated to speak out against him now. A woman's reputation is a brittle thing, easily broken and hard to mend. Presumably he had your sister's reputation in the palm of his hand, ready to crush it at the slightest provocation."

"That is what I feared." Darcy was relieved that she had taken his reassurance so well but struggled to keep his mind on topic. He knew she probably meant it as a soothing gesture, but her hand on his arm was anything but soothing. Her touch ignited a fire within him, distracting him from any serious contemplation. Was it possible that he was making progress in his suit for her heart? He sure hoped he was, because he couldn't imagine anyone else igniting the passion he felt when she was near. Her touch on his arm ignited a spark of optimism in his heart, and he felt the possibility of their love grow.

***

LOOKING AROUND THE DINING room, Darcy questioned his plans for the evening while he waited for everyone else to arrive. Without his aunt present to demand ceremony, they were free to relax and forego any formalities. It would be an attempt at something more relaxed. He had reached out to his aunt's solicitor via written correspondence to request information about his cousin's inheritance and the status of his aunt's will. There was something about Mrs. Stevenson that rubbed him the wrong way, but it was difficult to just send her on her way, with no additional information. He wanted to observe her during the dinner and had made a point about requesting that she and his cousin come.

"I see you have arrived before me." Miss Bennet's voice was cheerful and something he was pleased to hear.

Rising from his chair, Darcy bowed in greeting. "I did. I was eager to see you again."

Shaking her head at his desire to see her, Elizabeth teased, "Mr. Darcy, we only just spoke this afternoon. Not four hours ago."

"That does not mean I was not eager to see you. I am always eager to see you, even if you have only just walked from the room. Though I had a reason to want to see you."

"Really? Why did you want to see me?"

Reaching over, Darcy gathered the bundle of items that he had retrieved from Mrs. Collins and presented it to her. "I apologize that I forgot to give it to you at tea. I spoke to both Mr. and Mrs. Collins today. Even though your cousin remains a fool, your friend had saved and hid what she could from him."

Reaching out with unsteady hands, she took the shawl wrapped package. Darcy was not ready for the tears that sprung to her eyes. They hovered there, glistening on her long black lashes. "Thank you. These are some of my letters and my jewelry that Jane had given me. I had thought them lost."

"Then I am very glad that I was able to retrieve them for you." Darcy's throat tightened as he observed her expression, which was filled with appreciation and maybe something more. Her smile struck him, and for a moment, he couldn't think. He knew he needed to see her smile like that again.

His happy moment was cut short when Mrs. Stevenson came in with Anne, followed swiftly by his cousin. Dinner promptly began, the first course coming out as soon as they had all been seated.

As soon as the servants finished serving, Elizabeth turned to face Anne and offered her a warm smile across Stevenson. "Anne, how are you doing this evening?"

Anne smiled at Elizabeth, "I had a good day, I guess, but I was bored. I—"

"Anne." Mrs. Stevenson's severe expression made her sharp rebuke all the more biting.

"I am sorry. Fine, thank you." Though Anne did not frown, her face lost all expression, and she preceded to look down at her plate.

"Anne can say anything she wishes, Mrs. Stevenson." Darcy looked sharply at the companion.

Mrs. Stevenson inhaled delicately before looking at Darcy. "Yes, I know you are concerned for your cousin, but young ladies often need to learn what is appropriate for dinner with company." She paused and glanced at Miss Bennet before shaking her head and continuing. "As Anne's companion, it has been my responsibility to guide her in learning these things. I am aware of the task Lady Catherine assigned to me, and I will see to it." She turned back to her plate and picked up her knife, cutting into the meat with prim precision.

For the rest of the evening, no matter who tried to engage Anne in conversation, she refused to answer with anything more than a few syllables. Darcy looked across the table at his cousin. Theodore's furrowed brow and down-turned mouth revealed his deep concern. They would most certainly be needing to get Anne a new companion as soon as possible.

***

THAT NIGHT, DARCY CONSIDERED his conversations with Miss Bennet while he was trying to write a letter to his aunt's barrister. It had gone better than he thought. Much better if he was honest. Her conviction told Darcy that she believed him and felt compassion towards his sister's plight, which was a reassuring feeling. Most society ladies would have attempted to use the information to gain the upper hand in some way. Then there was that smile. He couldn't focus on anything else, as his mind was consumed by it. He had spent some time trying to go through papers and estate ledgers after dinner. Everything was in good order, which was to be expected with as controlling as his aunt was. She saw to her people and insisted on the best practices in both animal husbandry and crop rotation. Why anyone would feel the need to kill her was beyond him. He wondered if they would ever be able to figure out what had truly happened to his aunt.

Reeves came into the room, drawing him from his morose reflections. "Sir, I wanted to inform you that there is some rather dire talk about your dear lady."

"There is what?!" With a sudden jolt, Darcy rose from his seat and shoved his chair back, nearly causing it to topple over. His wild movements caused the papers lying on the desk to swirl around chaotically.

"I was in the servant's hall and overheard some talk. They are saying that Miss Bennet murdered your aunt because she was going to stop your elopement with her." Reeves spoke in a calm manner, almost willing his master and friend to react in a manner that would not harm the situation.

Darcy turned to pace around his aunt's study. It was a room with far too many ornate odds and ends for his taste, but he was grateful it had a space adequate for pacing. "Why would anyone ever say something so outlandish?"

"That is a good question. I asked the chambermaids who were speaking where they had gotten their information and they said that it was being spoken of by everyone. To have the free rein that it does, I would suspect one of the higher-level servants." Reeves failed to keep his face blank, showing Darcy just how reprehensible the act of malicious gossip being spread by a servant in a position of authority was.

Mind whirling, Darcy tried to ponder what to do. There were two problems with the gossip—it claimed that Miss Bennet murdered his aunt as well as claimed that she was willing to elope with him. Both were dangerous claims. Swirling around, Darcy froze and faced Reeves, his expression hard. "I know you are not standing there just to tell me of the problem. I know you never speak of a problem without having first come up with a solution."

"Well, one thought I had was that if you were engaged to her, there would be no need for an elopement. That might quash the risk to her reputation. However, that would also require you to step up your pursuit of her. How is that going, by the way?"

"Better than before, but not as good as I would hope. You know I had already hoped to be engaged to her by now, only you relieved me of my misconceptions." Sighing, Darcy slumped back in his chair, tired from his potent emotions and worries.

Reeves leaned up against the wall next to the door and said, "Might I remind you that you have yet to give her flowers, as I suggested?"

"True, though I wonder what flowers she likes."

"You really are helpless, sir. A gentleman is supposed to notice these things. What did you do on all those long walks? Stare at your shoes? What was she paying attention to?"

"I might have been staring at her shoes for all the good it did me. I was too flummoxed to speak and too ignorant to note anything but her smile and the way the breeze ruffled her hair and plucked at her skirt." The memory of his last walk with Elizabeth filled Darcy's mind, and he momentarily lost track of his surroundings. He had come upon her in a clearing and he couldn't help but notice how her green dress complemented the natural beauty around her. Her dress swirled around her, pulled by the playful wind, while she basked in the warmth of the sun on her upturned face. Sadly, when she saw him, her smile faded away. He barely spoke to her that morning. He was so taken with her beauty that he found himself completely tongue tied. Regretfully, he realized that he should have complimented her instead of staring, but the memory remained a cherished one. If only he had been able to express himself more clearly, things might be less complicated today. Looking at Reeves, he realized they had larger problems at hand. "What is your solution to the second problem?"

"It is less of a solution that you or I would like. More of an observation. There is an outside chance that whoever it is just dislikes her. Spreading gossip about Miss Bennet could be means to get her out of the way for some reason. However, most of the staff who know her have been sticking up for her. She is rather singular, your lady." Stepping away from the wall, Reeves reached out and started straightening the papers on the desk in his obsessive way. He never could stand a mess. It was one of the reasons that Darcy presumed he had gone into service. He truly enjoyed cleaning up after people.

Glaring at nothing at all, Darcy felt his emotions rise to a boil. "So you are saying that someone is spreading gossip about Elizabeth with the goal of hurting her?"

"Yes, it looks like it." Reeves watched his master's face turn dark. Darcy's need for justice and to protect those he loved was quite potent. He was normally a calm and even shy man, but once angered, he was a powerful force to be reckoned with.

Chapter Nine

Rhubarb and Wisdom

Rolling over, Elizabeth appreciated the comfort of a good mattress. Even if the room they had given her had been something like a servant's room, the bed was amazing. She raised her head and spotted a small figure by the tiny fireplace.

"Hattie, is that you?" Elizabeth sat up in bed and rubbed some sleep from her eyes. She had been up late thinking about the day's revelations. There were so many things that she had found out. Lady Catherine was dead. That had been a traumatic experience that she would never forget. Her cousin was a horrible man, though that had been something she had suspected on some level. Mr. Darcy loved her, and Mr. Wickham was a vile villain of the worst sort. It was no wonder she had been up late thinking.

Head popping up, the slender girl bobbed a quick curtsy. "Sorry to wake you, miss. I was only trying to return some items that we managed to get clean."

"Oh, that is no worry. I am an early riser; I enjoy rising before the sun so that I may greet it out in an open space somewhere. Thank you for bringing my things."

"My momma was the same. I would always wake to her soft humming as she cooked breakfast. There was a window that faced the sunrise, and she watched it every morning."

"That is a wonderful memory, Hattie," Elizabeth said with a smile. Getting out of bed, she stretched and felt the joy of feeling her body fall in line with the day. Glancing over, she spotted the cupboard where her clothes were. "Hattie, would you mind playing lady's maid? I would love to get ready for the morning but may need some help."

"That would be fine. Mrs. Graham said that I should help you, however you need me while you are here. Though I will tell you now, I have never had a task so grand before." Hattie smiled despite her warning, the grin stretching the generous helping of freckles across her rounded cheeks.

"I am sure that you will do just fine. In fact, I think I will speak with Mrs. Graham this morning about asking you to play lady's maid while I am here and maybe seeing if you can accompany me on my walks. If I do not get the chance to walk, I go a little mad." Elizabeth reached into the cupboard and pulled out one of her own dresses. It was only slightly damaged from its time in the mud and would do for a busy morning. It was a quick task to get dressed with Hattie's help and Elizabeth was soon walking down the hall with her.

She noticed that though Hattie was a new servant, she had not yet lost her sense of self, unlike some who had been in service for a while. She spoke with the rapid-fire chatter of a magpie, sharing details about the people and staff she knew in the area. Elizabeth found the information helpful. She had realized even at a young age that servants knew almost everything that was going on. People who were overlooked often saw and heard things that people did not realize.

"Bessie, the laundry maid, said she is much better this morning. Her cough is all but gone now. I told her she should have spoken to old Mrs. Wright sooner, but no one listens to me." Hattie talked despite the pile of linens she carried that nearly reached her nose.

"Who is Mrs. Wright?"

"She is an older widow who lives in a small little cottage on Rosings land. Making tinctures and other goods, she barters for supplies to get by. She knows a lot about what can help you if you are ailing. Mr. Collins called her a witch and an ungodly woman because she said she would not attend his service and listen to his blathering." Hattie's voice practically bubbled. As she walked, she spoke with a lively energy, her words matching the pace of her steps.

"I think I must meet her. She sounds remarkable. Standing up to my cousin is something that must be applauded." Elizabeth pondered while they wandered through the bowels of the house, taking stairs and halls that she never knew existed. It sounded like Mrs. Wright was possibly an herbalist. She might recognize the symptoms of Lady Catherine and help her understand what had happened to her.

"I like her. I have to take these down to the laundry, but Mrs. Graham should be in that office there." Hattie pointed to a door at the end of the hallway.

"Thank you for escorting me, Hattie. What are your tasks for the day? Do you think if Mrs. Graham says it is all right you could walk with me this morning? I would like to meet Mrs. Wright if possible." Elizabeth felt that a walk with the bright girl would be rather enjoyable.

"Mrs. Graham is the one who decides my day, so if she says it is all right, I can do whatever you would like," Hattie replied, her smile so wide that her eyes sparkled with joy.

Nodding her head in satisfaction, Elizabeth smiled at the girl. "Well then, I hope to see you later, Hattie."

"Yes, miss." Turning, she walked down the hall humming to herself and practically bouncing with energy despite her armful of linens.

Mrs. Graham sat at her desk, her eyes scanning the ledger with intense concentration. A cup of hot tea in her hand, the steam swirled before curling up and into the air. Looking up, she smiled at Elizabeth when she entered the room. "Good morning, Miss Bennet. How are you doing this new day? Was the bed adequate?"

"The bed was marvelous. Much better than the one I was sleeping in at Mr. Colins house, in fact." Elizabeth had no plans to speak to her cousin anytime soon, but she did not feel that it was a subject she would bring up to him.

"Was there something that you needed, dear? They will serve breakfast in a few hours, but if you need something to tide you over, I am sure the cook would be more than happy to give you something."

"I think that would be lovely, but I was wondering if I could borrow Hattie. I was hoping to go walking and greet the morning, but I should have at least a maid with me."

"She is a sweet little thing, and I think she would do well with a walk as well. We can spare her. She mostly just fetches and carries, helping around with odd jobs."

Elizabeth could see how she would be helpful with the supply of energy she displayed in abundance. "I was actually hoping to use her as my lady's maid while I was here."

"Now that is an idea. She is not trained, but she is smart." Sitting back in her chair, Mrs. Graham pondered the request, tapping a finger against her pursed lips for a moment. "I took the child on more as an act of kindness than as a genuine need and have often wondered what kind of future or training she could get. If you do not mind having her help you, I think that would be marvelous."

"I mostly make do with the help of one of my sisters back home. We must share a maid between us. It will be fine, I am sure," Elizabeth replied, smiling at Mrs. Graham before turning to go. The sadness of recent events weighed heavily on her, but she was determined to channel it into something positive by helping the girl. It was nice to get her way once in a while.

***

ELIZABETH WAS SITTING ON a bench in the small kitchen garden, enjoying the cool morning air and a hot scone, when Hattie came bouncing up to her, a grin on her face. As soon as the young girl reached her, Elizabeth noticed that she tried to restrain herself and show some dignity, holding herself still with difficulty. Her composure did not last long before she was bouncing on her toes with excitement. She practically vibrated with happiness.

"Mrs. Graham said I am to be your lady's maid-in-training for while you are here."

"Am I to take this to mean that you find the plan acceptable?" Laughing, Elizabeth watched the girl's head nod with enthusiasm. "Well then, I believe your first task is to come with me on my walk and help me introduce myself to Mrs. Wright. Unless you think it is too early?"

"No, she is an early riser. The sun is almost completely up. She will already be working on something." Walking ahead out on the path, Hattie took up a somewhat familiar tune, humming as she walked and gathering flowers as she went.

Elizabeth used the walk to stretch her legs but also to sort through the muddle in her mind. She felt she was surrounded by mystery. First, there was Lady Catherine's death, but there was also the discovery of exactly who Mr. Darcy was. She had gotten him and Mr. Wickham completely wrong. So completely wrong that she was almost sick to her stomach over the revelation. She had assumed that Mr. Wickham was all that was good and kind, noble even and, in reality, he was the vilest of men. How was she to trust herself when she had been so wrong?

Then, too, there was Mr. Darcy. He was not completely in the right, and he admitted to struggling against prejudice, but he was trying to improve. Was she any better? In the cold light of morning, she realized she had blamed his attitude on his wealth and privilege, making himself feel superior to her. She had never considered that he was also shy. What did that assumption say about her?

In the end, her feelings were tangled worse than the threads in Lydia's embroidery basket. Admitting to herself that the anger she felt towards him was built partially on the fact that she was hurt and not on facts. That was not a good feeling, discovering that she was at least partially petty. The more she truly knew about him, the more she found to like, and it was unsettling, to say the least. Taking a breath, she counted to ten and tried to force her uncertainty to leave her. Looking ahead, she saw she was drawing close to a very pleasant-looking little cottage. The stonework appeared to be in good condition and there were flowers all around it in neat little wheels of color.

"Mrs. Wright!" Hattie's merry voice called out, still full of energy even after the morning's duties and walk. "I brought you a visitor."

Elizabeth shook her head at the girl's exuberance. She reminded her of herself at that age. No care about how a lady should behave and with more interest in exploring the world and learning anything she could. Brash confidence and glee at the little things in life. A figure moved inside the cottage and then came to the open window.

"Hattie Harris, what are you doing out here this time of day? Have you left off your duties up at the big house?" The voice was kind despite the question of Hattie's activities. Elizabeth liked her immediately. She was not as old as Hattie had implied. Maybe her father's age? She had bright blue eyes surrounded by deep crow's feet and Elizabeth could tell right away that the woman spent most of her time smiling.

"No, Mrs. Wright, I am a lady's maid-in-training. Would you believe it? Miss Bennet wanted to meet you, so I took her here." Hattie grinned at the older woman, her white teeth showing in her open face.

Eyes that missed nothing scrutinized Elizabeth as she spoke with a voice full of laughter. "So you would be the Miss Bennet related to that buffoon of a rector? My condolences on the connection."

"Well, at least I am not the one married to him. He did ask, you know," Elizabeth answered the woman in kind, realizing that she was going to like her very much.

A melodious laugh filled the clearing. "Well, that is better. I believe much better indeed. Well, come in, I was just making a fresh pot of tea. Hattie, make yourself useful. Gather some of the rhubarb in the back while we are talking."

"Yes, Mrs. Wright." Grabbing a basket by the house, Hattie hurried off down a path that looked to lead to the back of the house.

"See that you do not get dirt on your uniform!" Mrs. Wright called after her. "She is a darling girl. It is good of you to put up with her energy. Come inside, the door is unlatched."

Elizabeth followed the kind orders and walked swiftly to the cottage and through the door. Pausing to let her eyes adjust to the gloom in the home, she looked around and was satisfied with what she saw. The home was tidy, although a little cramped. Drying herbs hanging from every available rafter made the entire area smell of the sweet and bitter of healthful plants. Looking to the corner where Mrs. Wright sat pouring tea, Elizabeth smiled to see that she had also appeared to have enough supplies and food laid away. Early spring could be hard in smaller communities, but it looked as if she lacked for nothing.

"Thank you for inviting me in."

Mrs. Wright's eyes softened at the sound of Elizabeth's grateful "thank you." She met the younger woman's gaze, and a warm smile spread across her face, causing her eyes to crinkle. "I hear there have been troubles up at the big house. I cannot say that I was ever on friendly terms with the grand lady, but she was good despite her sometimes pompous attitude. Made sure everyone had what they needed and would abide by no foolishness. Though I do not know what she was thinking, picking that cousin of yours to be the spiritual leader of the area." Shaking her head, she stirred her tea with a vigor that Elizabeth rarely saw.

Thinking back, Elizabeth shuddered to remember just what those troubles were. "I was there when she passed and though we never got on, I could bear no grudge towards her after all she suffered in the end. She was so very concerned about her daughter."

"It was bad then. Would you say possibly unnatural? I know there have been whispers, some about you even." Mrs. Wright's shrewd eyes studied Elizabeth. Not judging her for her actions, but possibly analyzing her mettle.

"I am not someone who would know much about medicine or tinctures, but I would say that something was wrong, and felt wrong in a way I had never experienced."

"Are you here for my help? Trying to protect your name maybe, or your reputation with gossip swirling like autumn leaves."

"Gossip will swirl how it wants. What I want to know is if someone hurt Lady Catherine on purpose, and if there is a way to know how. I will not allow someone else to suffer that way if I can help it."

Nodding her head and smiling, Mrs. Wright sat back in her chair and took a sip of her tea. "I would not help you if you were here for selfishness or because you wanted to look good for that strapping young man of yours," she explained. As if showing her approval, the old woman passed Elizabeth a cup of tea. "How did she suffer? What ailed her in the end?"

"Her color was off, she was drooling a lot and then foaming at the mouth, and at the end, she was shaking. She also complained about her head aching for days." Ticking everything off on her fingers that came to mind, Elizabeth tried to see what else she might remember that could help her find a solution.

"That does not sound like an ailment I have experience with, nor does it sound like any poison I am aware of in the area or found here abouts. I only know what herbs and plants are of benefit here. That fancy physician came by. What did he say?"

"He let us know it was most likely poison, but he could not name it." Elizabeth took a sip of her fragrant tea and loved the way the flavor played on her tongue. "This is a splendid blend of tea. Can I assume you blend it yourself?"

"Yes, I find it soothing. Passionflower is a favorite of mine for stress and shock. After your day yesterday, I figured you could use some soothing. I am sorry I am not much help sorting out the good lady's death."

Leaning forward, Elizabeth let her concern show on her face. "Can you tell me anything about what to look for in a poison? Anything?"

"Well, if we are talking poison, it doesn't have to be in a bottle with a skull on it." Mrs. Wright paused, watching Elizabeth's face closely, before exploding into a fit of laughter. Waving her hand around, she continued to laugh at her joke until she found a handkerchief in her pocket to wipe at her running eyes. Finally, she cleared her throat and giggled once more before continuing as if nothing had happened. "I know that some of the worst poisons are from plants. Roots, berries, leaves even if put in food or drink can do harm. Also, plants that are bright in color are some of the worst. If I were you, that is something that I would check. Lady Catherine was ever one for special tonics too. Was constantly ordering new ones brought in from lands all over the world. Dosed her daughter with them too."

"I have spoken with her daughter, and she is…" Elizabeth stopped, not wanting to be insulting and not knowing exactly what she should say. What was wrong with the girl?

"It happens sometimes like that in children. Some just seem to stay children. Never could tell why myself. Her health is unreliable, always catching something. If you ask me, she needs more sunshine and good food, not that fancy stuff that is always served up there. Not more of those tonics and potions."

Elizabeth smiled at the woman's zeal. "I have always been rather fond of sunshine and good food myself."

A commotion at the door pulled Elizabeth's attention away from the serious conversation to Hattie bounding up, spilling stalks of rhubarb on the floor in her exuberance. "I found some good ones for you, Mrs. Wright, but the rest will have to wait till they're done growin' some more."

"That is good of you, Hattie, dear. I can pick them myself, but any chance that I get to save my knees and back, I take. I am sure that Miss Bennet will be needed up at the big house soon enough. You take her up there quick like, we do not want her beau to get worried, now do you?" Glancing back at Elizabeth, she smiled at her discomfort.

Frustrated that everyone had known of his love but her, Elizabeth pushed back from the table and stood. "I do not know if he is my beau yet. Until yesterday, I was completely unaware of his feelings for me. I presumed he looked at me to find something about me that he disliked."

"It strikes some boys stupid like that. My Jimmy would chase me around, pulling on my braids for years before he realized that he liked me. It still took him another six months to tell me, though." Eyes turning dreamy, Mrs. Wright sighed and blushed at whatever she was remembering. "I thought he had gone daft. Starin' at me all fool like. Bout broke his hand with a hammer, lookin' the wrong way trying to help put up a barn. Once he got himself together and I forgave his crazy foolishness, we were engaged."

Watching Mrs. Wright speak of her Jimmy, Elizabeth wondered what it was like to feel that kind of love. The kind of love that would put a blush on your cheeks years after you were alone. She wanted that kind of love. Idly, she wondered if she could have that kind of love with Mr. Darcy.

Smiling at the kind woman, Elizabeth curtsied and turned to go back to Rosings with Hattie. "Well, all I can say is Mr. Darcy needs to get over his crazy foolishness soon or I may hit him with a hammer and see if that helps him on his way." She couldn't help but smile as she heard Mrs. Wright's infectious laughter trailing behind them.

Chapter Ten

A Most Significant Blunder

DARCY WAS DISAPPOINTED TO find that Miss Bennet was not in the room when he arrived to eat breakfast. He knew that she was an early riser and would have guessed that she would be there before him. Shaking his head, he went and poured himself some coffee, hoping it would help clear the fog from his mind. It had been a hard night full of odd dreams and long spells of wakefulness.

The possibility that someone might be throwing Miss Bennet in the way of suspicion in order to hide their own nefarious deeds made his blood run cold. He hated the fact that so much depended on factors that were out of his control. If he could use his practiced voice of authority the way he did to get things running smoothly back at Pemberley, he would, but he was wise enough to know that would not work here. There was a difference between calming the chaos when there was a fire at a tenant house and forcing someone to leave Miss Bennet alone.

He was just starting to make actual progress with her as well, which would explain the second dream he had. All he would say about that was that it was much more pleasant than the one where she was standing trial for his aunt's murder. A sound at the door had him looking up eagerly, only to be disappointed when it was just his cousin.

Theodore laughed at what Darcy could only assume was his expression of disappointment. "Well, I know I am not nearly as pretty as Miss Bennet, but you do not have to be *that* disappointed that it is me."

"Well, I need at least a second cup of coffee before I can face you in the morning. You very well know I was hoping to see Miss Bennet. Though it is maybe better that you are here first. I spoke with Reeves last night and he had some disturbing information."

Grabbing his own cup of coffee, Theodore took a seat at the table. "Your man Reeves would do well in his majesty's service. He's one to ferret out information at a prodigious rate. What has he learned now?"

"He has gleaned that there are rumors about Miss Bennet. That she murdered Aunt Catherine because Aunt Catherine was trying to stop us from eloping."

"Well, that will not do at all. Though you must admire the two-prong attack." Miss Bennet's voice at the door startled Darcy.

He had hoped to explain matters in a soothing manner to her, but she had quite snuck up on him. He could only be glad that he did not have a mouth full of coffee to spit out at the surprise. "Please forgive me, Miss Bennet," he said with regret. "I didn't intend to deliver the information in such an abrupt manner."

"Oh, Mr. Darcy, you know I am not a wilting violet. If I was, I would have been married to my cousin by now and all of this would be moot."

"Good God, say that is not so! Who wanted you to marry that bumbling buffoon?" Theodore sat forward in his chair, eager to hear the tale.

Darcy, on the other hand, felt sick to his stomach. The mere notion of Miss Bennet with that odious man left him feeling uneasy and revolted. "Miss Bennet, do sit down. Let me get you a cup of coffee."

Smiling at his offer, she sat down at the table near his own seat. "Well, first there was Mr. Collins himself who could not quite understand the simple English word no. Then there was my mother, who fears being tossed in the Hedgerows at the least provocation after my father dies. Which seeing that Mr. Collins tossed me out of his house without sympathy or ceremony, it is a real possibility. If I had been the wilting sort, I would have succumbed to the pressure and yet I am here unmarried."

"Let me say that I know of at least one gentleman who is eminently glad that you persevered," Theodore pointed out when it appeared that his cousin was once again struck speechless.

"It sounds like you had gained some manner of intelligence in my absence. I had heard this morning there were rumors, but not specifically what they were. Mr. Darcy, I'm curious to know your opinion on the problem." Looking at Darcy with expectation, Miss Bennet took a sip of her coffee.

"Do you mean besides the desire to run the fool spreading gossip to ground and let them know of my displeasure?"

Miss Bennet's melodious laugh filled the room and made Darcy's breath catch in his throat.

"Yes, besides that," she said.

"You were correct in saying that it appears to be a two-pronged attack. There are people here who know you and would say that you would never harm someone and deny the murder charge. The elopement, on the other hand, is something else. While a murder charge would put you in danger of a trial and sentencing, talk of an elopement attempt could damage your reputation. I do not like the idea of either scenario."

Theodore got up from his seat to go to the sideboard, while it appeared his companions were lost in thought. Returning with a plate heaped with thick slices of ham, eggs, and toast smothered with jam, he pointed out his own concern. "I believe it feels like someone is trying to keep us on the defensive. If we are trying to protect Miss Bennet, we will not necessarily be looking for the culprit."

"Do we believe, then, that this was intentional and not an accident?" Miss Bennet queried.

"This rumor has me leaning that way, yes. It has developed with far too much speed and is too specific to be the fruit of curiosity and rabid speculation." Theodore paused in speaking to take a bite of his meal. Ever the soldier, Darcy thought. His cousin knew it was never wise to skip a meal. Who knew when he would be prevented from eating because of a call to action.

Darcy rose as well to get a plate of artfully arranged bread and some of the ginger cake, along with eggs and the marmalade that was there. Going back to the table, he placed it wordlessly in front of Miss Bennet. Her widened eyes and blush were reward enough for his actions and after a quick bow, he returned and mindlessly gathered food for himself, too lost in euphoric reminiscing about her delicate blush to note what he had gathered. Sitting down once again, he noticed that he only put various kinds of eggs on his palate. He saw Theodore's shoulders shake in silent humor at his predicament.

"Did you have a good morning, Miss Bennet? I know you are an early riser, so I was surprised to not find you here when I arrived."

"Yes, I was up before the sun, but I went out with a maid for a walk and had a very interesting conversation with a nearby widow. A Mrs. Wright who lives not far from here," Miss Bennet explained as she spread a generous helping of marmalade on her bread.

"I think I saw her name on one of the ledgers. She gets a supply of firewood every winter, I believe." Darcy grudgingly took a bite of some of the scrambled eggs.

"Apparently, she sees to those in the area who are ailing by providing tinctures and the like. Her tea was certainly delicious. She is the one who told me that there were rumors, but we did not discuss them. I was curious to see if she knew of any local herb or plant that would give the symptoms that Lady Catherine displayed."

Theodore looked up from his plate and wiped his mouth before speaking. "That was a good idea, Miss Bennet. Did you find out anything that we could find useful?"

Elizabeth's fingers danced as she marked off each thing she had learned, explaining her knowledge. "She said that there were no local plants that would give those symptoms. According to her, Lady Catherine was always trying new tinctures and potions on herself and Anne, hoping to provide better health. She claimed that Lady Catherine would collect them from various far-off places. Oh, she also said that the brighter the color of the plant, the more likely it was to be poisonous." Reaching over, Miss Bennet picked up her coffee and took another sip.

"I had not thought of it, but yes, when I go over the ledgers, I often see expenditures labeled 'Medicinals' that look to be coming from as far as India and the far east." With a final bite, Theodore rose from his chair. "Maybe we should go through them to see what we find."

***

"THIS IS CERTAINLY MORE than I had pictured. Are we sure any of these concoctions even work?" Darcy looked around his aunt's dressing room. It was certainly not what he had expected. The room was lacking all the gilt edging and swathes of purple that he had always assumed his aunt would require. The largest shock was the massive table covered from edge to edge with bottles and sachets.

Miss Bennet picked up a bottle from the edge and held it aloft. Swirling it around, they both took note of the various bits of detritus floating in the mixture. "Are we sure that none of them killed her?"

"Without knowing what all of this is, there is no telling what it could do. Is any of it labeled?" Darcy took one of the bottles to the nearby window and held it up to the light. A faded pattern looked to be a handwritten label that was completely illegible. He knew his aunt preferred order, so there must be some kind of organization, but he could not see it.

Looking over, Darcy noticed Reeves standing quietly at the door. Ever faithful, he was conscious of the risk to Miss Bennet's reputation, should someone say they were spending time alone.

No need to fan the flame on that particular fire. When Theodore had decided to question the people who might have delt with any recent peddlers, it left Darcy alone with Miss Bennet. Though he was curious about Theodore's sudden idea and departure, he was appreciative of this opportunity to be alone with her. Gathering his courage, Darcy decided to ask Miss Bennet a question. "Miss Bennet, did you never think that I held any fondness for you?" he asked.

With a sigh, Miss Bennet stepped away from the table and made her way over to the trunk on the other side of the room. "I think you mostly confused me, Mr. Darcy. I had formed the conclusion that you did not care for me because of your comment, and I was trying to fit everything I saw into those parameters. When Mr. Wickham lied to me, it was almost easier for me, I think. I realize now that it hurt my pride that you found me so wanting. It was easier to feel that you were cruel to everyone and not just me. It made it hurt less. I could feel righteous indignation on his behalf and worry less about your opinion of me." Miss Bennet hesitated and worried her lip, then she looked him straight in the eye, her expression unwavering. "I also realize that I would not have been so hurt had I not felt something to start with."

Darcy's heart constricted with guilt as he contemplated the pain he had caused the woman he loved. His need to protect himself from ladies' expectations had become so ingrained that it was now an instinct to act the way he did. The last thing he wanted was to inflict any kind of suffering on her, on anyone. Was he unconsciously hurting others with his aloof demeanor without realizing it? "I know you do not want me to apologize, but I will say that I never intended to hurt you. I was completely unaware of the way I was being perceived. Though I am trying to be better, I am left wondering if my manner was hurtful to others."

"Well, how often do you call women tolerable in a crowd full of their long-time neighbors and friends?"

Darcy was glad she had resumed looking over the bottles and was facing away from him as he could feel his cheeks burn with embarrassment. "I believe that has been my most significant blunder."

Turning her head, Miss Bennet looked him in the eye, and with a pert smile, said, "Well then, it seems we have caught your issue in time. You are only sometimes proud and aloof, and hopefully we have caught it before you have descended into outright pigheadedness."

"Well, that is a relief." His surprise at her comment made him laugh. It was something that he was realizing he did not do enough.

"Mr. Darcy, I believe it is my turn."

"Pardon?" Darcy turned to see her laughing eyes.

"We are trading questions, remember?"

"Oh, by all means, ask your question." Darcy truly hoped that her question would not be as difficult as last time. Her inquiry about Wickham had been tough for him. He had a gut feeling that she was going to give him a run for his money. In a way, he felt that this was only fair. He had behaved in a manner to lose her faith in his intentions, so he needed to do what he could to alleviate her concerns.

"Why did you take Mr. Bingley away from Netherfield?" Miss Bennet's voice had grown serious as she questioned Darcy.

"He had matters to attend to in London." Darcy fought the desire to remove his cravat.

Miss Bennet's eyes had become hard and discerning, where only moments before, they had been laughing. "I believe that he needed to go to London, but he did not need to stay away. He had every intention of returning but did not. I believe that was you and his sisters' doing. Am I correct or have I misinterpreted things once more?"

Cringing at the fact that he had caused her to doubt her own understanding of things, Darcy forged on as he should, though it was with dread and not bravery. This could go badly. "You are correct in the belief that I used my influence on him to keep him away from Netherfield. His sisters also exhibited a determined effort to stay away from Netherfield as well."

"Then, once again, my question is why?"

"Since our days at Cambridge, Bingley has been a close friend of mine. Although I've had to deal with responsibilities since I was young, he's only just started to, and it's clear he's struggling to come to terms with it. He has a talent for finding the good in every situation, no matter how difficult. I think that is why we became friends. He shows me the lighter side of things when I am bogged down with responsibility. He is not overly careful with his attention, as I was trained to do at a young age. Bingley is like a bee drawn to the sweetest flower, always seeking out the prettiest girl in the room. He often talks of an angel one week only to find another at the next large gathering she is absent from." Darcy had a hard enough time talking easily to anyone at large gatherings. Finding his own angel was a concept he had never even considered until this moment. He had enjoyed the enthusiasm Bingley always showed, but he was beginning to see that there were flaws in that way as well.

Miss Bennet's fingers played absently with the lace on her dress as she gazed up at him, worry etched on her face. "Is he so callow, to disregard a woman's feeling in such a way? "

"Londoners are familiar with his behavior and understand it. Many young cubs like him behave similarly, with no great expectations from anyone. So he does not always think of how his gregariousness could be interpreted. However, in the country, things are different. His time with your sister was noted by the community and if he had stayed longer, there would have been serious expectations."

"Would that have been so bad?"

The wobble in her voice gave Darcy the great concern that he had misread something somewhere. He only hoped she would not hold a grudge against him for his actions. "Not if your sister's heart was engaged, and Bingley's emotions were as well. His sisters would have been a problem and maybe a member or two of your own family, but that would be nothing if they truly loved each other."

"Did you think that my sister's heart was not engaged?"

Thinking back, he remembered the older Miss Bennet's smile that she showed everyone. Sometimes he felt she smiled too much. He certainly had never found that much to smile about, but then he wore a mask most of the time. "She showed a generous attitude towards everyone and often smiled while conversing with Bingley, but I did not notice any signs of longing in her. I observed your mother's very forward declarations, and I feared your sister would be pressured into accepting a match that she did not specifically favor."

"And so you separated them because you did not see any love in them and my mother was so uncouth to talk about her hopes and expectations too loud among her friends?" Voice sharp and eyes hard, Elizabeth demanded the truth.

"Have you ever heard that separation makes the heart grow fonder?" Darcy spoke wistfully. He had definitely experienced the truth in that saying himself.

She nodded and said, "Yes," but her expression was pensive, her brows drawn together. Darcy wondered if his question perplexed her, or if she was possibly remembering an experience of her own.

"I advocated for some time apart, but I also trusted that if his love was resilient and steadfast, it would compel him to return to her despite his sisters' objections. Without that driving force, I did not feel he would have the backbone to stand up to his sisters on your sister's behalf. It would not have a pleasant existence. Bingley seems to have moved on. I cannot say for certain, however, he has not spoken of your sister for some time. If I misinterpreted your sister's feelings on the matter, I apologize, but I was, in my own way, trying to protect her from possible strife and ridicule." Finding himself playing with the bottle in his hands, he tapped it in his palm. It was likely that Miss Bennet was worried about her sister and that her sister had been attached to his friend.

Reaching back into the trunk before her, Miss Bennet spoke softly but firmly. "I would not wish a man so fickle in his affections on my sister. Though she has been somewhat morose of late in the long run, it would be better than having to live with Caroline Bingley without her husband's love and support."

Moving back to the table, he put the bottle back how he found it, only to notice that despite the clutter, everything was clean, there was no dust.

"Miss Bennet, did you notice everything is free of dust? Someone has been cleaning. My aunt would never dust, so that meant someone else has been seeing to it."

Miss Bennet was kneeling next to a trunk, sorting through the items inside. From where he stood, it looked mostly to be clothing or fabric. She glanced up at his comment. "You are right. It is possible that someone will know more about all these mysterious bottles. Most of this is old clothes and keepsakes. Though I have found several journals."

The sound of rushed footsteps had them both turning to the door to see what was about. A flustered Mrs. Graham came rushing in and Darcy knew yet another thing had gone wrong. "Mrs. Graham, whatever is the matter? You look like you have had a fright."

"Sir, I must tell you that the maid who was assigned to Miss Bennet's room brought me the most alarming thing. Now I know Miss Bennet, and I know Hattie who swears that it was not there this morning when she was putting away Miss Bennet's clothes. It is not right, but I know how it looks."

"Whatever did the maid find?" Elizabeth spoke up, her voice full of concern for the frantic housekeeper.

"She found this." Reaching into her pocket on her apron, she pulled out a small bottle. Turning it over in her palm so they could clearly see the label, she held it out to them.

Their culprit had stuck again. Someone had obviously gone into Miss Bennet's room and planted a bottle to make her look guilty of murder. There, on Mrs. Graham's work-worn palm, was a bottle that clearly said hemlock.

Chapter Eleven
What Could Happen in a Day or Two?

ELIZABETH'S BLOOD TURNED COLD as she became transfixed by the bottle in Mrs. Graham's possession. The plain brown bottle looked so innocent, and yet what it represented was ominous. Someone had gone into her room and put it there. Someone wanted her to look like a murderer. She did not know what disturbed her more—that she would look like the culprit of such a heinous crime or that there was an actual murderer in the house. Someone who was targeting her.

Feeling the need to say something, anything, Elizabeth finally managed to open her mouth, "I would not even begin to know where to get hemlock."

"I know that this is not your doing, Miss Bennet. You would never hurt someone maliciously." Mr. Darcy's expression was one of earnest entreaty. Reaching out, Mr. Darcy took the bottle from Mrs. Graham, examining it as if the bottle could tell him who planted it.

Free of the offending item, Mrs. Graham reached over and pat Elizabeth's hand in a show of maternal comfort. "You do not worry, dear. I know it was not you that brought that bottle into the house. Hattie went through your room putting your clothes away earlier and it was nowhere to be found."

Though Elizabeth smiled vaguely at Mrs. Graham's show of comfort, her mind was whirling. They had put hemlock in her room, but at least they had not put it in her tea. When she nearly burst out laughing at the odd idea, she forced herself to halt and focus on her breathing. Taking a deep breath, she closed her eyes and focused on the sensation of the air filling her lungs. Relaxing for a moment allowed her to step back from the building panic and think. Eyes widening as she remembered something, she turned to Mr. Darcy to point it out. "Now that I think about it, I think the physician said that he knew she did not have the symptoms to match hemlock poisoning. Why would the presumed killer use a bottle of hemlock to make me look bad?"

"You are right. It is not logical."

"Someone who has been pushed to the point of murder may not be in the right frame of mind to exhibit logic." Elizabeth found herself hugging the journals that she had found to her chest as if needing some comfort, though it was all becoming too alarming for her complete comfort.

It was to this scene that Colonel Fitzwilliam came into the room with a stack of papers in his hands and noted all the concerned expressions. "What else has happened?"

"Someone has planted a bottle of hemlock in Miss Bennet's room and one of the maids found it just now." Mr. Darcy held the bottle of poison up for his cousin to see.

"Well, that is certainly a bold move." Reaching out, the colonel took the bottle of poison from Mr. Darcy and handed him the papers. "These came for you from Aunt Catherine's barrister. To have been sent by express, I thought it might be important."

"Thank you." Taking the papers, Mr. Darcy immediately began reading the correspondence. His brow furrowed as he read.

Wanting to distract herself from her growing sense of dread, Elizabeth turned to Mrs. Graham. "Mrs. Graham, who was it that cleaned in here? It is immaculate, so someone must have helped."

"Sarah, she was a wonderful maid, always neat and tidy, always helped Lady Catherine with all her medicinals."

"Was? What happened to her? Is she no longer at Rosings?" Elizabeth felt the edge of a memory tugging at her. Something about a complaint that Lady Catherine had made before her death.

Mrs. Graham shook her head at the issue. "Lady Catherine dismissed her that morning, or possibly sometime in the night. The morning that she passed. It was a pity as she was such a good worker, but Sarah left immediately. She has family in London, and she went on the early coach."

"That is it. Lady Catherine spoke of her maid saying that she was unwell and wanting her to rest. She said that she had dismissed her." Pressing a hand to her temple, Elizabeth forced her mind to recall the horrible morning. Was it only the day before that it had happened? "Lady Catherine said, 'My fool of a maid tried to convince me to stay abed, and I fired her for her impertinence.' Her maid, Sarah, knew she was unwell. Somehow, she knew something was wrong with her."

The colonel snapped to attention when given that information. "We need to talk with the maid. She could have vital information about Aunt Catherine's death. It is possible that she fled because she had caused her death, or she may simply have information about Aunt Catherine's last days. Either way, we need to find her. Mrs. Graham, do you have her direction?"

"Yes, I have it somewhere in my paperwork."

Turning back to Mr. Darcy, Elizabeth realized that his concerned expression had only gotten worse while they had discussed the maid, Sarah. "Mr. Darcy, is everything all right? You appear rather concerned about your correspondence."

Running his hand through his hair, Mr. Darcy let out a sigh. "Aunt Catherine's barrister says that he received an alarming correspondence from her shortly before her death. He states it is not something that he would wish to trust to a letter and requests that I hurry to London to discuss matters with him. He also explains the arrangements that are in place for the inheritance of Rosings may not be what we think and once again asks that I come to see him as soon as I am able."

Miss Bennet sensed the importance of the information they received and believed it required immediate attention. "Well, it sounds like you and the colonel are going to London today. It is a good thing that it is not so very far from here."

"You cannot be serious! Someone just went into your room and planted a bottle of poison, and you're suggesting that we abandon you to the clutches of a murderer?"

Eyes narrowed, Elizabeth faced the man across from her. She tried to tell herself that he was concerned for her and did not intend to be acting in a heavy-handed manner. She was only partially successful. "Do I look like I am in the clutches of a murderer, Mr. Darcy? I will be perfectly fine in your absence. Mrs. Graham and Hattie will look after me and I was thinking that I should spend some time with Anne. The poor thing just lost her mother and cannot but feel a little lost right now."

Mr. Darcy had the decency to look embarrassed for his reaction, if not cowed. "Miss Bennet, I did not mean... I would never presume to control your actions. I only would wish for you to remain safe and happy. I...I...I will stop talking now."

"What my fumbling cousin is trying to say, Miss Bennet, is that he cares for you deeply and the thought of you in any danger strikes him to his very core. Even the possibility of you being in danger of experiencing a hangnail would worry him. So the idea of leaving you in the same building with a murderer struck him deeply and left him quite befuddled." Colonel Fitzwilliam smiled fondly at his cousin, who had begun to massage one of his temples.

Elizabeth was moved to forgive the man for reacting so strongly. Now that she knew the intent behind some of his statements, and how deeply his feelings ran, she could not help but smile at them. She understood his bumbling statements better. Though she was not ready to admit the truth to herself quite yet, when he said things as he did, she felt a fluttering that was entirely too distracting. Despite any mental protestations, she was much closer to liking him that she would have believed at that point.

Going over to the suffering man, she carefully pulled his hand away from his face. Looking into his eyes, she said, "Thank you for worrying about me. I will endeavor to be fine. You must remember that I am not easily intimidated. Look how well I was able to contend with Caroline Bingley."

"She could not even comprehend half of your comments. You handled her with the grace of a queen and the skill of an expert archer. Every comment hit it's mark, even if she did not see you shooting holes in her arguments." Darcy chuckled, smiling warmly at Elizabeth who had forgotten that she still held his arm. "No matter what you say, I will worry. I can do nothing else."

Giving him her best pert smile, she responded, "Both of you go. Time may not be on our hands. Do not worry for me, Mr. Darcy. What could happen in a matter of a day or two?"

***

THE ROOM WAS A pleasant one, Elizabeth decided. It was less ostentatious than the more public spaces of Rosings. She watched Anne and Hattie interact, and she was glad she had asked Hattie to come. Elizabeth could tell that Anne was lonely. Of course, she would be—she socialized with hardly anyone. It did not look like there were many activities to keep her occupied in the room. What disturbed Elizabeth was that she did not see evidence of Mrs. Stevenson anywhere.

Elizabeth may have never had a companion herself, but was not that the point of the position? Across the room, Elizabeth monitored the chatting going on while she took inventory of the room. There was a bookcase that looked very forlorn. It was not dusty, per se, but the books looked unread and forgotten. A shelf held some mementos and old toys. There was a large picture window that looked out over the gardens. It was a lovely view and Elizabeth would enjoy it. She was simply confused. There was an entire corner of the room that was simply blank, as if everything there was unimportant and taken away. If this was the room that Anne spent most of her time in, what was she doing?

The sudden sound of crying had Elizabeth dashing back to Anne to see what was amiss. "Whatever is the matter?"

"She was just talking of her little puppy, Buttons. He died last week. She was rather fond of him, Miss Bennet." As she spoke, Hattie comforted Anne with a gentle arm around her shoulders.

"Buttons was my friend, but he died, Miss Bennet. Momma was my Momma, and she died too. It makes me sad." Anne wiped her face with a handkerchief.

"I am sorry to hear about Buttons. Tell me about him."

"He was the best friend ever, always soft and wiggling. He liked to lick at my fingers and play with my beads. But he got sick. He would not eat, and he kept making messes. Last week he was just wanting to lay down, and then he started shaking and he would not wake up." Anne looked up at Elizabeth, her face solemn. "Mrs. Stevenson came in and said he had died and to stop whining about it. She made the maids take him away and all of his things, even his bed."

As Elizabeth thought about the situation, she recalled a time when she had lost a pet and how devastating it had been. Her heart ached as she wondered who could be so heartless to someone mourning the loss of their beloved puppy. Let alone someone who was like Anne. "I am so sorry, Anne. That is very sad. I never had a puppy, but I always wanted one. They make my momma sneeze, so I could never get one."

"I was able to hide some of his stuff. Would you like to see?"

The poor girl's beaming smile at her saved items was bittersweet to Elizabeth, and she could not help but smile broadly in return. "I would love to see, Anne."

Running over to a chest in the corner, Anne started taking out winter blankets and then, finding what she wanted, came back clutching at a small bundle. "This is all I was able to keep. Do not let Mrs. Stevenson see it, though. She would want to take it away."

Taking the small bundle from Anne, Elizabeth opened it up to find that a small, chewed on blanket was wrapped around a little stuffed dog. There was also a little ball and, oddly enough, a broken bead bracelet. "Did Buttons like playing ball?"

"Oh yes, we would play together all the time. I would roll the ball and Buttons would chase after it and bring it back. Then he would wiggle his behind up in the air, waiting for me to roll it again." Anne's smile was wobbly as she remembered her fond friend.

"Was this Buttons's bracelet? It is broken."

"Well, it is my bracelet, but he loved playing with my bead bracelets ever so much. I lost most of the beads when he broke it a while ago. So, I saved it with his other things," Anne spoke, holding the stuffed dog to her chest.

Elizabeth felt that she really was more like a child in her sorrow. Picking up the red bead bracelet, Elizabeth laid it on her open palm. The design was certainly odd. Nothing like anything she had seen before, and the beads did not look so much like any beads she had seen either. They were not uniform, and each had a small black dot on a red body. "Anne, where did you get this bracelet?"

"Momma got it from one of those faraway places. She said it was supposed to bring me health." Shrugging, Anne went to put her treasures away.

It appeared to Elizabeth that Anne did not think it was very important where a bracelet came from. Elizabeth did not know what it was, but something about that bracelet, the whole situation really, struck Elizabeth as odd. She wondered why it was bothering her, but she could not put her finger on it. Maybe it would come to her later.

Elizabeth had returned to her room that evening and was looking through one of the journals she had found in Lady Catherine's things. She had brought two of them to her room and soon realized that she had found the first and the last journal. Figuring she would find more relevant information in the most recent book, she sat down on the one chair and began reading.

Much of the information did not appear to be of any great importance. It was mostly about her running of Rosings and a mother's fear for her daughter. It was clear that her daughter's differences from others weighed heavily on her mind. She also noted that she cared very much for her nephew, Mr. Darcy. It was not something that Elizabeth had observed herself, but she felt that her daunted powers of observation were not as skilled as she once assumed.

Closing the book, she leaned her head against the tall back of the chair. She really felt that she might not know as much about the people she observed as she had always felt. Even her assumption about Mr. Bingley was, at its root, incorrect. Mr. Bingley was a grown man, able to make his own decisions. Mr. Darcy may have played a role in influencing him, however, his own actions proved he was inconsistent in his attention. Poor Jane—her affections had truly been engaged, but Mr. Bingley was unworthy of them.

Her faulty logic was perhaps best demonstrated by Mr. Darcy. She had interpreted his actions as concrete evidence of his emotions. Only she had not been correct in her assumptions. She had entered a loop that was full of fallacies. Just because he was staring at her did not mean that he found fault with her. She now knew that he looked at her out of a more positive emotion. An emotion that he called love.

Elizabeth next considered Mr. Darcy's emotions and discovered that they did not bother her in the slightest. Did that mean that her emotions were reciprocal? Not necessarily. However, Elizabeth realized that she certainly felt more than she would have believed possible. Two days ago, she would have been fine commenting on how much of a disagreeable man Mr. Darcy was. But now she knew she would not, could not say anything against him. Though awkward and severe at times, he had good intentions, even if he did not always manage the best outcomes. Who was able to say that they got it right all the time? At least he was trying to do good things and improve. Did realizing that change her feelings for him?

She had always thought him a fine figure of a man and now that she felt the person behind his careful expressions was a good one, she admitted that she liked looking at him. Had she been waiting to give herself permission to like the man? That was ridiculous. She did not like the idea that she had disliked him merely because she believed he disliked her.

Refusing to contemplate the physical pull she had been feeling, Elizabeth instead tried to contemplate his evident wishes. He had completely admitted that he wished to marry her. How would that look? Would they argue all the time? Would he hide in his study from her impertinence?

She had realized growing up in Meryton that most boys did not like smart girls. For a long time, she had convinced herself that marriage was not for her. She was content, she supposed, to help raise her nieces and nephews. Or, if necessary, become a governess somewhere. She had given up any expectation that a man of quality, of worth, would ever be interested in her. Could that be why she assumed his actions were negative? If so, she was ashamed of the behavior. The more she reasoned on it, the more she realized it was true. She had gone into the situation feeling that he would never give her notice and his unthinking words had tipped her over the edge into some very poor assumptions.

With her misconceptions cleared, Elizabeth contemplated the idea of them marrying. They argued often, but Lady Catherine said they were debates. She told herself that Mr. Darcy enjoyed matching wits with her. Just how many men could she match wits with? Her knowledge and love for reading different subjects made her stand out from most women of her time, which was not well received by the men she knew. She enjoyed reading nearly everything from the classics to journals on agricultural reform. She had even read Fordyce sermons, though it was the one book she would willingly use to kindle a fire. What would it be like to discuss the notions that always ran through her head with someone besides her father? In the end, the long day caught up to Elizabeth, and she drifted off, sitting in the chair by the tiny fire with Lady Catherine's journal on her lap.

Elizabeth had been dreaming about a little boy with wild brown hair bringing her flowers. She felt a presence beside her, large and reassuring, and somehow she knew he was her husband, only she could not see his face no matter how she tried. His warm arm drew her to his side, and she nestled into his warmth, happy, in a way that she had never known. It was a lovely dream until the door to her room was unceremoniously flung open and banged against the wall.

Sitting up, she glanced around, immediately wishing she had that comforting presence back. In the doorway stood Mrs. Stevenson with a look of satisfaction on her face. A man stood beside her, wearing rumpled traveling clothes and a few too many pounds. He had an imperious air that reminded her of Lady Catherine.

"Here she is, my lord. The woman I believe murdered your dear sister. The maid found hemlock in her room only this morning." Her voice was accusatory and cold as she blamed Elizabeth.

Looking Elizabeth up and down, the man dismissed her with a flick of his eyes and turned back to Mrs. Stevenson. "You say that my sister had brought her in the morning she died?"

"Yes, my lord, there is a rumor that she had discovered an elopement plot and was putting a stop to it. I do not know what your nephew was thinking, installing her at Rosings. I can know of no decent reason for her to be here." Mrs. Stevenson's ingratiating comment hung in the silence like a funeral bell. Being a woman herself, she understood the delicate nature of one's reputation and was eager to tarnish Elizabeth's.

The narrowing of her eyes as she implied vile things set Elizabeth's teeth on edge. Looking at the woman casting doubt on her virtue, Elizabeth held her head high. The petty woman would not intimidate her. She knew who she was, and she suspected that the woman before her was more than simply annoying. She was possibly very dangerous. It was obvious that she had something against Elizabeth, but was it more than that?

Coming forward, the rumpled gentleman glared down at Elizabeth. "You can have nothing to say in your defense against such evidence, young woman. I will not have my sister's killer under her roof."

"Lord Matlock, I presume?" As Elizabeth stood up, she curtsied gracefully, taking a moment to study him before speaking. "I find you very much like your sister. She, too, liked to assume things about me without giving me the privilege of answering. Despite that, I found I liked her well enough. I am sorry for your loss, my lord."

"Buttering me up will do nothing. I know your sort. Turning the heads of young men with your feminine wiles. I will not have your manipulative ways bring harm to my family." Turning, he left the room, his strides long and powerful. "Have the footman bring her to the front hall. The magistrate should be here soon."

"Of course, my lord." Although Mrs. Stevenson might have tried to smile kindly, there was something menacing about the way it came across.

Movement in the hall had Elizabeth trying to see into the dark corridor. She noted Reeves talking to a figure. He caught her eye and bowed with a flourish before turning to go. The figure turned, and she could recognize Gregory.

"Footman, take her downstairs and guard her until the magistrate comes to take her away. We would not want her to escape justice."

Coming into the room, Gregory bowed. "Miss Bennet, if you will come with me. May I suggest you bring a shawl? It is rather cold at night still."

If Mrs. Stevenson wanted to see her dragged away, it was not to be so. Elizabeth had too much dignity and too many friends. She would behave like the lady that she was. Taking up the thick woolen shawl that was lying on her bed, she wrapped it around her shoulders. On impulse, she decided to bring the journal she had been reading. She could probably use something to keep her mind occupied. "Let us go Gregory, there is no use dawdling."

Elizabeth held her head high, despite the woman's angry gaze, and walked out of the room with Gregory by her side. She heard the huff of frustration come from Mrs. Stevenson, who had started following her. Elizabeth could not stop the smile that crept onto her face. She was on her way presumably to the nearby Hunsford's gaol, and yet she found it funny to be aggravating the bitter companion. Her mother had always said that she was contrary.

It had not taken long for Elizabeth to be taken to the town gaol by the magistrate, who was the small town's mayor. He reminded her of Charlotte's father, Sir William Lucas. Though he was a gregarious and happy conversationalist, it confused him to have been woken up to escort a young lady on orders from an earl. He talked of having a daughter her age who was expecting his first grandchild and though he was nice, it was an odd conversation to have in the front of a wagon under the light of the half-moon.

The look on his face when they accused her of murdering Lady Catherine was one of shock and disbelief. Despite his reservations about the Earl of Matlock's claims, he was a good-hearted man who obeyed his orders. The woolen shawl that Elizabeth wore on their brief journey was a welcome relief from the chilly night air that threatened to seep into her bones.

Crushing his hat in his large hands, the man shook his head. "I am sorry that the conditions are so poor. I had wanted to have you come stay with my family, Miss Bennet, but Lord Matlock insisted I put you in here. We only use it to house the disorderly drunks until they sleep it off. It is not fit for a lady like you."

The town gaol stood alone, its squat walls somehow bleak and foreboding. The stone that made up the structure looked to be sturdy, though obviously very old. It was only one room with one door and no chimney; it was going to be a frigid night. There was no glass or shutters in the roughhewn rectangle hole that served as a window. Metal bars would not keep out the cold or wind and simply blocked any hope of escape. Not that she had any intention of escape. She would endure. Mr. Darcy would return soon enough to set things straight.

Forcing herself to step into the room, Elizabeth peered around, trying to take in every detail. It was, without a doubt, the bleakest room she had probably ever been in. The room was empty except for the hay on the floor and the musty, rank smell that permeated the air wrinkled her nose. It was not even the clean dry hay she saw in the stables at home. There was a bucket in the corner that Elizabeth had a sinking feeling about. "Mr. Cleaves, do not worry about it. I know you would choose something else for me if you could. I will just have to make do for a time. Though I have a request for you, if you do not mind?"

"I will help if I can, miss."

"If it is not too dear, do you have a sheet or blanket at home that I may wrap up in? It is a frosty night and I do not think I will manage well with only my shawl." Elizabeth did not want to think about what was crawling in that hay. If she could wrap herself up in a blanket, she could try to stay clean. Well, at least cleaner than if she lay on the hay, she did not think clean was a possibility tonight.

"That I can do. The lord said that I had to put you in here. He did not say that I could not help you out while in here. I will return right quick. I must lock you in, though." His face was awash in guilt.

"I understand Mr. Cleaves. I respect a man who knows his duty and I hold none of this against you."

He quickly returned from his nearby home with his arms full. "My wife sent over some things as well as the blanket. A small stool and a sheet to go with the blanket. She said you might like this bonnet as well. She advised you to keep your head covered. It might keep you warm, but she said you wouldn't want nothin' getting into your hair."

"Your wife is a wonderful woman. I will take this all with gratitude." Grateful for the small white cap, Elizabeth put it on right away. It covered all her head and though she knew it was a dowdy cap, she was glad that she had something to protect her hair. It took some time for Elizabeth to create herself a little area against the wall near the door. She cleaned the area of what straw that she could and wrapped herself in the sheet and blanket. She contemplated sleeping on the stool, leaning against the wall, but dreaded the thought of tumbling off into the hay. Sitting on the bare earth, she leaned against the wall, resting her face against the cold stone. Was it only that morning that she had been talking to Mr. Darcy? What had she said? What could happen in a day or two?

Chapter Twelve

Blackmail!

DARCY SAT IN HIS room at his home in Mayfair and found that he could not sleep. He had left Miss Bennet at Rosings with a killer. What was he thinking?

He and Theodore had come on horseback to London with two separate goals, and it felt as if they had made no headway with either. He had gone directly to the barrister's office to find that he had been called away on a family emergency, but he was told that he could return in the morning. Theodore, on the other hand, had spent his time searching for the missing maid. He had gone to her lodgings only to find that she was applying to employment agencies. This information led him on a merry chase, looking at all the employment agencies he could find looking for her. Sadly, they had failed to get a description of the woman and only had her name.

The only ray of hope that had come about from Theodore's search was that he had spoken with one of the offices that said she would be returning the next day for an interview. Theodore had planned to return early the next morning and wait for her to show up.

Darcy felt he was a failure for leaving Miss Bennet to go on a quest that he was failing at. He had nothing to do but wait until he could attempt to see the barrister in the morning. The office did not open until ten, and this frustrated him as well. He had sent a note around to Georgiana, who was staying at Matlock House with her new companion and Lady Matlock. Hopefully, he could see her tomorrow morning.

All his frustration was mounting, but oddly, he knew that was not what was keeping him awake. It was the memory of her. The stray curl that danced around her face, taunting her with its refusal to be tamed. It would lie against her cheek and Miss Bennet would constantly brush it back behind her ear, only to have it spring out again minutes later. She drew him to her, and he did not know if he had any hope of her feeling the same way. Would she ever grow to love him back?

There was a sinking feeling in the pit of his stomach that told him he must hurry, that there was an urgency he did not know of. He tried to brush it away and told himself it was merely a figment of his imagination. What he was doing in London was important, he knew that, but he felt he had left the most important thing back at Rosings.

He had no ability to protect her from this distance. Miss Bennet would say that she did not need to be protected, that she was fine on her own. That did not, however, stop his need to see her well. She had the remarkable ability to refuse to be intimidated no matter what the world threw at her, but that did not keep her safe. He prayed she would be well until his return, that God would protect her and keep her safe. He would feel uneasy until he returned and laid eyes on the precious curl and the woman who had entranced him.

***

THE MORNING ARRIVED GREY and abysmal. It matched Darcy's mood in nearly every way. He had slept poorly and woke with a crick in his neck. Having left Reeves behind, he managed on his own, but he missed that man's way of lifting his spirits.

Sitting at his table, he clutched at his cup of coffee like a drowning man clutched at a piece of driftwood. He felt as if he needed the dark brew to even keep his eyes open. When he could finally sleep, his dreams had been horrendous. Visions of Elizabeth in danger and calling to him for help haunted him even now. He had attempted to eat some toast but had lost his appetite for anything else.

Across from him sat Theodore, happily munching away at eggs and sausage. The sight of it nearly turned his stomach. "How can you eat at a time like this?"

"Darcy, I am a soldier. I know how important it is to eat food when it is available. Supply lines fail and battles erupt. I have gone without and so when there is food, I eat it," Theodore chirped merrily; he had always been a morning person.

Movement at the door had Darcy swiveling his head to see who came in. Georgiana smiled timidly at him and spoke with a delicate voice that reminded him of his mother. "I hope you do not mind, but I wanted to see you. When I heard you were in residence, I asked to be brought over."

Putting down his nearly empty cup, Darcy got up to hug his darling little sister. "I never mind seeing you! I was uncertain I would be here long enough to make a visit or else I would have come to Matlock House myself. How are things working out with Mrs. Ansley?"

"She is splendid. I would have brought her with me this morning, but she is suffering from a cold. Are you certain you are well, brother? You do not look at all yourself." Peering up at her tall brother, he imagined she could see the exhaustion in his face.

"He is merely mooning over his lady love. I do believe he has failed to sleep much at all last night." Theodore winked at Darcy over Georgiana's head.

"Love? Are you in love, brother? Tell me everything." Going over to the sideboard, she selected a muffin and sat down at the table.

Admitting defeat in the face of both expectant faces, Darcy began. "Her name is Miss Bennet. She is a gentleman's daughter from—"

"Hertfordshire! I wondered if there was something there. She is the lady who walked three miles to tend her ailing sister at Netherfield." Georgiana's face was aglow with excitement that Darcy had not seen for some time. The joyful girl that had been damaged by Wickham's treachery was finally glimmering back through the cracks of her somber timidity. Miss Bennet was already helping his sister, and they had not even met.

"How did you know?" he questioned.

"You wrote about her several times in your letters. The only other woman you had ever written to me about was Miss Caroline, and that was only to tell me how annoying she was and how you had managed to avoid her company that day."

Pausing his consumption of his breakfast, Theodore spoke up again. "Yes, our dear boy is quite lost to cupid's arrow. Now if only he can court her, he may find happiness."

"I thought you were at Rosings. Have you been back to Hertfordshire? Why would you not court her? What is amiss, brother?" Georgiana looked at him, her blue eyes confused.

In order to explain himself, he stated only the basics. "Miss Bennet was visiting her friend that is married to our aunt's rector. I had been seeing her in the area and meeting her on walks. I realized that I loved her and decided to propose."

Theodore's chuckle at his explanation drew Georgiana's gaze and her grin. His mirth came through when he spoke to her conspiratorially. "What he is leaving out was that he never talked to her on the walks and often got in arguments with her. Stared at her often and overall, he proceeded in an addled manner. Poor Miss Bennet was under the impression that he disliked her. Would you believe that he was going to propose thinking she would accept his hand with no indication of his emotions beforehand?"

Biting her lip, Georgiana appeared to be fighting a smile at his expense. "Not well done at all, brother. You must let her know you hold her in esteem."

"Things have gotten rather complicated. But despite that, I believe she now knows of my affection." Darcy tried and failed to keep from smiling.

"Complicated how?"

"I sent something with the post. Did you not get it? Aunt Catherine has died."

"No, I did not know. I was going to read my mail when I returned to Matlock House. What happened?"

"That is why Theodore and I are here. We think she may have been poisoned. The maid who may know something came to London and we are trying to find her. I am also trying to speak with her barrister. It looks like there is something going on with her will and the inheritance of Rosings."

"How horrible. Poor Aunt Catherine. How is Anne?"

"Did father not tell the household? I sent him a letter telling him of what happened." Theodore spoke seriously for the first time, cutting off Darcy's own response.

Blushing, Georgiana looked down before replying in a low voice. "He stays away from Matlock House. He has been spending time in the country at house parties or at his clubs in London. I overheard Aunt Matlock telling one of her friends that she was ever so much happier in her marriage after she had produced her spare, as it meant that she no longer had to see the man."

Darcy shook his head. He had once told himself that he would settle for such a marriage because that was what the people of his class did, only he had realized recently that following society's standards would never give him the love that he craved in his life. His aunt and uncle may be content to find their happiness outside of their marriage, but that would never be something he could condone. No, their kind of marriage was not for him.

"I will write a message for mother if you would take it back with you. She should know as well." Theodore's grim expression spoke more than his words did of his opinion of how his father treated his mother. Standing from the table, he left the room to write the note. Darcy noticed that his plate was all but licked clean.

Focusing on his sister, he took careful notice of how she looked. Despite the events at Ramsgate, she maintained her usual polished appearance and met his gaze with newfound strength. Eager to find out about the improvement, he asked her, "How are you, Georgiana? I have written to you, but I always feel as if I have not seen you in months when I have been away."

She squared her shoulders as if remembering a new stance on life. "I am doing better. Mrs. Ansley has helped me to understand more of the way the world works, and I think I have gained some confidence. I was not wholly to blame for Ramsgate, but I know now that I would not fall for the same ruse again. Mrs. Ansley says that I have more power than I may think."

"That sounds like something Miss Bennet would say. I did not want to leave Rosings, but Miss Bennet would not have it. She is very courageous in the face of adversity. That does not mean that I will not worry, though. Just like I will always worry about you and your wellbeing." Darcy smiled at his little sister. She was growing up from the little girl who had looked up at him over their father's grave, lost and alone. She looked so much like their mother.

"Have you been worrying about your Miss Bennet?" she asked him before taking a bite of her muffin.

"I could not sleep for worry last night. Then, when I slept, I dreamt of her in peril. It was not a good night." Running his hand down his face, Darcy went back to the table to get his coffee. Drinking it all in one big gulp, he went to get himself more.

Theodore came back into the room in a bluster, a note in his hands. "Here you go, poppet. I think we will soon get to the bottom of everything about her death. Mother will bring you to Rosings soon for the funeral, and I look forward to seeing you then. I must go if I am to catch that maid." Leaning down, he kissed her forehead and left the room.

"It sounds as if I will need to look through my wardrobe to find something suitable for mourning. Or maybe go shopping for something, as I have grown taller lately," Georgiana smiled at her brother. He often loved to treat her with shopping trips, always with the excuse that she had grown so she must have something new.

Darcy smiled, happy that he had the opportunity to see his sister while in London. With all the stress and worry he had been dealing with, it was nice to have a moment of peace with her. He was still worried about what Elizabeth was dealing with back at Rosings, but he hoped she was fine. Hadn't she told him she would be fine? After all, what could happen in a day or two?

***

DARCY GLANCED AROUND THE sitting room they had shown him to. It was obvious that the barrister was trying to impress his wealthy clients. He wondered if the man bought his furniture in the same place his aunt did. There was far too much gilt edging for his own taste, but he assumed it sent a message. He had arrived early, so now he had to wait.

"Mr. Darcy?" A voice at the far door drew Darcy's attention. A gaunt man with sharp eyes was watching him from where he stood.

Standing, Darcy quickly approached, hoping to gather whatever information he could and return to Miss Bennet. "Yes, I have come about my aunt's affairs."

"Yes, Lady Catherine de Bourgh. If you will come with me."

Several dark paneled corridors led Darcy into an office that was well lit and tidy despite the piles of papers on the desk and book-lined walls. "You said in your letter that you were concerned about something."

Sitting down at the desk the man, a Mr. Steele, if Darcy remembered correctly, smoothed out the paper in front of him before speaking. "Yes, Lady Catherine sent me paperwork the week before her death that changed quite a few things regarding her will and established things about her daughter Anne."

That did not sound so odd to Darcy. He would often change his will as his investments shifted. He had also put up safeguards for Georgiana and her dowry. "And that was unusual?"

"For your aunt, yes. Some of my clients change their will regularly. They get mad at an heir one week only to make up the next and thus their wills will change as swiftly as the seasons. But your aunt had left her will unchanged for the last fifteen years." Looking up, he judged Darcy, seeming to measure how he would take the information to follow. "I have never met your cousin Miss de Bourgh and until recently, the only information in the will stated that Rosings went to whomever she married. She wrote of you filling that role often, actually."

"Yes, she was quite fond of that idea. I, however, was not." Darcy's grimace was quickly noted by Mr. Steele, but he did not comment.

"The most recent correspondence spoke of her hand being forced in some way to act to protect her daughter. It implied blackmail in the wording."

"Blackmail! Who would want to blackmail my aunt?"

"She did not say, but she asked for me to research having her daughter declared incapable of overseeing her own affairs and having her made a ward of you and your cousin—a Colonel Fitzwilliam. Lady Catherine asked that I do it all quietly. She stated that she would prefer to avoid the paperwork if she could, but she said that by doing so, she would lope someone off at their feet." Mr. Steele allowed Darcy to take in the information's magnitude.

Darcy crossed his legs, drumming his fingers on his knee as he pondered the implications. Someone had been blackmailing his aunt. It would stand to reason that the person who was blackmailing her would not like being stymied. They most likely retaliated in the most severe fashion. "I believe someone murdered my aunt, Mr. Steele. The information you have implies that she was in the midst of a battle of wills with a blackmailer. To me, it appears quite clear that the person who poisoned my aunt was that individual. You said that she did not want you to file anything yet. How do things stand right now with my aunt gone?"

"Anne inherits everything, or rather, her husband does. However, from the implications in the letter she sent me, I am assuming that she is not necessarily..."

Darcy could sense that the man was having a hard time politely stating that there could be something amiss with Anne. "Mr. Steele, I will trust you with my family's secret. My cousin is not well and having her marry anyone would be a cruelty. A childhood illness left her changed. She will never be able to live a normal life."

Eyebrows drawn together, Mr. Steele shook his head in confusion. "Why, then, did your aunt want you to marry her?"

"I think she knew that I would never treat her badly and I could manage both estates. Considering my cousin's current health condition, it is unlikely that she will live to be an old woman. I am unsure if she ever considered my need to have an heir. I have long known that she was desperate to help her daughter and saw me as the only way. She would never take my advice about other ways to care for her. I only wish that she would have confided in me about the blackmailer." Leaning back in his chair, Darcy thought about his aunt. He had always pictured her as a loud, arrogant woman who demanded to have her wishes met, but he was finding that she was also a mother afraid for her only daughter. Maybe he should have tried harder to get her to see how they could work together to help Anne?

"I worked with her via correspondence for over twenty years, seeing to a number of her investments in her stead. Your aunt was a proud woman who firmly believed in her own strength."

Nodding his head, Darcy acknowledged the comment. The man was right. It was hard to push someone into agreeing with you when they were like his aunt. "Did you make much headway on what Aunt Catherine asked? I would like to see my cousin protected.

When will she come under the protection of my cousin and myself? Technically, she is now an heiress, and I would hate for someone to take advantage."

"I have made some headway and I will continue to assist you with the matter. There are several things that will need to be considered. Who will oversee Rosings for Miss de Bourgh, for example?"

"I would like to suggest a few things, but would you mind if I return after the funeral to discuss matters?"

Tapping on the desk, Mr. Steele pondered things momentarily. "Of course, there is no issue that needs immediate action. I will handle things without input for now."

"I can't stay away from Rosings," Darcy said, his voice firm. "Not when there's a killer there who needs to be caught." Getting up, he turned to the door only to be stopped when Mr. Steele spoke up.

"I hope you can get whoever killed Lady Catherine. No one should be able to get away with murder without consequence." The older man's grim countenance revealed his displeasure at the murder of Lady Catherine.

"Yes, I hope so too." Darcy left the room, eager to get back to Rosings. He wanted to see Miss Bennet, confirm that she was safe. He acknowledged that Miss Bennet was not the only reason he rushed through London. Elizabeth was frequently on his mind, but he knew there were other things he needed to consider. He also wanted to stop whoever had been threatening his cousin and aunt. He only hoped that Theodore had found the maid and they could be off.

Chapter Thirteen

Isn't That What Love Means?

Elizabeth awoke in the foggy grey morning feeling that it was very fitting, as it reflected her state of mind. She felt muddled and dull after a night of fitful sleep. Every sound had startled her, keeping her from sleeping deeply. As she listened closely, she could hear faint rustling sounds emanating from the hay in the far corner of the cell. Even using her vivid imagination to picture a cute little country mouse had not helped in the slightest. Looking around, she realized that sleeping against the wall had given her a crick in her neck.

She was glad she had the foresight to tuck a handkerchief into her sleeve the night before when she suddenly began to sneeze. She knew that she had a hardy constitution, but much more time in the cold cell and she would get sick. Standing, she stretched as best she could while staying wrapped in the blanket. Trying to work the kinks out, she began pacing in the small space that was provided. Five steps to the wall and five steps back. If she was willing to walk on the filthy hay, she would have had more space to roam, but she refused to get the filth on her if she could help it.

Instead of dwelling on the bleakness of her situation, Elizabeth forced her mind to contemplate the puzzle she had available. Fact one, someone murdered Lady Catherine. All of the events following her death led Elizabeth to believe that her death could not have been an accident. Fact two, someone was attempting to shift the blame on herself. The bottle of poison in her room spoke to that fact. There was also the fact that she was not quite languishing in a cell. She believed that someone wanted her out of the way. It would make sense that the person who committed the murder would be happy to have someone else take the blame. But was there a bigger picture? Did they want her gone for another reason? Was there more at stake?

Though she had no evidence, she wanted to suspect Mrs. Stevenson. Elizabeth felt like Mrs. Stevenson had a grudge against her, even though she couldn't recall any specific incident that would cause it. Despite her best efforts, Elizabeth could not fight her nagging feeling of unease about the woman. But unease was not evidence. She recognized that without evidence, she couldn't expect anyone to take her seriously, and her concerns would go unheard.

Elizabeth's mind had just started drifting towards the more pleasant avenue of wondering when Mr. Darcy would return when she heard a sound on the other side of the door. It was Mr. Cleaves, coming with something in his hands. Elizabeth realized she had been pacing for some time as the sun had risen farther than she expected.

After some juggling, he unlocked the door and came in. "I have brought you some breakfast, miss. Careful now, the bowl of porridge is hot, and I have some tea in the flask. Me missus is right upset that you are out here, she is. Our Nelly is friends with one of the maids at Rosings and she said that you are the kindest thing, always remembering the staff's names. I just do not think you could have done what they say."

"Thank you for the food and your belief in me. I am being accused of something that I did not do." Elizabeth's voice was scratchy, and it alarmed to hear its gruffness. Elizabeth took the food he offered and put it on the stool as a makeshift table. She was glad to have something warm, for her throat was sore.

"I see all sorts in here, but you are not the sort that should be here. I will say that much. You can expect me to return in the middle of the day to check up on you. I run the milliners in town, so I cannot say exactly when I will come." Leaving, he relocked the heavy door before walking away.

Elizabeth could not help but shudder at the sound of the lock turning. While she believed she was always up to the challenge, this situation proved to be tougher than she had expected. No matter how much she tried to convince herself otherwise, the feeling of being trapped persisted while she waited for release. She was cold and achy, and she needed a bath. Refusing to give in and cry as she wanted to, Elizabeth sat down at her makeshift table to eat.

She was momentarily flustered when she couldn't locate a spoon to eat her porridge. He wrapped a small square of fabric around the bowl to keep the porridge warm, and the spoon was inside. She was happy that he had remembered to bring her a spoon with the meal. Merely imagining how she would attempt to eat it without a spoon was degrading. Despite that, the porridge smelled divine. Though she typically didn't like porridge, this morning she craved its warm, comforting taste, and it looked as though Mrs. Cleaves had drizzled honey over the top. Taking a bite, Elizabeth sighed with the simple pleasure of warmth on her throat as she swallowed it down.

Once done with the porridge, she uncorked the flask to drink the tea. It was far too sweet for Elizabeth's taste, but it was wonderful on her throat. She settled once again with her back to the wall, the light from the barred window above her filtering into the gloom of the small room. She picked up the journal that she had brought and started reading, hoping to decipher anything that could have contributed to the murder of Lady Catherine.

"Miss Bennet? Are you in there?" Hattie's little voice came from the other side of the wall and pulled Elizabeth out of her reading.

Standing up and rising on her toes to look through the open bars, Elizabeth saw Hattie. Worry lines creased her face as she clutched a small bundle in her hands. "Hattie, whatever are you doing here? Does Mrs. Graham know you have come? Did you walk all the way from Rosings?"

"I am an excellent walker. Mrs. Graham sent me in a way, I guess. She told me she wanted to have me drop something off in town and said that I was free to see anyone I wished while I was here. Mr. Reeves said he had something to see to here as well and has walked with me. I brought you some of the cook's fresh biscuits for you. There is also a flask of water. Can you reach it?"

Elizabeth reached out of the window through the bars. It was awkward, but she managed to get the small, wrapped bundle up and through the bars. Grateful for Reeves's willingness to walk with Hattie, she acknowledged him with a nod as he appeared behind the girl. "Thank you, Hattie. It is so kind of you to have brought this for me."

"Are you all right in there, Miss Bennet? I would be ever so scared to have to stay in there." Hattie's small voice quivered.

"I am well enough. I will not say that it had been pleasant, but I very much appreciate the water and biscuits." Elizabeth swallowed her fear and made a conscious effort not to frighten the girl.

Nodding her head at Elizabeth's courageous attitude, Hattie smiled. "I am so glad you have Mr. Darcy to come rescue you. You can be sure that he loves you too much to leave you here. He should be back soon to get you out, I am sure of it."

"I would like to say that I do not need to be rescued, but I think I am rather in need of some help. How did you know that Mr. Darcy loves me?" Elizabeth pressed her face into the hard bars of the window in an effort to see Hattie better. She was curious to know how the girl had sorted it out while she had struggled with the concept.

"I saw how he looked at you. All smitten like. My pappa would look at my momma that way when he thought she wasn't looking. Like the sun wasn't as much a gift to him as she was." Hattie grinned up at Elizabeth through the bars despite the seriousness of the situation.

"And here I was with no idea. I feel very foolish to not have noticed. His family will not welcome me warmly if I'm correct. If they are anything like Lady Catherine, it will be an uphill battle. That is definitely going to be something worth witnessing. Hattie, what are your thoughts on how it will turn out?"

"If you can face being in here, I am sure you can face a bunch of silly old folks with too much money and not enough sense. How bad can they be? Not any worse than staying in there. Besides, your Mr. Darcy is awfully nice. I am sure he would not make you face them by yourself. Isn't that what love means? Not doing things alone." Tilting her head, she looked up at Elizabeth, her face open and unaware of the magnitude of her message.

Speaking as if she had not just been given something of such significance to think on, she said, "You are very right. You get back to Rosing and stay safe."

"Yes, Miss Bennet," Hattie replied before trotting off towards Rosings. It was a long distance, but not above three miles. Elizabeth would not hesitate to go the distance herself on foot, but she would have worried if the girl was on her own. For the first time, she found she understood her mother's flutterings. She walked all over the countryside with complete confidence in her ability to stay safe. She would have to apologize to her mother when she saw her.

Sliding down the wall, Elizabeth heard the rustling of hay behind her, indicating more movement by what she hoped was a mouse. She took twenty deep breaths and let the panic wash over her before regaining control and shutting it away. The cool stone on her forehead was a grounding force that she relied upon to bring her breath back under control. She would not succumb. Once back under control, she sat with her back to the wall and opened the bundle and, opening the water, she wet the scrap of cloth that had come with breakfast to wipe her face and hands with. It was the best that she could do for now.

Picking up the journal, she once again began to read. It had not been long when she noticed a change. The writing was not as smooth and looked almost rushed. Sitting up and away from the wall, Elizabeth paid closer attention.

Once again, she confronted me about Anne and her differences. She spoke of the ridicule Anne would face in society. Spoke about her lack of skill and her childlike reasoning. If Anne were well, she would be the most splendid pianist. She would be able to do anything required of a debutant. How dare that woman disparage my darling Anne? It was, however, a mistake to threaten her employment. She knows too much.

The journal moved back to discussing the new roof and problems with a boundary dispute between two different tenants. Not wanting to miss anything, Elizabeth continued to read, skimming over Lady Catherine's apparent obsession with her new mantel piece. Looking for more evidence of the 'she' Lady Catherine had written of. The further Elizabeth read into the journal, the more often there was a comment about the 'her' or 'she.'

She has demanded an increase in pay in order to not write the gossip papers about my poor Anne. For now, I have no choice, but I will find a way to be free of her demands.

Little Anne's dog has died, and she was so cruel about it. I cannot allow that woman around my daughter any longer. I have written to Steele about putting Anne under their care. If forced to, I will see her documented myself to protect her. It would take the wind out of her sails, but I do not wish for that for my daughter. If I could just get Darcy to agree to marry her. No one could touch her as Mrs. Darcy. Why he insists on refusing, I can never understand. Marriage would never confine Darcy the way it would a woman. He could have whatever mistress he wanted and claim her children as Anne's. He remains stubborn, and I may have to settle for a less favorable option.

The last few pages only talked about her suffering the last few days of her life. It hurt Elizabeth to know of her suffering and that her struggle was all for her daughter in the end. The woman's behavior may have been challenging, but she was undeserving of the harm that followed.

Chapter Fourteen

To Rescue a Fair Damsel

Darcy admitted that he should have spent the night in London, but he couldn't shake the feeling that Elizabeth needed him. He finally made it to Rosings sometime after dark. He had pressed on at the last coach stop. Theodore was escorting the maid back to Rosings with the hope that she could look over Aunt Catherine's room to spot something, anything that would tell them what had happened to her. Darcy hopped down off his horse, Castan, and handed of his reins to the stable boy.

Before he could turn away, the boy urgently stopped him. "Mr. Darcy, you must find Reeves. He told me to send you to him the moment you arrived. It is Miss Bennet."

Without hesitation, Darcy turned and broke into a full run. His dreams had left him with a sense of foreboding about her safety, and now his worst fears were coming true. After nearly knocking over two maids and a footman, he found Reeves.

Seeing the panic on Darcy's face, Reeves dispensed with pleasantries. "Your uncle arrived last night, and the first thing Mrs. Stevenson did was accuse your lady of murder. Lord Matlock had her taken from the house in the middle of the night and put in gaol."

Darcy stood frozen, his mind whirling. "Of course, he would be foolish enough to take her word for it. He is a man with a lustful eye for women, and Mrs. Stevenson is an attractive woman with sharp features. All she had to do was bat her eyes." He wanted to confront his uncle and question his sanity and, yes, possibly do bodily harm to the man. He wanted to rush to Miss Bennet and free her from where they had confined her and wash his hands of the whole sordid mess. But how to do both at once? He would have to choose.

There really was no choice. Elizabeth would always be his choice. Darcy longed to take her away from this oppressive corner of the world and into the sunshine at Pemberley, where they could start anew. The thought of her soft skin against his, the feel of her delicate hand in his, was all he could think about as he plotted his next move. He wanted to make sure she was happy and well taken care of. How would she ever trust him if his own family was so callow as to accuse her of murder and throw her into gaol?

Noting his employer's hesitation, Reeves spoke up. "Wait for your cousin to confront your uncle and the shrew. He will not be able to deny you both. I have been asking around and the magistrate is none too happy to be holding Miss Bennet. If you have any information at all pointing to her innocence, I am sure he will release her."

His decision made, Darcy turned back towards the stables only to be pause when Reeves called after him. "Do not take your horse. She will not wish to ride back to Rosings astride with you. Have a carriage or phaeton at least! And bring a maid, for heaven's sake!"

Darcy found the energy to grin at his valet's commands as he rushed. Whenever Reeves directed his actions, he couldn't help but wonder who was really in charge. In the end, he always turned out to be correct, so Darcy did not see the need to gainsay him. It would make more sense to confront his uncle with Theodore to back him up. Though heaven help him if the man got pigheaded—it would not end well for him. Taking the stairs two at a time, he dashed for the stable, only to have to wait for the carriage to be made ready.

Remembering the need for a maid, he called out to the footman Gregory, who was nearby. "Gregory, I am going to try to get Miss Bennet released, but I was told to bring a maid for propriety's sake. Do you know where I may find one that is available?"

"I know my niece Hattie would be more than happy to help you, sir. We have been right worried about Miss Bennet. Only a fool would think she would have anything to do with a murder plot—" Gregory stopped, as if realizing that he had just insulted Darcy's uncle. "Uh, that is to say…"

Waving off the man's anxiety, Darcy said, "Think nothing of it. I have called him worse and you do not want to hear what I have been calling him in my head. If you would fetch Hattie, I would be more than happy to bring her with me."

With a sharp bow, Gregory rushed off to find his niece. Darcy began to pace, fighting the guilt he felt. How long had Elizabeth been in that cell? Was she cold? Hungry? Scared? That worry brought him up short. At one time, he had hesitated to court her because of the scorn they would face because of what he saw as the unequal footing they would come to the relationship with. But really, what did he care about those who would scorn him?

People already disdained his quiet nature and sanctimonious thoughts as he once heard it said. He did not let those naysayers stop him from acting in the way that he felt was right. Miss Bennet was a force to be reckoned with and never shied away from a challenge. She had walked three miles to tend to her sister, who she suspected needed her. Despite his wealth, she had never fawned over him. Elizabeth looked at people for who they were, not how many land holdings they had. Her energetic nature and kind spirit drew people from all walks of life to her. She was the ideal mistress for Pemberley and would see to its people and lands with grace and humor. Thinking of how she was probably handling the whole situation made him frown at his previous doubts.

If he was at all correct, she would be handling the entire issue like a queen, with dignity and self-assurance that he found most people lacked. Strangely, the image of Caroline Bingley in a similar situation popped into his head and he fought a grin. There would be screaming and sobbing and throwing things. No dignity, no decorum and most definitely there would be a ruined ridiculous hat. In his mind, he could see one of those tangerine peacock monstrosities covered with muck. Maybe there was something to the whole finding humor in things. It was certainly better than wallowing in his fears and guilt.

"We are ready, sir," the stable hand spoke up from beside Darcy.

The voice shook Darcy from his musings, and he lifted his gaze to the boy before responding, "Good. Thank you. I will just wait for the maid, Hattie, and we can be off."

"I am coming, Mr. Darcy!" The youthful voice came from the top of the stairs leading to the kitchen. The girl's arms were full of a blanket of some kind and a small bundle. "I got a blanket from Mrs. Graham in case Miss Bennet is cold and a little something to eat."

Hattie's thoughtfulness and attention to detail impressed him. Elizabeth had found an amazing friend in the girl. Helping her up and into the carriage, Darcy quickly tapped on the roof and they were off.

***

IT DID NOT TAKE long to get to the place where Elizabeth was being held. As soon as the carriage slowed, Darcy flung open the door and jumped out, his stride eating up the earth that separated him from the woman he loved more with every breath he took. Reaching the window that separated them, he called out, "Elizabeth!"

"Mr. Darcy?" Her head popped up into his view and he forced himself not to growl at the sound of her voice. It was hoarse and painful sounding. The darkness of the light left him wanting to see more of her than the moonlight would allow. He only saw her in shadow, and he wished for more light in order to take in her condition and wellbeing.

"Elizabeth, are you all right?" Had the damp and cold of her confinement taken a toll on her health in just a day?

"I must admit that I have been better, but I believe there is no lasting damage." Her comment would have been more reassuring if she did not follow up the brave statement with a fit of sneezing and a hoarse cough.

Darcy could not help reaching through the bars. He cupped her cheek and found it cold. Wondering if that was better than finding her feverish, he reassured her and himself by saying, "I am going to get you out of here."

"That would be rather lovely. I find the accommodations rather lacking. I do not believe I would suggest anyone else stay here." Elizabeth's eyes twinkled as she spoke. He had not moved his hand away from her face, and she had not pulled back. She leaned into it.

Darcy hoped that she was not so very unwell. Could you be truly sick if your eyes twinkled as hers did? Turning, he addressed the coachman. "Find the magistrate. Tell him I have information that will exonerate Miss Bennet."

Watching the man as he rushed off, she spoke up, "I am glad to hear that you made progress in London, but there is no need to rush." Her statement lost some of its impact as she took a step back and sneezed repeatedly.

"I hate that I could not prevent this. Can you ever forgive me?" Resting his head against the bars that separated them, he felt his self-recriminations build.

Shaking her head, Elizabeth spoke, "No matter how you feel about me, you cannot stay with me all the time. Bad things happen. I could sprain my ankle on a walk even if we were walking together. While I am feeling well enough, I cannot fault you for what happened. I have blamed you for plenty of things that I have now realized I had no reason to, and I will not blame you for something like this. I cannot forgive you because I never blamed you. Now it is my turn to ask a question." The clouds seemed to part and allow the moon to grant him just enough light to see her smile. That incredible smile, though subdued, was still there, despite everything. She wet her lips before continuing. "When did you decide you liked me?"

Closing his eyes, Darcy contemplated the path he had traveled to love the woman in front of him. There was only a wall between them right then, but sometimes it felt like much more. "I cannot name the day or hour that I loved you, but I had a startling revelation once I returned to London. The day I realized Bingley was thinking less of your sister, but I only thought of you more, I somehow knew. I think it hit me like a bolt of lightning. I knew then that what I had deemed to be a mere fascination had been the first stirrings of love. When I first met you, I found you captivating because of how different you were from other women in society. Your singular self at Netherfield captivated me. You were genuine and considerate, and yet you held your own against Miss Bingley without being overt or heavy-handed. From our debates, I knew you were well read. Do you know how hard it is to have a decent conversation about anything? No one I knew enjoyed reading and debating as I did until I met you. Only it took me a while to appreciate the depth and breadth of what I felt."

Darcy might have continued if not for the magistrate rushing up. "This fine young man says that you have information that will help release Miss Bennet?"

"Yes, I went to London to speak with my aunt's barrister. He let me know that someone had been blackmailing my aunt, and she was trying to stop them. There is every reason to believe the person who murdered my aunt was also the blackmailer."

"That could all be well and true, but one could argue that Miss Bennet could be the blackmailer. I do not believe it, but I have to look at things logically."

"Miss Bennet met my aunt after the blackmail started," Darcy countered.

"That will do. I have hated having to keep the poor lady here and I am happy to release her into your care." Rushing to the door, he unlocked it.

Darcy was right behind him. He took in the filthy conditions of the cell from the light of the lantern the magistrate carried. Refusing to dwell on his mounting anger towards his uncle, he embraced Elizabeth, heedless of her disheveled state. Wrapping an arm around her shoulders, he guided her out. Although he knew she was a strong woman who might not welcome his help, he couldn't resist being there for her. She had consumed his thoughts so completely in his time away from her. His arm around her was less about what she may need, but his desperation to know that she was well and safe.

Hattie was waiting by the carriage with a blanket in her arms. "I told you he would come and rescue you, Miss Bennet. He has been that worried for you."

"Hattie, you are a dear for coming. Mr. Cleaves, I want to thank you for the kind care you showed me while I was here." Pausing, she stepped away from Darcy and took the blanket away from her shoulders, handing it back to him with the white monstrosity on her head.

Darcy's heart filled with warmth as she came back to his side without hesitation. He knew he should thank the man who had released Elizabeth, but was resentful of the fact that she had to remain in such conditions. "Thank you, Mr. Cleaves."

Hattie came over and replaced the blanket that Elizabeth had given up with the one that she had brought. In no time at all, they were in the carriage and heading back towards Rosings. Darcy tried not to be elated that Elizabeth was leaning into his side. She had been through a traumatic experience and her needing support did not necessarily mean that she was beginning to return his feelings.

"You did not wish to thank Mr. Cleaves," Elizabeth spoke with her head on his shoulder.

"He had you locked up in that filthy cell. I find very little to thank him for at the moment."

"He brought me that blanket and cap to protect me from the filth in that cell. He brought me food and hot tea in a flask. It was not his desire to have me contained there. That was your uncle's doing at Mrs. Stevenson's instigation. Mr. Cleaves did what he could while operating under the constraints your uncle gave him. I think that strictly speaking, he should not have released me if he was not so unhappy with having me there."

"Well then, I will concede that he deserved the thanks. However, it will take me some time to align myself to the fact that you were forced to endure that."

"It was little more than a day and I am sure there will be no lasting effects. Thank you for your support and indignation on my behalf. It is nice to have someone worry over me." Elizabeth spoke almost sleepily from where her head rested on his shoulder. "What did you learn in London? Did you and the colonel find the missing maid?"

Remembering the larger but not more important problem of the murderer on the loose, Darcy recalled the issue that he had left Rosings to discover. Forcing his mind away from the weight of her body leaning into his, he responded to her question. "I spoke to my aunt's barrister. He let me know that someone was blackmailing her."

"I have been reading her journal, and she said that there was a 'she' that was threatening Anne. She wanted you to marry her to protect her but said she had another option, a less favorable option to stop the blackmailer, but never said who it was." Another round of sneezing had Elizabeth sitting up.

Handing her his handkerchief, Darcy frowned as she made a face and grimaced in pain. He wanted to pull her in to his lap and hold her tight, giving her warmth along with his security and love, but knew that he could not. It was not yet time for that, but he hoped that it was a time that would come soon enough.

Hattie spoke up from where she sat across from them. "We are almost back to Rosings and you can get clean and warm and get some sleep in a bed, Miss Bennet."

Elizabeth shook her head. "Is the colonel back yet, or did you come ahead of him?"

"He should be here soon enough." Darcy had a sinking feeling he knew the direction her thoughts were headed.

"We need to talk about what we have found. There is a murderer at Rosings and they must be stopped. Who knows what their next move will be?"

Though it was too dark to see her expression, Darcy could tell from the tone of her voice that she would have that stubborn glint in her eye. Her nose would be scrunched in that adorable way. There would be no putting her to bed to rest. She was on a mission.

***

DARCY STARED INTO THE fire, his mind miles away and at the same time right next to him. Miss Bennet had insisted, as he suspected, to not go to bed. Mrs. Graham had bundled her away the minute she had seen her and presumably given her some hot sweet tea and a good scrubbing, if the woman's muttering meant anything. He had waited in the hall for her to reemerge. Eventually, after a while, she came out clean and wrapped in a thick shawl. He had noticed that her hair was still damp, though it looked as if Mrs. Graham had put it back into a tight bun. As he suspected, she had wanted to stay up and discuss their issues. She had gone with him to the sitting room that he shared with Theodore. Reeves was standing watch to act as chaperone.

It had not taken long for her to fall asleep waiting for Theodore to show. Sitting in front of the fire wrapped in a blanket had been too much for her worn condition. She was asleep there on the settee, curled up with her breath coming out in little puffs. As he gazed into the fire, he pondered how his life would be enriched if he could witness such beauty every day.

He wished for a day when he could see her asleep every night and watch her every morning. The privilege to watch the expressions flit across her face and guess at her thoughts. Maybe one day he would get to wake her up on chilly mornings by snuggling up to her and giving her a kiss. That was how his cousin found him—sitting in the chair next to Elizabeth while he watched her sleep.

"What happened in the two hours I was behind you?"

"Your father happened. He had Elizabeth thrown into the gaol on the word of Mrs. Stevenson. She said that Elizabeth had killed Aunt Catherine. Elizabeth spent the majority of the time we were away in that horrid gaol. I managed to convince the magistrate that she was not the guilty party and got her released."

"I wondered where he was. Should we confront him tonight, do you think?" Theodore queried.

"I think Elizabeth would like to be part of the discussion. She said that she read in Aunt Catherine's journal that there was a 'she' threatening Anne, explaining that it was one of the reasons she so wanted me to marry Anne. She thought I could protect her somehow." Darcy still had problems with what her aunt had wanted of him. Her assumptions that he would be content with such a marriage disturbed him. Or had she simply been so worried that she did not care?

"She also thought you would simply take a mistress for anything that Anne could not provide. And that you could claim some mistress's child as Anne's. She had a very odd view of holy matrimony." Elizabeth sat up from where she lay, rubbing her eyes. Her voice was husky and sounded almost painful.

He knew his aunt had been worried about Anne, but what kind of life would that have been for her, or him?

Who would have the audacity to push his aunt to such a point?

Chapter Fifteen

What Do We Know?

Elizabeth awoke in stages first, realizing that she felt warm and safe. She noted she found that greatly comforting for some reason, driving her mind to search for why she would be happy to feel warm and safe. Then the memory of the cell hit her, and she realized she was free of the small dirty space and, once again, safe. She was not in bed, though. Voices off to the side were a soft murmur that she focused on. It was Mr. Darcy and the colonel speaking about their situation.

"She also thought you would simply take a mistress for anything that Anne could not provide. And that you could claim the mistress's child as Anne's. She had a very odd view of holy matrimony." Looking around the room, Elizabeth sat up and rubbed her eyes. It was very odd to Elizabeth to think that Lady Catherine would condone Darcy keeping a mistress in opposition to her daughter.

"Yes, I believe that most people miss the fact. I am sorry if we woke you, Elizabeth. How are you feeling?" Mr. Darcy looked contrite, his eye's filling with worry.

Elizabeth found herself smiling faintly at his concern for her. Somehow, she had the feeling that despite their differences, their similarities were the right sort. That he was the kind of man to care for her wellbeing spoke volumes to her.

She had a lot of time to think in that little cell and had realized several things. One of which was that despite feeling that her feelings were not as strong as his, hers were growing steadily. Taking stock of how she felt, Elizabeth recognized that her voice had sounded hoarse. She also felt slightly achy, but she would not complain of such minor ailments. "I am well enough, Mr. Darcy. I would have woken eventually. Have we started coming up with a plan?"

"For one, we are going to wait to confront my father until the morning. I would like to apologize, Miss Bennet, for my father's actions." The colonel spoke in a deep, authoritative voice from his high-backed chair across from herself and Mr. Darcy. His countenance lacked the usual merriment he exuded.

"You are not responsible for your father's actions any more than I am responsible for my mother's. We can merely try to be the people we believe we should be." Elizabeth pressed her hand to her throat. Despite drinking tea with honey, the sore throat that began earlier in the day still lingered.

"You are kind to say so, Miss Bennet, but know I condone none of his behavior and I am sorry for what he forced you to experience." The colonel still looked grim and oddly contrite. Elizabeth realized that there was more to his character than the lightheartedness she had previously observed.

Mr. Darcy stood and went to the bellpull. "Why don't I ring for some tea, and we can discuss all our findings?"

"Tea sounds delightful." Elizabeth hoped that the warmth of the drink would soothe her scratchy throat. "I do not remember what Mr. Darcy said about your search for the maid. Were you successful in your endeavors, Colonel?"

"I found the maid while she was looking for employment in London. She was willing to return with us and look over Lady Catherine's things to see if there was anything in her many medicinal potions that looked off. Or maybe she could explain what they were," he explained.

"Did she shed any light on Lady Catherine's ailment? Are you suspicious of her?" Darcy asked after speaking with the maid to ask for tea.

Leaning back in his chair, the colonel seemed to ponder his response. "My gut tells me she is innocent. She was not trying to hide in London. Genuinely concerned, she paced back and forth, biting her nails, when she got the news about Aunt Catherine. She told me that Aunt Catherine was very ill, leading up to her death. Very early in the morning on Thursday, she started experiencing some sort of stomach ailment. She also complained of pains in her head and eventually lethargy. The maid said that she was very concerned about her, but that Lady Catherine stubbornly refused to call for a physician. She stated she had been growing weaker, but insisted on putting Miss Bennet in her place."

"And, of course, Aunt Catherine dismissed her when she continued to fret over her condition. I want to feel bad for Aunt Catherine. The effects of being poisoned caused her to suffer greatly. However, her behavior towards the poor maid is making it difficult for me to do so. In fact, a lot of her behavior is making it hard for me to feel bad for her," Mr. Darcy spoke with a frown.

Elizabeth could see how he would feel that way but could not think of what to say to reassure him. When the tea arrived, she let out a sigh of relief and savored the warmth spreading through her body. She was charmed when Mr. Darcy first served her a cup. It was exactly how she liked it. It dawned on her that he would have had to be watching her closely and paying attention to even how she made her tea. She knew for a fact that her father did not know how her mother took her tea and they had been married for over twenty years. Her parents' bitter and indifferent marriage was always in the back of her mind, making her cautious about commitment. She felt a sense of relief wash over her as she realized she wouldn't have to worry about those sorts of things with Mr. Darcy.

She watched him take his tea over to the small desk in the room's corner and draw out a piece of paper. "Let us think of this in a logical manner. What do we know?"

Stirring her tea idly as she thought, Elizabeth spoke up first. "Poisoned on Wednesday, Lady Catherine's life ended on Friday morning. It was not hemlock despite what that bottle showing up in my room might imply."

"Aunt Catherine suffered many stomach ailments, a headache starting very early Thursday and became progressively weaker. She was also jaundice at her death," the colonel added.

Darcy began writing before looking up and saying, "She was being blackmailed about something to do with Cousin Anne. What kind of threat could someone make to Anne?"

"As much as I am growing to like her and getting to know her has been enjoyable, you have to admit that she is not quite right. Does your father know of her condition, Colonel? Would he have had a problem with her peculiarities?"

Frowning, he responded, "You know, I am not sure he does. He hates visiting Rosings and Anne never leaves. I know we do not talk about it. I think he just assumes that she is sickly, not different."

Taking a sip, Elizabeth swallowed before speaking. "What would he do if he found out that she was different? I know Lady Catherine was afraid for Anne somehow. She never said what exactly she was afraid of, almost as if she feared putting it in writing could make it come true."

"I do not think that simply knowing she was different would have caused him to do anything, but if he was embarrassed enough, he could do something drastic," the colonel added.

"We are talking about the man who had Miss Bennet confined on the word of Mrs. Stevenson. At this point, I am not putting him above acting harshly." Darcy's voice carried his frustration and discontent with the way his uncle had acted.

"So, there is a possibility there was a threat someone would do something that would cause Lord Matlock to act, harming Anne in some way. This is all supposition, of course, but it makes sense to me. Though I wish there were fewer gaps in our reasoning." Once finished speaking, Elizabeth took another sip of her tea. All the conversation was not helping her throat one bit.

"My question is, who would blackmail Aunt Catherine? It could be anyone at Rosings or the surrounding area," Darcy spoke up from the desk, though his eyes lingered on Elizabeth.

Cocking her head to the side, Elizabeth spoke up. "Not anyone. Remember, she said 'she' in her journal?"

"So that reduces the suspects by half." The sardonic comment came from the colonel.

Elizabeth hesitated, trying to decide whether to say what she was thinking. Worrying her lip, she finally gave in and put forth her thought. "I know this could merely be my reaction to her instigating my incarceration, but I have never liked Mrs. Stevenson. Could she be the culprit?"

"She is close enough to Anne to have the information that would be necessary to blackmail Aunt Catherine, but unless we find a signed letter from her detailing her murder plans, I am uncertain how we could prove anything," came Mr. Darcy's response.

The colonel crossed his legs at the ankles and looked to be thinking before speaking up. "Has anything odd happened lately, anything out of the ordinary?"

Elizabeth tried to remember everything she had learned while talking with Anne. It did not seem like there had been any large changes to their routine except for the death of her dog, Buttons. Was it possible that was significant? "Did you know Anne had a little dog that she played with? It died last week. Mrs. Stevenson had everything from the dog immediately removed and gotten rid of. I am not sure if that means anything, but I was certainly upset when I heard about it. Anne was very upset about it. She had hidden away some of the dog's things as mementos and she is afraid that Mrs. Stevenson will take what few things she has." Elizabeth knew her tone was harsh, but she really disliked that woman. Would it be wrong of her to hope that she was the culprit? At least it would explain away her anger at the woman. Elizabeth was a cheerful person and had handled even Caroline Bingley with a certain amount of humor, but she could not find a way to do that with Mrs. Stevenson.

Looking over his list, Mr. Darcy looked uninspired. Frowning, he rubbed the back of his neck and handed the list to his cousin. He commented, "Why do I feel like we should have more on this list by now? We will most likely bury Aunt Catherine in the next few days and begin to work on what to do with Rosings. It would be reassuring to have the murderer taken care of before more people show up for her funeral."

Taking the list, the colonel glanced at it before handing it to Elizabeth. He downed the last of his tea before saying, "We have two things that we can do tomorrow. The maid can look over all those bottles to see if anything is off. I also suggest we find a way to search Mrs. Stevenson's room. Who knows what we could find? I am with Miss Bennet—there is just something about that woman that I cannot like."

Elizabeth looked over the list and felt as disappointed as Mr. Darcy was acting. It was not a very inspiring list of clues they had gathered. She wished for more as well. They had thrown her into gaol, for heaven's sake; she wanted to have more to show for it. Though Elizabeth admitted that Mr. Darcy's penmanship was excellent, seven phrases on a blank sheet of paper were not much.

Murdered on a Wednesday

Not hemlock

Stomach problems, headache, weak, and jaundice

Threats to Anne / Blackmail

Afraid for Anne / Threat from Matlock

She

Little dog died

Looking at the clock on the mantelpiece, the colonel spoke up. "I think we should reconvene in the morning, and we can see what we find with our two endeavors."

"Do you think we should confront your father in the morning?" Darcy questioned the colonel.

"No, let us see if we can get any evidence to show him first."

Elizabeth got up and deposited her empty teacup on the tray. Heading to the door, she turned to say good night, only to be stopped by Mr. Darcy.

"Miss Bennet, would you permit me to set one of the footmen outside of your door tonight?"

"Although I feel foolish for feeling this way, I can't help but feel relieved by your offer and would like to accept it. I must begrudgingly admit that I am uneasy with the idea of a wandering murderer who does not seem above framing me. Now that I am back, who knows what they may do?" Biting her lip, Elizabeth tried to stop the lurid images from filling her mind. Her imagination could sometimes run away with her. She could only hope that none of the horrible imaginings would prove to have any foundation in reality.

***

THOUGH MRS. GRAHAM HAD her bed nicely warmed with hot bricks, Elizabeth still found herself chilled before she got under the covers. She closed her eyes, trying to shake off the memory of the cold, damp cell and the sound of hay rustling in the dark. Despite telling herself that there could not be rats in the hay, something was stirring within it. She grit her teeth in frustration. It was over, but she still felt the chill in her bones.

Rolling onto her side, she curled into a ball. Forcing her mind from things she would rather not think of, Elizabeth found that she quickly found Mr. Darcy on her mind. It surprised her to think that her thoughts had turned to him for comfort. Had it only been two days that had passed since her world had been irrevocably altered? Not even a week ago, she had been under the impression that Mr. Darcy disliked her as much as she disliked him. Only now she was wondering if that had even been true. If she was honest with herself, she had been attracted to Mr. Darcy from the start and she acted mostly out of hurt from his dismissal.

Did it make her a small person to believe that knowing Mr. Darcy made her realize just how poor of a man her father was? She had written to her father when everything had first happened and told him about being thrown from Mr. Collins's home, yet he had not responded. If she had to guess, her letter was sitting in the stack on his desk. Mr. Darcy would never be so lackadaisical about his family, responsibilities, or correspondence.

Mr. Darcy was desperate to look out for her, she could tell, and that meant something significant to her. Her own father had laughed when she told him of Mr. Collins's overtures and the way that he had leered at her. He found it humorous and did not feel the need to act on her behalf. Compared with Mr. Darcy's concern for her wellbeing, she knew she had found a man who see to all her needs and even her whims. Had her feelings changed so dramatically towards the man that she was actually considering his suit?

Her heart said she wanted to consider it. She may not feel that the emotions she felt matched the love he spoke of, but he was still more of an option than she would have ever suspected. He was proving to be a thoughtful and considerate person. In fact, her intellectual leanings were something he found intriguing about her. That in itself was huge. She had once assumed that she would never marry. She would not give up reading and learning for the sake of being a wife. Had she actually found the one man that wanted to discuss Greek philosophers and agricultural developments with her?

Her eyes widened in the dark as she realized that the feeling of his presence near her had been a comfort as she fell asleep on the settee that evening. In fact, she felt a sense of security wash over her as soon as he arrived, after her harrowing experience. What was it that Hattie had said? 'Wasn't that what love was, not doing things alone?' She had felt so alone in that cell. The memory of it still made her shudder, but thinking about Mr. Darcy made her feel not so alone.

Gradually, she came to the realization that the chill that had seeped into her bones had dissipated. The mere memory of Mr. Darcy had a warming effect on her. As she reminisced about Mr. Darcy, her body was filled with a sense of security and comfort that was enough to lull her to sleep. With a blissful smile lingering on her face, she drifted off into a peaceful slumber.

Chapter Sixteen

Emeralds, Amethysts, and Topaz, Oh My

Getting up and ready for the day was a relief after a long night of nightmares. Taking a sip of coffee, Darcy stared out the window in the sitting room. They had chosen to meet there and avoid the chance of meeting up with Lord Matlock at breakfast. There was plenty of food gathered on the table in the corner, but he was too unsettled to eat. He felt the need to see Elizabeth.

Despite having talked to Miss Bennet more in the last several days than ever before, he still felt like there was so much more to say. His longing to see her continued to intensify, while his worries for her safety lingered in the back of his mind. Did she get sicker in the night? Did she wake up feeling refreshed or groggy from a night of tossing and turning?

His pacing around the room paused when he sensed movement at the door. Turning, it was as if all his muscles unclenched, and he felt relief wash through him. Elizabeth stood in the doorway and he could breathe again.

She appeared less pale than the night before. That was good, right? The dress she wore was a lovely dark blue that must have been something she had borrowed from the trunk. It flattered her form nicely.

Elizabeth fought back a yawn before grinning at him. "Please tell me you have coffee, Mr. Darcy."

"Yes, ma'am, sit down and let me get you a cup."

"You know, if you continue to bring me coffee and tea, I will become spoiled." Elizabeth looked up at him from the seat that she had taken, a blush creeping across her cheeks.

"Ahhh, you have discovered my plan. I want to spoil you." Bringing the cup of coffee to her, that he had made sure was just how she liked it, Darcy was thrilled to see her eyes widen and her blush deepen. Seeing how adorable she looked when he indulged her, he knew he had to make it a daily habit. "Isn't that natural? To want to spoil those who are dear to you. I still remember my father bringing mother her tea every morning, even when she was sick. Especially when she was sick. Doesn't your father treat your mother somehow?"

"No, I do not think he even knows how she takes her tea. They both seem to regret their decision to wed. At best they are indifferent acquaintances who happen to share a last name and abode. More often they endeavor to annoy one another at every turn and we daughters pretend their antics do not mortify us," Elizabeth spoke softly and looked away.

Darcy wondered if her family was one of her hesitations when it came to his courtship. He had a happy example of love that he remembered from his childhood, but she had the opposite. His parents had been an aberration for their class, a love match. He had always assumed that he would never find a love like theirs, but he felt that maybe with Elizabeth he would have what he had always wished for. Reaching out, he caught her hand where it twisted in the fabric of her dress. Holding her palm in his, he waited until she gathered her courage and looked him in the eye. "I believe you were the person who said we can merely try to be the people we believe we should be. You are a remarkable woman and regardless of whether you and I develop into what I would wish, you will live a life full of love. You cannot help but to show love and compassion to others."

"You really will spoil me, Mr. Darcy." She squeezed his hand.

Darcy had lost himself in her gaze until he was disturbed by the throat clearing behind him. Looking up, he spotted his cousin grinning behind him. He wondered if he was blushing. Surely not.

"Are you eating breakfast or were you waiting for me?" Theodore spoke with a straight face, but his shoulders shook with mirth.

"We waited for you so we can plan our morning's adventures." Darcy glared at his cousin but found that there was no actual heat in it. He was too happy at the moment to feel anything but joy at the fact that he held Elizabeth's hand in his.

"I was thinking we should look over your aunt's room with the maid first. That way we could know perhaps what to look for later on," Elizabeth spoke up but did not remove her hand from Darcy's warm embrace, despite the pointed look by Theodore.

"That makes sense. Let's eat so we may be about our business. My father is a late riser and if we are quick about things, we can confront him with proof when he finally ambles down." Making his way to the food table, he grabbed a plate and started putting together a substantial breakfast.

While his back was turned, Darcy took the opportunity to bring Elizabeth's hand to his mouth so that he could kiss it. Watching her, he gauged her reaction, ready to stop if she acted upset, but he found that was not the case at all. Though a vivid blush quickly painted her cheeks, she bit her lip and smiled at him. "They have more ginger cake this morning. Would you like me to get you some?"

Elizabeth cleared her throat before saying, "Yes, please, and some eggs as well."

Darcy left her sitting on the settee drinking her coffee to go get her breakfast. Gathering her plate together, he brought it to her and then got his own, this time making sure that he got more than eggs for himself. A member of the staff, possibly Reeves, had arranged small tables throughout the room, presumably because they kept taking meals there. Whoever had thought of it had his gratitude, as it was quite convenient as they prepared for whatever the day held for them.

***

IT WAS NO TIME at all, before they were once again in Lady Catherine's room full of bottles and packets, but this time they were there with her maid. She appeared to be somewhere in her late thirties or forties possibly and wore a neat brown dress. She was a no-nonsense woman who must have had the patience of Job to have been able to put up with his aunt for any length of time.

Looking around the room as they entered together, the maid spoke up, "Your aunt liked to get any new nostrum or medicinal that she heard of, hoping that it would either help her or her daughter. The peddlers who contacted her, in my view, knew that she had the means and used her concerns to their benefit. She was persuaded to purchase an unnecessary amount of potions and protective jewelry."

"What was she hoping to combat? I had never known that she was ill," Theodore questioned as he stood near the entrance, taking in everything in that way that he did.

"It started out as a cough one winter and then she had trouble sleeping, but what she took for that seemed to make it hard for her to concentrate and get anything done and things all started rolling downhill from there. I was with her ladyship for close to twenty years," the maid replied, wringing her hands.

"And yet she let you go so easily?" Elizabeth was upset over the idea of releasing a servant of twenty years over mere concern for her health.

"She had been acting oddly recently and then, when she started getting ill, she was almost in a panic. It was not the first time she dismissed me, but I would usually take my time about my arrangements on leaving and she would change her mind before the next day was over. It was why I left so quickly. I was getting too tired to deal with her fits and frustrations anymore. I had decided that I would look for somewhere else that would be easier." Going over to the table, she glanced at the many containers before rubbing one of her arms as if catching a chill.

"I can find no system in all the bottles. Did she really know what she was taking? Is there an order to all of this?" Darcy efficiently managed his estate, and he used many different systems to do so, but he was unable to comprehend the table covered with bottles as a system.

Gesturing to the bottles as she spoke, the maid explained what she knew. "She had her method, though I am not sure it was the best. The bottles on the left were older. Either she found they did not help her, or she did not like how they made her feel. The bottles on the right she used more often. She seemed to know which one was which, but I am not sure. The ones in the back were to help her sleep, while the ones in the front were various other ailments."

Studying the table before him as if it held the secrets to the universe hidden somewhere amongst the bottles, Darcy queried the maid, "Does anything look off? Maybe it is different than it should be?"

"No, I do not see anything in the wrong place. Is that what you mean?" she responded.

Darcy would have commented, but he was too distracted. Elizabeth's concentration made him notice the adorable line between her eyebrows. She was remarkable. How could he not want to spend a lifetime staring at that little line?

Suddenly Elizabeth's eyes widened, and she gasped. "Or maybe, what did she use the most often? Something that she would for sure have taken in the days leading up to her death."

Going to the bottle in the back row on the far right, the maid picked it up. Uncorking it, she looked in and frowned. "Lady Catherine took some of this every night. She had gotten to where she needed some every night in order to sleep. It was supposed to be clear, if slightly milky, with no sediment, but something is floating in there."

Going to the ornate side table that had a decorative bowl on it, Theodore took out the dried flowers, dumping them in a pile on the floor in frustration. He wiped it down and once it was clean, he went over to the maid and took the bottle from her. Carefully dumping it into the shallow bowl, they all leaned closer to see what the innocuous bottle had revealed.

The liquid was tinged slightly pink and small bits of red something were floating harmlessly around the bowl. Tapping the side of the bowl and watching ripples form and cross in concentric circles, Elizabeth pondered, "It looks as if we might have found what poisoned Lady Catharine. Though I do not want to test the theory."

Darcy had acted as a magistrate before in Derbyshire, but there had never been a murder that he had to oversee. A theft here and a few property damages there, once even a case involving stolen chickens. Nothing remotely as serious as a murder. "Should we contact someone? Possibly let someone know what we found?"

"I sent a letter to the coroner for the county of Kent, but I do not know when he might make it this way. My suggestion is that we document our findings, at the very least, so we have a record of what we discovered. I believe we have no safe way to test the substance to verify the presence of poison," Theodore spoke from where he stood, his voice grim.

Tapping on her chin, Elizabeth said, "Do you think Mrs. Wright might suggest something? I know she is quite knowledgeable about plants and herbs. She might know what that red stuff is."

"I think that is a good idea," came Darcy's response.

Darcy walked down the hall with Elizabeth with Reeves in tow. He felt there must be some conversation. Feeling the need to say something, he blurted the first thing that came to mind. "You appear better this morning. Were you able to sleep well last night?"

Elizabeth's light laugh answered him before she did. "I did sleep well. Better in fact than I feared I would."

"Why did you laugh?" Darcy was learning that she laughed often and at times without restraint. This laugh, however, had him wondering what instigated it.

"Mr. Darcy, while I understand you meant it as a compliment, saying that I look better this morning implies that I didn't look good last night. If you had said that a week ago, I would have assumed that you meant to point out some deficiency on my part. However, I know you better now. I believe I can now see that you said that not out of derision but out of concern for my wellbeing. It suddenly struck me as funny that most things in life are simply a matter of perspective. So, Mr. Darcy, I was laughing at myself and what a difference a few days can make." She looked up at him and flashed a smile.

It was one of her many smiles, and Darcy was cataloging them all. This one was playful, and it made him feel that she was sharing a joke with him. "You are correct on several accounts. I was worried about how you are faring. I think it is true that time and perspective change a lot. We have been speaking more now than we ever did back at Netherfield. I am learning more about you, who you are, what you like and what you dislike." Darcy hesitated, wondering if the words he was about to speak were too daring. The pull to continue was too strong, and he found himself unable to resist. "If you do not mind me saying so, I am finding new depths to you and to my love."

As if by some mutual agreement, they stopped at the door that hid Mrs. Stevenson's room. Theodore had said that she had gone down to Mrs. Graham's office to come up with the meal plan. It was, strictly speaking, Anne's responsibility now, but she had undertaken the task. It was fortunate that she would be away because it gave them time to search her room unhindered.

Stepping forward, Elizabeth opened the door and walked into the room. Her movements were silent, though they knew that the woman was away. Darcy followed her with care and nodded to Reeves, who would stand in the open doorway.

"Unless we find a sign that says, 'This is how I did it, signed Mrs. Stevenson,' I am uncertain how to go about proving anything." Elizabeth's hushed tone echoed and carried in the room, filling every corner. Though it was possible, it only seemed that way because of the strain he felt trying to search the room.

Darcy could not help but snort at the perfect way she had said what she did. He did not know how they would prove anything himself. "That would be convenient."

Opening the wardrobe, Elizabeth went through the lady's clothes and Darcy was relieved that he did not need to himself. Turning, he found a table against the wall with knickknacks scattered about it.

Opening a jar, he found cold cream but no poison. Time passed, and he found nothing that was suspicious.

"Mr. Darcy, come see this," came Elizabeth's voice from behind him.

"What have you found?" Going to her side, he kneeled next to her.

When he came over, Elizabeth was pulling clothes out of the bottom of the wardrobe. Once she removed the last pair of boots, he noticed the base had a line around the edge that looked off somehow. "I think that there is a compartment here." Running her hands around the edges, she seemed to find some kind of catch because there was a click and then the base came away.

What it revealed was disappointing but still significant. There, in the wardrobe's bottom, was a cache of jewelry. Emeralds, amethysts, and topaz sparkled at them in the dim light from the window. Elizabeth reached in and pulled out a necklace at random and held it in the light. "Oh, my."

"I think that was Aunt Catherine's. There is a painting of her and my mother at Matlock House when they were maybe slightly older than Georgiana. Aunt Catherine was wearing that. I would assume that she would have given it to Anne." Darcy had searched for anything that could have been used to poison his aunt or to implicate the murderer and found nothing, though he was pleased to have uncovered a thief.

"I think we should take all of this out of here. She should not have access to it, to be able to hide it again." With a sense of purpose, Elizabeth retrieved a large square of fabric and began to transfer the jewelry onto it.

"You are correct, it needs to go in one of the safes." Helping her gather the rest of it, he tied a knot in the bundle and stood from where they knelt on the floor. Holding a hand out to help Elizabeth up as well, he was happy that she took it without hesitation.

Walking over to Reeves, he held out the bundle to him. He knew Reeves had an expression of bored indifference but would have been listening to the entire conversation. Reeves had once told Darcy that you could not stay ahead of your employer and their interests if you did not keep an ear open to everything that related to them. "Reeves, go take this and put it into the small safe in the sitting room I share with Theodore."

"And while I am gone, who shall act as lookout?" Reeves's arched eyebrow conveyed his skepticism as he looked at Darcy. They both knew he was commenting more on the lack of chaperone.

"It will be fine. You will be back in mere minutes. What could happen in that short a period?"

"Careful, the last time I said something like that, I ended up in a cell overnight," Elizabeth called from further in the room.

Frustrated, Darcy growled at Reeves, eliciting a smirk. "Fine. I have not found anything myself and I really do not know where to look. My attempts to be useful in this endeavor have been unsuccessful. I will stand in the doorway until your return and allow Miss Bennet to search on her own. She has been more successful, anyway."

Giving Darcy an ironic bow, Reeves turned and left to put the jewelry in the safe. Hearing Elizabeth move around the room, Darcy turned to watch her busy movements. Leaning against the threshold, he idly waited for Reeves to come back.

"We must have some conversation, Mr. Darcy. You cannot simply watch me; it is not seemly. A woman could begin to think that you were searching for her faults." Finishing with the bedside table, Elizabeth got on her knees next to the bed to continue her search for incriminating evidence.

"How do you keep coming up with places to look? I ran out of ideas within minutes."

"Obviously, your younger sister is not prone to stealing your things and trying to hide them in her room. I have plenty of experience finding hiding places both for my own things and searching in my sister's rooms."

"Really? I can say that was never a problem I had. Then again, I do not think Georgiana would have had any use for my best cravat." Darcy could picture Elizabeth searching her sister's room with single-minded determination.

Laughing, Elizabeth began looking for loose floorboards around the bed. "While Lydia always wanted my best bonnet. Though I will say it was always easy to find my bonnet as she always hid it in the same spot."

Pondering that information, Darcy reasoned it could be the perfect time to bring up their almost game. "Did you have a question that you wanted to ask this morning, Miss Bennet?"

Leaning back from her search on the floor, she pondered for a moment. "What do you want from life?"

"In addition to wanting to have you by my side in reality, not just in my dreams?"

"Yes, besides that." The blush on Elizabeth's face ran straight up into her hairline.

"I do not want grand parties or the bustle to see and be seen. The hustle and bustle of London drains me, and I feel uncomfortable at parties where I'm surrounded by strangers. I know what I want is not normal for society, but I cannot help wanting the small things other people ignore. A happy home, time to read, good things for the people of Pemberley. I want to have children who are free to explore their own passions and interests, not just to fulfill some family legacy. I want to spend time with them and watch them grow and get to teach them things." Darcy looked into Elizabeth's eyes when he found the courage to after revealing all that he had. He saw her eyes widen in surprise, and something else that he could not quite place. "What? You seem surprised. I know what I want is not what most people in my sphere do, but you did ask."

"I mistakenly had assumed that the reason you were so full of disdain at the assembly when I saw you there was that you felt we were all beneath you. It turns out that I was wrong. I do not know why I had assumed you would want to spend time among your peers attending balls. To know that you want small things in life as well is something that I did not expect, but should have. Frankly, it is a relief."

"As well? What is it that you want for your life?"

"Until recently, I saw little for my future. Unlike my older sister, I do not possess her stunning beauty. I know I don't fit the mold of the ideal wife that men are searching for. I laugh when other women might titter, and I read too extensively in subjects most woman ignore. Marrying only for security or status is not something I'm willing to do. I hold to my opinions too strongly and do not give way to a man merely because he believes his gender makes him correct. I had always assumed that I would be the maiden aunt if things went well and if things went poorly, I thought I would make a tolerable governess."

He watched her sit there and admit to living a life without the dreams that he had always believed were held by women. Was it possible that she had resigned herself to a life without love or marriage? Yes, her sister was classically beautiful, but that did not mean she was not without her own beauty. A beauty that pulled at him in every way possible. "You overlook the fact that not all men are on the hunt for woman like your sister. She is lovely in her way, I suppose, but too bland for my tastes. Your laugh is one of my favorite sounds in the world. I enjoy discussing books with you. I love your spirit and confidence when we debate. Your love and nurturing nature make you the perfect candidate for the role of aunt. I hope that when you said until recently you meant you were hoping for more for yourself now. Possibly because of some recent development?"

Turning away, Elizabeth hesitated, looking under the mattress instead of responding. "I have only recently started to hope for more. In fact, I worry my hopes might run away with me. Hopes of children and of love—"

Darcy did not hear the rest of her confession. It had been a mistake to overlook his duties as a lookout in order to watch the woman he loved. A blinding pain in the back of his head had him staggering to his knees and then collapsing on the ground in a heap. There he lay, unaware and unable to react, when booted feet stepped over his prone form to accost Elizabeth.

Chapter Seventeen

I Would Never Make an Agreeable Companion.

Elizabeth hesitated to respond how she knew she should. It was a lot to admit to a man that his words had opened you up to the possibility of love when there had been none before. She was realizing that the bleak future she had accepted was receding with every conversation she had with Mr. Darcy. Reaching out, she ran her hand under the mattress and felt around to distract herself from the words she knew she must speak. Elizabeth's hand ran across a lumpy packet and she began to pull it out. "I have only recently started to hope for more. In fact, I worry my hopes might run away with me. Hopes of children and of love—"

A thud behind her startled her and had her swiveling around with whatever it was in her hand. There on the floor behind her was Mr. Darcy, apparently unconscious, and stepping over his inert form was Mrs. Stevenson, a candlestick in her hand. It looked to be the candlestick from the hallway, and it looked to be dripping blood. Probably Mr. Darcy's blood. Elizabeth's fear was replaced by a sense of controlled fury, empowering her to face whatever came her way. Clenching her fists, Elizabeth felt the small lumpy bag in one hand while she could feel her nails cutting into her palm in the other.

"I am tired of you failing to comply with my wishes," Mrs. Stevenson spat, her narrowed eyes and drawn brows giving her an intimidating appearance.

Elizabeth noted she was once again talking down to her. She seemed to do so whenever there was not someone else around. "I was unaware that you had wished me to do something. Had you asked something of me and I not hear it?"

"I wanted you to rot in that cell, but it appears that your knight in shining armor had to return and let you out. If you had left well enough alone, I might not have had to act further. Yet here you are in my room, touching my things. It really is not proper, Miss Bennet. Did your mother teach you nothing?" Shaking her head, she clearly ignored the fact that she was the one holding a bloody candlestick.

Trying to appear non-threatening, Elizabeth remained on the ground, though she went from kneeling to crouching. Hoping that voluminous skirt hid the difference, she spoke in attempt to distract Mrs. Stevenson. "I always knew I would never make an agreeable companion. I cannot seem to fit in the mold society expects of me. As for my mother, she was never a slave to my education."

Moving fully into the room, Mrs. Stevenson paced. The candlestick left drops of blood where she walked in a gory display of her commitment to her cause. "Have you no notion of apologizing for coming here and threatening what I have built for myself? Do you not see how hard I have worked? I would think you would appreciate how hard it is for a singular woman to make any headway in the world."

Elizabeth refused to apologize for trying to find the culprit behind Lady Catherine's murder. It would appear that her hunch had been correct. Standing before the pacing woman, she responded, "I recognize how cruel the world can be to a woman. My own mother can expect only charity once my cousin inherits. Her failure to give birth to a son means she cannot stay in the home that has comforted her for most of her life. My father has failed to provide much at all for any of the woman in his life. If I do not marry Mr. Darcy, I cannot expect much besides the role of governess to my sister's children or someone else's."

"So you see how I have had to work at making a comfortable life for myself. I married well and yet when my husband died, I had not bore a son and his brother kicked me out of my home with merely a tuppence in support. I saw an opportunity to provide for myself without compromising my dignity by marrying another unpleasant man." She spat the last word with disgust.

Elizabeth fingered at the bag in her hand in agitation. She wanted to go to Mr. Darcy and yet she also feared drawing Mrs. Stevenson to his prone form. Reeves should be returning soon, she hoped. Maybe if she kept her occupied, Mrs. Stevenson would complain until someone could come and contain her. She obviously saw her actions as her means of providing for herself. "I understand the fear of not knowing how you will be able to provide for yourself. It is a fear I have danced with before. Did Lady Catherine threaten your plans as well?"

"All she had to do was comply. I did not ask for so very much. Only enough to manage somewhere small on my own. But she grew stubborn."

"Some mothers are protective of their children and unless I miss my guess, you threatened Anne. What did you expect?"

Whirling around, she gestured at Elizabeth with the candle stick, flicking her with blood. "I expected her to comply. It is not like her daughter is a normal member of a productive society. Her dreams of that girl marrying Darcy were cruel and ridiculous. Maybe she needs to be in an asylum. Did you ever think of that?"

Elizabeth flinched when a drop of blood hit her cheek. "You threatened Anne with being sent to an asylum. How would that have been possible?"

"I overheard an argument between Lady Catherine and her brother. It was easy to realize that he abhorred looking weak by society. Aspirations of grandeur and all that. I knew he did not know the depth of her simple-mindedness. All it took was a threat to expose her to the gossip sheets, and I had her. I told Lady Catherine I would then go to Lord Matlock and advise him of her need for additional help and my willingness to sweep it all under the rug. I know she loved the girl. She should have complied with my wishes."

Elizabeth wanted to vomit. She knew how badly treated people were in those institutions. To think of Anne there. No wonder that Lady Catherine had been so upset. They both turned to look at Mr. Darcy when he groaned. While Elizabeth hoped that his injury was not as bad as she feared, Mrs. Stevenson frowned.

Noting that frown, Elizabeth desperately tried to draw the woman's attention to herself. "What was your plan once Lady Catherine died?"

"It is not possible for Anne to run the household. I would do it and she could be a puppet. Or I could always arrange a marriage and an accident, though that plan has me marrying her husband, which I cannot like. It has been something I have been planning, but you and Mr. Tall, Dark, and Grumpy have been getting in my way."

"How were you planning on getting away with so many more murders?" Elizabeth knew that time was running out, and it appeared to her that Mrs. Stevenson was getting antsy. If she was ready to act, Elizabeth would have to act first.

"Oh, I would not murder anyone. In fact, for all intents and purposes, I haven't. You murdered Lady Catherine and when Mr. Darcy found you trying to plant poison in my room, you killed him and then yourself."

Taking an unobtrusive step forward, Elizabeth told herself to look for an opening. "It sounds like you have quite the thorough plan."

"What can I say? I have always thought on my feet. Now to do something, before he wakes up and becomes a threat." Mrs. Stevenson turned to look at Mr. Darcy.

It was too much; she had to protect him. "But Mrs. Stevenson, you have not asked me how I will stop you."

Swinging back around to face a closer Elizabeth, Mrs. Stevenson opened her mouth to speak. "I have the weapon. There is no way—"

Acting on instinct and fueled by the fury she felt, Elizabeth pulled her arm back and let her fist fly towards the bitter woman's face. The impact was a shock that sent pain running up Elizabeth's arm. The crunch of Mrs. Stevenson's nose breaking under Elizabeth's fist was as satisfying as it was disturbing.

She drew her hand back, and the feeling of triumph was deflated slightly as she clutched it to her chest in pain. "Ow!"

Mrs. Stevenson dropped the candlestick to clutch at her misaligned face. "My nose! What have you done?"

"It is no more than you deserve. You are a despicable woman who did not appreciate what you had. You have blackmailed, lied, and murdered. I cannot understand how you assumed to get away with such abominable behavior." Even as she spoke, Elizabeth still clutched at her hand. The pain was significant, and she hoped she had not damaged it too badly.

Ignoring the pain, she reached down to grab the candlestick before Mrs. Stevenson came to her senses. Now if only she could hold her at bay long enough for Reeves to get there. Edging around the angry woman, she put herself in between Mr. Darcy and the threat. It also put her between Mrs. Stevenson and her escape. She did not want the woman getting away. Who knew what would happen?

Elizabeth was weary of the angry woman who had glared at her with utter hatred. That did not mean that Elizabeth was not willing to hold her ground. She was willing to protect the man who loved her and that she was developing feelings for. In fact, seeing him laying so still and being afraid for him had made her realize just how much she truly felt for him.

"You have no connections, no wealth, no talent. Mr. Darcy cannot truly want you. You are a nobody. And yet you think to stop me?"

"You may view me as a nobody if you wish, but I will stop you. You have done enough harm." Tightening her grip on the candlestick, Elizabeth readied herself for an attack.

"I should say so. Miss Bennet, would you mind checking on Mr. Darcy while I contain Mrs. Stevenson?" Reeves spoke up from behind Elizabeth.

Hearing Reeves's words from behind her almost made her collapse with relief. Still, she waited until he had torn the bed sheets into strips and was tying Mrs. Stevenson up before she dropped the candlestick and went to Mr. Darcy. Worried for him, she dropped to the floor, where he lay groaning.

He lay face down, providing her with a view of his bleeding head. She was happy to see that he was not bleeding profusely, as she had feared. Getting up, she went to the bed and grabbed some of the remaining linens to fold up and press to the back of Mr. Darcy's head. Her gaze swept the area and finally rested on the small packet she had obtained just before things went awry. A few red beads had fallen out. She stared at it momentarily before reaching out and picking it up. It must be important if the woman had hidden it. Wanting to keep her hands free, she shoved the packet in her bodice. It was not so large to be noticeable.

Rushing back to Mr. Darcy, he looked no worse in her absence but also no better. She pressed the folded cloth to the back of his head and grimaced when he groaned at the pressure on his wound. Despite his exclamation of pain, he did not exhibit any signs of waking.

"Miss Bennet, if you would, I think we should get Colonel Fitzwilliam and the physician. I need to stay here and watch Mrs.

Stevenson or I would get him myself." Reeves, though appearing unflappable as ever, forced Mrs. Stevenson into a chair in the room's corner.

"Yes, of course." Elizabeth knew she needed to be strong, but it almost hurt to leave Mr. Darcy there on the floor and bleeding. Giving in to the impulse that consumed her, she leaned down whispered to him. "I will return, Mr. Darcy. Stay well until I return. I want to tell you of my hopes, but you must wake up and be well to hear them."

Standing, she rushed down the hallway and to the stairs that would take her to the servant's hall. The colonel had gone to get Wright and should be back, but she was uncertain where they would be. She decided to at least let Mrs. Graham know they needed to send for the physician and a footman would be helpful. Finding Mrs. Graham's office empty, she continued on to the kitchen to look for her.

Mrs. Graham was talking to the cook, but looked up when Elizabeth came rushing in. "You look a fright child. What is going on?"

Ignoring the impulse to straighten her hair, Elizabeth explained. "Mrs. Stevenson hit Mr. Darcy on the head. He is unconscious and bleeding. We need to send for the physician, and we need to send a footman up to help Reeves contain her."

"So, you found out who it was that murdered Lady Catherine," Mrs. Wright spoke up from behind Elizabeth. She must have come up to the house at the colonel's request to look at what they had discovered but was clearly glad to hear that they had found the killer.

Recovering from her startle, Elizabeth turned and clutched at Mrs. Wright's hand. "I am so glad you have come. Mrs. Stevenson has hit Mr. Darcy over the head. I was hoping to send for the physician, but your being here is almost fortuitous."

"She did what?" Colonel Fitzwilliam thundered.

"We were searching her room, and she came up behind Mr. Darcy and hit him in the back of the head with a candlestick."

The colonel's scowl turned fierce, and Elizabeth could see how he would be formidable on the battlefield. "Did she get away?"

Shaking her head, Elizabeth continued, "No, I managed to keep her there until Reeves returned. He is holding her there until I could return with help."

He took off running down the hall before Elizabeth had even finished speaking. Elizabeth watched him go and hoped that he would be of some help. There was little enough she knew to help with a head wound and it was possible that he would have experience they could use from his time on the battlefields in France. Besides, he would be able to contain Mrs. Stevenson with ease.

"It will be well, you will see." Taking Elizabeth by the arm, Mrs. Wright shepherded her into the kitchen and had her sit at the great table there.

"He was so still, Mrs. Wright." Clasping her good hand over her eyes, Elizabeth endeavored to rid her mind of the image. All that had transpired recently flooded her mind and taunted her with the horror of it.

Mrs. Wright whispered to one of the kitchen maids before turning to speak to Elizabeth. "Was there no sign of him waking at all?"

A teacup quickly appeared in front of Elizabeth, and she took a sip of the warm brew before responding. "He was groaning before I left." Elizabeth put the teacup down with a clatter and looked up at Mrs. Wright and Mrs. Graham, who both stood nearby. "We should hurry back to him. I cannot simply sit here drinking tea while he bleeds."

"We are accomplishing what we need to accomplish, Miss Bennet. You have had a shock and need time to gather yourself. Meanwhile, the maids are gathering supplies for me to use for a poultice. I am also finding out information I will need to treat him. We will see to him once you have finished your tea. Was there very much blood? Was he bleeding freely or was it sluggish?" Taking Elizabeth's damaged hand in her own, Mrs. Wright sat next to her and began rubbing a salve into the abused flesh.

Despite wincing when the kind woman manipulated her hand, Elizabeth spoke through the pain. "It looked as if at first he had bled more, but by the time I was able to see to him it was sluggish, and I applied pressure to it with some folded up linen." Elizabeth looked down at her hands and found them shaking. Frowning, she realized she had not noticed before how affected she was. No wonder they had given her sweet tea and had her sit down.

"Then you did just as you should." Getting up from the table, Mrs. Wright went over to gather the things the maids were providing and began doing something with it that Elizabeth could not fathom at the moment.

Mrs. Graham patted Elizabeth's shaking hand. "I have sent one of the grooms to go get the physician, but there is no telling how long he may be. Between the good colonel and Mrs. Wright here, we will see to your gentleman until he arrives. So how was it that a little thing like you was able to stop a woman welding a candlestick?"

Blushing at the unladylike method she had used, Elizabeth simply replied, "I punched her."

Laughter erupted around the room and various members of the staff spoke of how they had all been wishing to take the pompous woman down a peg. They piled congratulations and thanks on her trembling shoulders. Somewhere deep inside Elizabeth something unwound, and she could finally smile.

Chapter Eighteen

The Miscreant is Dealt with

Darcy's head ached something fierce. He sensed movement around him and tried to open his eyes and found that was a mistake. The blinding light sent his pain to new levels, and he slammed his eyes shut and groaned in regret. Trying to figure out what exactly was going on, he tried to use his other senses to decipher what had put him in his painful predicament. The ground was cool under his face, and he realized he was lying on the floor. The sound of arguing made him wince, but he tried to listen to what was being said. Maybe he could figure out what had happened.

"I do not know what to tell you. I came into the room and that horrible Miss Bennet hit me. Mr. Darcy was already on the floor when I arrived. I demand you release me!" A woman's voice was annoyingly shrill.

"Not likely. You can say what you wish, but I believe none of your lies," Theodore said in an angry tone. "Gregory, go grab another footman. The burlier the better. Remove this woman from Rosings and have her taken to the gaol in town to be held until the coroner arrives."

"Yes, sir."

Darcy was beginning to put the pieces together. He had a few memories of searching Mrs. Stevenson's room, talking with Elizabeth, but then nothing. Something must have happened, and his pain spoke of some kind of injury. Where was Elizabeth? Was she all right? His terror on behalf of Elizabeth sent him reeling. Pushing himself up off the floor, he felt his pulse pounding in his head and the room spinning around him.

Strong hands helped him lean against a wall. "Whoa there. If you move too much, you will get the bleeding started back up."

Darcy's fuzzy mind told him who was speaking. "Reeves? Where is Elizabeth?"

"Yes, sir, Miss Bennet is fine. Better than you, actually."

Relief rushed through his sagging form, but he was still full of questions. "What happened?"

"It appears that you are absolutely horrible as a lookout. You were not watching the hallway and Mrs. Stevenson came up behind you and conked you on the head."

"I did no such thing!" Mrs. Stevenson's screech had Mr. Darcy wincing.

"You will hold your tongue, or I will have you gagged." Theodore once again spoke from somewhere nearby. "Welcome back, Darcy. I am glad you never had aspirations of joining the regulars. I hear you are a horrible lookout."

"I cannot remember what I was doing. But I will admit to never wanting to join the military, so maybe it is a good thing." Darcy kept his eyes shut tight and tried to concentrate on not vomiting.

"That will happen when you get knocked out. Though I have a guess of what you were watching instead of the hall," Theodore chuckled.

Darcy could sense a bustle going on, even with his eyes closed. It sounded like Gregory and at least one other man with heavy footfalls had arrived to take Mrs. Stevenson away.

"Unhand me!" she screeched.

The noise stabbed at Darcy, and he gritted his teeth, though that did not help with anything beyond making his head hurt. A scuffle erupted, and it tempted Darcy to open his eyes to see what was going on, but he refrained.

"I told you I would gag you if you did not hold your tongue," Theodore griped at the woman.

Darcy could hear her being dragged away and found he was satisfied to know that they had found the woman who had killed his aunt.

"Well, she seems to be a lively one," an unfamiliar voice spoke up.

"Mr. Darcy, are you all right? Should you be sitting up?" Elizabeth's wonderful voice had him opening his eyes to confirm for himself that she was well.

"I am fine." Darcy found that his voice was a mere whisper. Even with his eyes open merely a sliver, the pain was intense.

"And your being fine is why the light seems to give you pain. Silly boy, you should have kept your eyes closed. Though I suppose you had to see your lady love," came the unknown voice once again.

"Yes, I did." Darcy had not been scolded so thoroughly in quite some time.

"Mr. Darcy, do close your eyes. I will still be here even if you shut your eyes. I will not disappear. Mrs. Wright is correct for scolding you. Let her check you over and see if she can help you."

Elizabeth took his hand, and her reassurance settled him, grounding him in a way that he had not expected. He closed his eyes but held tight to her small hand. He felt delight worm its way into the tumult of his emotions. It was so much better to focus on than the pain and confusion. Darcy held still for the probing and clucking of the heretofore unknown Mrs. Wright. The entire time, he tried to remember not to crush Elizabeth's delicate hand.

"Now that the miscreant is delt with, can we move my baffled cousin to his room? It will be darker there and I am thinking quieter. If he is concussed as I suspect, then he will want both."

"He should be fine to make it to his rooms, though I suspect it will be rather unpleasant for him. I will want to apply a poultice once he is laying down."

Darcy managed to keep from tossing up his accounts when he was brought to his feet, but only just. It was hard to put one foot after the other and he leaned rather heavily on his cousin, and the footman he had found. It became a blur of endurance and the desire to not disgrace himself in Elizabeth's eyes.

Finally, he was in his bed, having been helped into night clothes by Reeves. The dark was heavenly, as was the cushion under him. It was heaven until a candle sputtered to life.

"On your stomach, young man, so that I may see to your head." Mrs. Wright's command brooked no nonsense or refusal.

Giving in to her stern command, Darcy rolled to his stomach. "Yes, ma'am. You wouldn't happen to have any relatives in Derbyshire by chance? You sound quite like my housekeeper."

"Not that I am aware of, but you never know. The bleeding has mostly stopped. I will leave the poultice on for now. Mrs. Graham has the tea I want you to drink whenever you are awake. A full cup, well steeped four times a day. The physician should be here soon enough, but I doubt he will have many concerns. You woke up fairly quickly, and your eyes are reacting to the light. That is always a good sign. What you need is a good rest."

Darcy would not argue with that sentiment, though he was only slightly successful trying to settle in bed in a way that would not hurt his sore head. However, when Reeves placed a folded cloth that was filled with ice chips on the wound, he sighed at the relief. "Thank you, Reeves."

"Of course, sir."

"Where is Elizabeth?"

"She is fine, sir. Spending time with Miss de Bourgh and Hattie. The world will still be here even if you rest. I am sure you will feel much better after you sleep."

Darcy wanted to give some form of witty retort but was unsuccessful. His muddled mind demanded rest, and he fell asleep while trying to figure what to say in response.

***

Upon waking, Darcy no longer felt as if his head was the location of an epic battle, merely a skirmish. At some point during his slumber, he had rolled over and the change in position was putting pressure on his head wound. He quickly learned that gritting his teeth sent shards of pain down his spine. He lay there trying to figure out how to fight the pain without whimpering like a child. Giving up on trying to sit up in bed for the moment, he stared at the ceiling above him.

So much had happened the day before. He felt that somehow, he was missing moments from just before he was so easily felled by a candlestick. He hazily remembered finding some of the jewelry that Aunt Catherine must have given Anne and sending Reeves off to put it in a safe. Then he was talking with Elizabeth about something. Something about, was it Pemberley? He had a feeling that children were involved in the conversation, but he wasn't sure why.

He felt as if he was missing something important. Whatever it was, he felt a new hope. Which was odd because he did not even remember what they said exactly, but he felt that somehow the conversation he was missing was full of a possibility for the future. He lay there smiling for some time, simply basking in the hope that he may very well end up with love in his life yet.

"I see you are awake, sir. Are you faring any better having gotten some rest?" Reeves's voice came from the side of the room where he was setting down a tray.

Attempting to sit up in bed once again this time, he succeeded, but did not do so without groaning. At least he had remembered not to grit his teeth. "Yes, the pain is receding some, but still keen to make its presence known. Have you brought me the tea Mrs. Wright commanded I drink?"

"Yes, sir, you are to drink at least a full cup before attempting to move out of the bed. She is rather singular, that woman." Handing Darcy a cup of the tea where he sat in bed, Reeves made sure that he was steady with it before he stepped back.

The tea was bitter, but Darcy drank it down, hoping to find some relief. He wanted to speak with Elizabeth, but he wouldn't be able to do that with the way his head felt. "What is the state of things?"

"Mrs. Stevenson has made her way down to the town gaol. I will say that she handled it with a decided lack of grace. She will not be receiving the treatment Miss Bennet did, that is for sure."

"Oh?" Darcy felt a surge of curiosity. He had heard nothing beyond the fact that Elizabeth was being confined. The only thing on his mind was her release, so he didn't process any additional details anyone might have shared.

Reeves noticed Darcy's curiosity and grinned at him. Full of mischief, he spoke conspiratorially with Darcy. "Miss Bennet was as dignified as a queen when they took her. Polite to even your uncle and especially the magistrate that was called upon to confine her in the night. That, combined with the good name she had earned by being polite to staff, is what influenced the magistrate to give her whatever comforts he could. Food from his own table and extra blankets, even hot tea. Mrs. Stevenson's screaming and demands will get her nothing but the crust of bread and water the law demands. She has been cruel to too many people to expect sympathy."

It was easily something he could picture, both the fact that Elizabeth acted with dignity and that Mrs. Stevenson did not. Neither was surprising. Finishing the tea, he swung his legs to the side of the bed and sat there for a moment. "How long was I asleep?"

"A number of hours. They will serve dinner soon. Would you care to take a tray in your room?"

"I want to go down to dinner." Darcy realized he sounded like a petulant child who wanted to eat with the adults, and so he added, "Lord Matlock will assuredly be there and you know how bad he can be."

When Reeves quirked his eyebrow, Darcy was determined to show the man that he could indeed make it downstairs. He forced himself to his feet. After teetering slightly, he straightened and headed towards his door. He would sit through the dinner. It was not like he would exert much energy. He stopped when he heard Reeves speak behind him.

"Unless you want to wear your nightclothes, I really should find you something to wear," Reeves spoke laconically. Even with his back to the man, Darcy could tell his valet was fighting a smile at his foolishness.

"Maybe I would start a trend, going to dinner in my nightclothes. You do not know everything, Reeves. I will prove you fallible at some point." Darcy went to the nearest chair and sat down with a slight groan. Allowing himself to relax momentarily, he waited to let Reeves help him dress.

***

MAKING IT DOWN THE stairs was an event that was better off not described to anyone, but Darcy was finally down the stairs and in the sitting room, waiting for dinner to be announced. It looked as if someone had kept the lighting to a minimum, for which Darcy was eternally grateful. His head, though better, was still making itself very known.

Across the room, Theodore sat drumming his fingers on his leg. Most likely, he was impatient to get to his food. "So, how is your skull? Are you feeling any less muzzy headed?"

"My head is certainly making itself known, but it has improved. The tea Mrs. Wright commanded I drink seems to have helped some."

"You know, I have often wondered if we would have defeated that French menace already if we put a woman like that in charge of things. It would even be more effective if we just sent them after him. They could lecture him into good behavior in a trice." Theodore chuckled, probably imagining the swath of motherly commanders moving across France.

"It would not work as lovely as the notion is. Women like Mrs. Wright would merely tell you that they have actual issues to deal with and they would not go trapesing after fools who should have learned to share as a child." A melodious laugh accompanied Elizabeth's pert statement.

Noting Miss Bennet's entrance, Darcy tried to stand and greet her. Seeing his struggle, she shook her head and came to sit near him. He was not overly upset at that turn of events. Not upset at all.

"Miss Bennet, I am glad to see you. Although I want to apologize for being asleep for so long." They were supposed to be working together, and he slept the afternoon away. He was certainly not going to be much of a conversationalist with the way his head was.

"It is not your fault someone bashed you in the head with a candlestick. You needed time to rest and recover. I spent some lovely time with Anne. I think she is doing well despite her mother's death. Though I think she misses her. I even think I may have discovered what poisoned Lady Catherine."

"How did you do that?" came Theodore's quick response from where he sat.

"What?" Darcy's own comment came much slower.

Though not exactly cheerful, Elizabeth's smile was still present on her lips, albeit with a somber undertone. "Before Mrs. Stevenson came in, I had found a small packet of something hidden under her mattress. When I got the chance, after the drama was over, I looked in the bag. It was full of what looked like little red beads. But it made me remember Anne's dog."

Darcy's head drooped onto the seatback, unable to hold itself up while he ruminated. "Her dog? The one that died?"

"Yes, the dog died recently, and Anne had told me he loved chewing on her bracelets. Shortly before he died, he had broken one of her newest bracelets, chewing on the beads. Anne had saved the bracelet, or what was left of it, for sentimental reasons. I checked and the beads match." Elizabeth produced several red and black beads from somewhere and held them out for them to see.

Theodore, on the other hand leaned forward before he asked. "But how could a bead poison someone?"

"It looks like a bead, certainly, but I think it may be a seed. I considered the possibility of cutting one in half experimentally to compare it to the bits in the liquid we found, but as I am uncertain of its properties, I did not want to risk it."

Reaching out, Theodore took the beads, or possibly more accurately seeds, from her and examined them. "I certainly have never seen their like before."

"Anne said that Lady Catherine got the bracelet from some far-off place. I had asked Mrs. Wright if she knew of any local plants that would give the symptoms we observed, and she said there was not anything here that she knew of. She pointed out that nature uses bright colors to signal danger, as poisonous things often have the most vibrant hues. Anne's dog died shortly after chewing on the bracelet and breaking it. If it ingested a seed and then grew ill, and Mrs. Stevenson observed that, she could have used that knowledge to her advantage. Why else keep a stash of the seeds under her bed?" Elizabeth spoke calmly of the conclusions that she had come to, her reasoning put forth in an orderly manner.

Theodore watched the fire dance and flicker in the fireplace before breaking the silence. "Unless we can get her to admit to her crimes and logic, we may never know exactly what transpired, but this is highly probable. Well done, Miss Bennet."

Darcy observed his cousin as he pondered. He had remained quiet as they discussed the poison, but that was mostly because of the aching in his head. He knew Theodore well enough to note that he was coming up with some kind of strategy. "What are you thinking, Theodore? I can see it on your face. You are in your military mindset."

"The coroner should come soon to take things in hand. While he may be content with our findings, I remain dissatisfied. Though we found the killer, there is still a feeling of dissatisfaction that I cannot quite shake. I want to know the details surrounding Aunt Catherine's death, including the motive and method of her murder. I was considering writing an old friend of mine who had the uncanny ability to get people to confess. He was very useful in ferreting things out for my battalion."

"Though I am not against you writing to your friend and gathering more information, she confessed in a fashion after she had knocked out Mr. Darcy," said Elizabeth.

"Did she?"

"She stated that Lady Catherine would have been fine if she just gave her what she wanted. Or something like that. She never said how she did what she did, though. Her confession detailed how she had threatened Anne, hoping to obtain the resources necessary to live comfortably on her own. She had threatened having Anne sent to an asylum. Her plan had been to tell the gossip sheets that Anne was addled in someway, and that she would tell Lord Matlock that she would smooth it over by having her placed in an asylum."

"That conniving witch!" thundered Theodore.

"Apparently, the threat did not work out the way she had wanted, and she changed her goal to running Rosings with Anne as a puppet figure."

"I seemed to have missed a lot while I was unconscious. I am glad that Reeves was there to bring her under control," Darcy spoke.

Elizabeth's eyes darted in a way that made Darcy wonder. "Well…" she started.

"What? I was under the impression that Reeves lent a hand?" Darcy prompted.

"He did, but that was after I had gotten the candlestick from her." Elizabeth looked down, a blush gracing her cheeks in the low light.

"How did you get the candlestick from her?" Darcy was curious about why she would blush so.

Picking at a snag in the fabric of her seat instead of looking up, she muttered, "I found the need to punch her. I think I might have actually broken her nose."

Theodore's laugh was unrestrained and though Darcy thought it was quite fitting himself, all the noise made his head throb. Beyond the slight humor, Darcy felt guilt at allowing Elizabeth to be put in that situation. "I am sorry, Miss Bennet. You shouldn't have had to deal with her alone. If only I had been there to help. I do not know what I was thinking, failing at my duty to watch for her."

"I think I know what you were doing." Theodore's muttered comment was audible to everyone, causing Elizabeth to blush even deeper. Once again, Theodore was laughing, but this time it was at Darcy's expense.

Darcy tried glaring at him but found that any extreme emotional expression hurt his head rather fiercely. His attempt at planning some kind of retribution was suspended by the arrival of a servant announcing dinner. They stood and headed into the dining room. Darcy's gratitude that his uncle had not shown up was short-lived. Just as he was seating Elizabeth next to him at the table, his uncle burst into the room with a loud bang.

"What is that vile murderess doing at my sister's dinner table? Darcy, do not tell me this is your doing." His uncle's growl from the doorway caused everyone to freeze in place.

Chapter Nineteen

I Never was Partial to Fancy Hothouse Flowers

Elizabeth was stuck halfway between sitting and standing. The man was once again disturbing her peace. Sitting down, she refused to allow him to make her uncomfortable.

Theodore did not get up to confront his father, and yet he did not cower beneath his bluster. "Are you sitting down to dinner, father, or are you insulting Miss Bennet?"

Stepping forward, he placed his fisted hands on the edge of the table and glared. "I thought that woman was taken to the town gaol. I ask again why she is here."

Darcy stood straight beside her and placed his hand on her shoulder. "She is my guest and after the way that you had her put in the gaol merely on the word of Mrs. Stevenson, I am ashamed of my connection to you."

Huffing in indignation, Lord Matlock countered, "Mrs. Stevenson is a respected member of this household. Why would I not believe the lady?"

"You had no evidence, nor did you consult others to see if her viewpoint was flawed or biased. If that is how you handle your estate,

I question your efficacy as a member of the ruling class." Mr. Darcy's voice was cold and condescending.

She had considered Mr. Darcy cold and condescending at Netherfield, but she must have been kidding herself. This icy disdain was so much greater when compared to the way that he behaved back in Meryton. What was more was that he used it against someone in defense of her. He had not sat down, nor had he moved his hand from her shoulder. Reaching up, she placed her hand over his where it rested on her shoulder.

"We have proven that Miss Bennet was not the perpetrator of that crime. In fact, it was Mrs. Stevenson who was framing Miss Bennet and who blackmailed and then murdered Aunt Catherine," Theodore commented from his seat, leaning back slightly in a nonchalant pose that visibly angered his father.

"Oh, and I suppose that the conniving strumpet is the one that proved it to you. Even now, she is trying to manipulate you." Unwilling to admit defeat gracefully, Lord Matlock pushed forward blindly.

"Mrs. Stevenson proved herself the murderer when she admitted it to me after she knocked your nephew unconscious with a candlestick. If you had any genuine concern for your nephew, you would ask after his wellbeing, not castigating him for your own ill-conceived notions. As for the paragon whose word you trusted, we have traded places, so to speak, as she is now residing in the gaol awaiting the coroner to come investigate and, of course, trial." Elizabeth kept her voice dry and without inflection. There was no reason to sink to his level.

The man stood dumbfounded. He had obviously believed himself incapable of being proven wrong. After a moment, he moved to sit down without a word. As if everything would be fine if he ignored the fact that he had caused a scene. Claiming the head of the table for himself, he nodded to the servant standing in the corner to start bringing the food.

Mr. Darcy sat down next to her but not before squeezing her hand and giving her a wan smile. It was obvious to her that he was in a significant amount of pain and should lie down instead of dealing with all the excessive amounts of drama. As she ate in silence, she couldn't help but notice the way the sounds of forks and knives clinking against plates echoed in the empty room. Maybe it was better for Mr. Darcy that there was no talking.

"So, Miss Bennet, where do you come from? Who are your people? Anyone I would know?" the earl spoke as the soup was being taken away. As they waited for the next course to arrive, he fixed his gaze on her from across table.

Wiping her mouth, Elizabeth barely hesitated before answering. "I am from Meryton, and I doubt you would know any of my connections."

"I am sure if you are attempting to win my nephew, you must have some connections worth noting. Anything less would be laughable."

"No, actually, I have no lofty connections. Though my family has possessed Longbourn for five generations, it is entailed away from the female line and my many times cousin, Mr. Collins, is set to inherit. Before you question it, I will tell you that my mother's family has connections to trade. So, no, I have no connections that you would ever deem acceptable, and yet here I am." Elizabeth felt no compunction over her confession. While she may cringe at her family's behavior at times, she never felt shame in regards to their social class or personal identities.

"Then the rumor I was told must be incorrect. There is no way someone with connections to my family would deem you appropriate to bring within its sphere." His doughy face turned petulant, acting like a spoiled child who whined and complained when a toy he threw got mud on it.

Darcy lay his own serviette down, ready to engage his uncle. "I do not know what rumor you heard, but I greatly wish to bring her into my sphere, as you say. I would ask to marry her at this moment if I had felt that I had won her over already. The mere thought of her being far away from me is enough to make me ache for her presence. While you, on the other hand, I am wishing farther away by the moment."

"How can you wish to marry her?!? Devil it, she has been in the town gaol. Think of your position in society. Think of Georgiana. How will she ever be accepted by society if you bring a grasping mushroom into her midst?"

"You were the one that put her there, may I remind you!" Then, grabbing his head, Mr. Darcy took a breath, obviously pained by his injury when he raised his voice. Taking another breath, he spoke again, this time in a measured voice that somehow retained its power without increasing its volume. "She is kind, good-hearted and clever. She reads, can have intelligent debates, and is cognizant of modern agricultural developments. Her worth is beyond that of corals, and I wish to marry her because she is the best woman I know. She could be the helpmate that I have always wanted. The woman my parents always told me to search for."

"My sister always was sentimental and too easily swayed, but I would have thought your father would have taught you something about your role in society. You have a name to uphold. At least when he chose his marriage partner, she was appropriately lofty. You are the grandson of an Earl."

"The significance is irrelevant if I'm not happy with the life I lead. Yes, I have a name to uphold. But what you do not understand is that I want the Darcy name to stand for more than bloodlines. I want it to stand for love." Darcy may have been speaking softly, but his glare was unflinching and cold.

"Love! No one needs love in their life. It is a foolish fairy tale that simple doesn't exist. You cannot be so weak-willed, Darcy. I won't let you ruin our family's reputation." Lord Matlock's anger was palpable as he shook his head in disagreement, and his face became increasingly red.

Elizabeth leaned back in her chair, watching the man as he worked himself up into a lather. She wondered if this obstinacy was an inherited trait; he was certainly very similar to his sister. Maybe it was a learned behavior? She refused to allow him to browbeat Mr. Darcy, so she spoke up. "He may wish to marry whomever he chooses. He has reached his majority. Running his estate single-handedly for years, he has proven himself to be a capable decision-maker, always considering the welfare of himself and others. He is not your son or a Fitzwilliam. In fact, he is the head of his own household. You may be his uncle and even an earl, but that ultimately has no great meaning in his life if he does not wish it to. He is a gentleman, and I am a gentleman's daughter. Ultimately, there is nothing separating us except our decision on the matter."

Elizabeth's statement did not go over well with the earl, and he pushed himself back from the table and stood. "I demand you to promise that you will not bring my nephew down by marrying him. Tying yourself to him could only be a degradation to you both. You will not be acknowledged by anyone of note. I will not acknowledge you, nor will my family acknowledge you. You will gain nothing from me by attempting this farce."

"Why would I hope to gain anything from you? You are not someone I would wish to have acknowledge me. You are not my father nor my relative. Your behavior is not something I hold in esteem. I am not attempting to impress you in any way. Who I choose to court or marry is wholly unconnected to you. I will promise nothing to a man who holds his opinions on society over the happiness of his nephew."

"Well, I see how it is." Lord Matlock looked to be about to say something else when he was interrupted by his son's hard voice.

With the face of a seasoned soldier sizing up an enemy, hard and unrelenting, the colonel spoke. "You have heard their say, father. You will not win this battle, nor the war. I believe you should focus on dealing with what you came here to do. How are the plans proceeding for your sister's funeral?"

His mouth flapped open and closed like a dying fish as he struggled to process the statement. Lord Matlock stood frozen in indecision before once again ignoring all that had transpired and moving on.

As if by moving forward, he could avoid the necessity of admitting his poor behavior or the fact that he lost. Sitting back down, he took a gulp of wine before speaking. "The bishop is sending someone for her service, which will be held this week."

From there, the dinner progressed smoothly without the discord it had started out with. Lord Matlock was not happy, but was completely unwilling to admit defeat at the hands of those in the room. Elizabeth found that the stress of the day made the food unappetizing, but she was grateful for the absence of conflict for once.

***

THE NEXT MORNING, ELIZABETH had woken up early and went for a walk with young Hattie before meeting up with the gentlemen for breakfast. Darcy's color had improved, which reassured her more than she would want to admit. They had all retired soon after dinner the night before. Mr. Darcy needed to lie down, and she was tired after dealing with the distressing day. It appeared that the night's sleep had helped Mr. Darcy recover somewhat. She looked over at him and judged him to be looking better than the night before.

She sipped her coffee, enjoying the bitter brew and the way the warmth permeated her being. Ever since her night in the gaol, she had enjoyed the warmth of the hot beverage even more. She watched the cousins chatter about arrangements for the funeral and having the countess and Georgiana come sometime the next day. The way that they interacted spoke of how close they were.

"Miss Bennet, what happened to your hand? It is rather bruised." Mr. Darcy spoke with concern from where he sat next to her.

Putting her cup down, Elizabeth winced as she gazed down at her hand, noticing the discoloration that had spread across her knuckles. The sight of the deep purple bruising made her stomach turn. She could almost hear the sound of the impact that had caused it, the sickening thud of flesh meeting flesh. "Yes, well, apparently punching a villain in the face has consequences I was unaware of at the time. It hurt rather more than I would have thought." The colonel's bark of laughter caused her to laugh as well. She had always reasoned that it was better to laugh than cry.

"I am so sorry you were forced to act as you did. I am sorry for putting you in a difficult situation at Rosings, where you had to protect us both," Darcy spoke quietly into the laughter, bringing it quickly to a halt.

Elizabeth felt bad that he worried but wanted to get him to understand something important. "Mr. Darcy, I am not a wilting hothouse flower. I am more of a wild bloom found along a trail. I can endure more than most. My courage rises at any effort to intimidate me. I do not regret my actions and I do not want you to either. I am proud of my ability to do what I must in order to protect us both. If you are still worried, you can take on the next murderer we face."

The colonel looked back and forth between the two, smiling at the latest developments. Mr. Darcy looked at her strangely, and she wondered what he was thinking. She knew she was not the typical woman, and she hoped he loved her enough to accept that. His love had a magnetic effect on her, and she was irresistibly drawn to it. Her heart stuttered in her chest as she waited for his response.

"I never was partial to the fancy hothouse flowers."

"No? I am sure that there are plenty of hothouse flowers that would love to be preferred by you." Elizabeth was not so ignorant of high society that she did not know they considered him a wonderful catch.

"Anyone else would satisfy them just as much. Flashy flowers are attracted to what I have, and they do not care about who I am." His gaze was direct and full of meaning.

"How do you know I am not after what you have? I hear Pemberley has a rather wonderful library."

"Well, as long as you are not opposed to company on occasion and are willing to debate what you read, I am more than willing to share." Shifting his chair in order to face her directly, Darcy looked at her. His lips twitched and Elizabeth realized he was attempting not to smile.

"I am not opposed to a good debate about what I have read. As long as you are not afraid of a woman with strong opinions." Elizabeth swallowed hard as she recognized the enormity of what was happening. She stared at Mr. Darcy, unable to blink or tear her gaze away, her heart pounding so hard it felt like it might burst.

Taking her hand, Mr. Darcy kissed the bruise that was forming on her knuckles where she had punched Mrs. Stevenson. He did not let go of her hand, instead bringing it to his chest and placing it over his heart, where she could feel his heart racing. "You are not a woman who would toy with my heart, with anyone's heart. Your words and conviction in standing against my uncle have given me more hope than I had thought possible. Over the past few days, I have learned that my past actions have hurt you and damaged your confidence in me and my intentions. I want you to know that am trying to learn from this and I am trying to find a way to do better by you and everyone else. I considered asking once again for you to marry me, but I want to do this the right way. My feelings for you and your connections are nothing to be ashamed of, and I'm eager to show you that. You deserve the honor of being courted openly. Would you allow me the privilege of showing you, of showing the world how much I esteem you, ardently admire and love you?"

"Are you asking me for a formal courtship, Mr. Darcy?" Elizabeth's heart raced as their fingers intertwined, sending a shiver of excitement down her spine. Mr. Darcy's pulse was as rapid as hers, and his grip on her hand was firm yet gentle, conveying his eagerness to express his feelings. Elizabeth couldn't help but feel exhilarated, as if they were the only two people in the world, lost in their own moment of bliss.

"Yes, Elizabeth, I wish to conduct a formal courtship with you."

"Over the last few days, I have spent a lot of time reflecting on things. I believe if my pride had not been so injured, I might have seen you in a different light. I've started seeing you in a new light that accentuates your best features, and I'm intrigued to learn more about you. The possibility of spending more time with you without having to worry about a murderer is delightful. So yes, William, I wish to enter a formal courtship with you." Her grin was so bright that it lit up the room.

Chapter Twenty

Almost Anticlimactic

Darcy could not believe how wonderful his morning was progressing. He had woken to significantly less pain. The physician had shown up shortly before he had gone to sleep the night before. He said that there was not much to be concerned with. His head had stopped bleeding and did not require any stitches. Though his head hurt, and the light was still bothering his eyes, the physician assured him it would pass with time. He suggested Darcy should continue to drink the tea Mrs. Wright had left.

The best part of the morning was looking at Elizabeth and realizing that she was open to what was developing between them. Despite the debacle that occurred in the last few days, she had become interested in knowing more about him. Or maybe it was because of it? As they worked to settle the matter of his aunt's death, they found themselves with more chances to see each other. They spoke openly and honestly. He knew he had found out more about Elizabeth, about who she really was. It was likely that she had learned about him as well. It might just have been enough to counteract his terribly poor start with her.

He believed that he could have asked for her hand, and she may have even agreed, but he wanted to make sure that she knew the depth of his affections. He had recently come to realize that he had acted terribly in Meryton, and he hoped to make amends and prove to her that he was capable of being the kind of man she deserved. The need to prove himself to both of them was like a constant buzz in his head, a nagging feeling that never went away. Or maybe that was the concussion?

Watching his uncle utter those phrases the night before had made him realize the kind of man he could easily become if he wasn't mindful of his actions. He promised himself that he would never become remotely similar to his uncle.

"What are you thinking of over there, Mr. Darcy? You are wearing such a serious expression." Elizabeth's voice pulled Darcy from his musings.

Darcy looked at the woman who held his heart in the palm of her hand and smiled. She was sitting with Anne across the room and they were playing one of the games she loved. "Just marveling at what a difference a few days can make. Revelations can bring about a profound shift in one's perspective and change the trajectory of their expectations."

"That is true. It's amazing how opinions can change, and hearts can be touched so quickly, something I didn't know until recently." Elizabeth tilted her head and watched him with a serious look in her eye before turning to Anne. "Anne, do you mind if I talk with your cousin for a time?"

"Of course, you make him smile. He needs to smile more." Anne smiled up at Elizabeth as she stood. Her grin wide and unencumbered, despite how wan all the black she was wearing made her look. Darcy could tell that she was better for having company, though she often was staring at nothing for periods of time.

"Hattie, would you take my place in the game with Anne?"

"Of course, Miss Bennet, you go talk with your gentleman." Picking up the piece that Elizabeth put down, Hattie sat in her spot as Elizabeth walked away.

Darcy watched Elizabeth approach him, unaware of the magnitude of his smile or the way it affected the woman he loved. "How is Anne? Is she coping with all the change going on?"

"She seems to be fine, despite how horrible everything has been. But you, sir, need to be careful with that smile. Had you smiled like that in Hertfordshire, woman would have been throwing themselves at your feet."

"I only care for one woman and I do not want her at my feet. I want her beside me." Darcy was happy when Elizabeth chose to sit next to him on the settee instead of in the chair across from him. He took her hand and kissed it where the bruise lingered. Then, refusing to let go, he held tight and rejoiced when she leaned her head on his shoulder, settling in at his side.

"Will this do?"

"Yes, it will do nicely." They sat in silence for a while, simply enjoying the peace together before he spoke up again. "Theodore and I have decided to continue to keep his father in the dark about Anne until the barrister has settled things. Putting her as a ward of us both, I think, is the best idea, as it should prevent fortune hunters."

"How will Rosings be managed?"

"I am trying to get Theo to resign his commission to settle here and manage the estate, keeping the profits for himself. I do not need another estate."

"You say that like you already have too many."

Elizabeth's soft chuckle sent a thrill down Darcy's spine. "Well, I have five. That should be enough for anyone, I would think."

"What?" Elizabeth sat up abruptly and looked him in the eye. "I thought your estate was Pemberley, in Derbyshire. I never knew about the other four."

"Oh yes, I have two estates in Scotland and two other small ones—one in Devon and the other in Cheshire. I have always tried to downplay my holdings. My father had hopes for lots of sons, so he obtained estates for them, but it was not to be. He was heartbroken when my mother died. He never remarried, or had any more sons, and they all ended up coming to me."

She settled back into his side with a sigh. "Well, I guess that is all right, but you simply must take me to Scotland. I have always longed to travel."

"My dear, we are not engaged yet. I think you are putting the cart before the horse. We are merely courting." While still grieving his aunt's murder, he found comfort in the weight of Elizabeth's head on his shoulder. Somehow, despite all the problems with finding the murderer, his sore head included, everything was just as it should be.

Darcy felt like he was on top of the world; everything was falling into place.

"I suppose that is true. Though it is all a matter of timing," came Elizabeth's reply.

"Brother, could you be sitting with the remarkable Miss Bennet?" Georgiana's voice came from behind him.

Turning around, he spotted Georgiana in the doorway. He gave Elizabeth a quick squeeze before rising to greet his sister. "Georgie! I did not expect you so soon. How was your journey? Where are our aunt and your companion?"

"It was fine, boring, and dusty as always, but fine. Aunt Matlock and Mrs. Ansley are refreshing themselves after the journey, but I wanted to see you. I know we are know we ladies are not to go to the actual funeral but I am happy to be here to support Anne. Now introduce me to Miss Bennet." Georgiana hugged Darcy but then shifted so she could see Elizabeth. Her shy enthusiasm had Elizabeth laughing as she joined them.

Taking Elizabeth's hand, he once more kissed the bruise. He would have to find another excuse when the bruise faded. "Georgiana, darling, this is Miss Elizabeth Bennet. Miss Bennet, this is my darling little sister, Georgiana Darcy."

"It is truly a pleasure to meet you, Miss Bennet. My brother has mentioned you more than once." Her soft voice held enthusiasm.

"Has he now? I hope he was kind in his description of me. He tells me you play the piano. I play as well, though poorly. Who are your favorite composers?"

Georgiana's smile was glowing. Darcy knew she had always wished for more siblings and especially a sister. Looking at the two most important women in his life, he was happy to note that they both smiled broadly, happy to meet one another. Elizabeth was pulling her into a conversation better than anyone he had ever seen, and he knew then he'd been right to always think Elizabeth would be wonderful for Georgiana.

***

Dinner was an uncomfortable affair even before the coroner finally arrived. His aunt was pretending to be indifferent to her husband, who had still not gotten over not getting his way. Though Mrs. Ansley and Elizabeth were chatting softly with Georgiana, Anne appeared to be terrified of her uncle, Lord Matlock, and refused to speak at all. Something must have transpired between Theodore and his father, because Theo was quieter than usual and kept glaring at his father across the table.

When the coroner arrived, Darcy felt it was almost a relief. In the end, he did not know what he expected from the man's arrival. He knew coroners worked for the crown and that it was their job to investigate suspicious deaths, but he hadn't thought about how they went about doing that. He expected the process to be more involved than the man simply asking questions and nodding. It had not taken long before he declared himself satisfied with their findings. He stated he would arrange Mrs. Stevenson's transport to London to stand trial for her crimes. After informing them they might be called to testify at the trail, he left without ever looking at the evidence they had gathered. It all felt almost anticlimactic.

They had gathered once again in the sitting room, though this time Georgiana and Mrs. Ansley had joined them. Which meant that Elizabeth was sitting near him but had failed to rest her head on his shoulder. He tried not to pout but was uncertain of his success.

"The funeral will be tomorrow?" This was from Georgiana, who was sitting next to Mrs. Ansley on one of the settees.

"Yes, everything is in order and now that the coroner has come and gone," Darcy spoke but kept his eyes on Elizabeth. It was a habit he was not necessarily interested in breaking.

"I will need to leave shortly afterwards. I have to be getting back to London. My family there is expecting me, and my uncle is sending his carriage." As Elizabeth spoke, she glanced at him. Her eyes spoke to him, saying something that he could not decipher.

"I believe your London relatives live near Cheapside. Is your sister with them still?"

"Yes, Jane has been staying there to get away from my mother's harping, not that she would ever complain." Elizabeth looked pained when she spoke of her sister, Jane.

Darcy knew Elizabeth could not shake her worry for her sister, who was still nursing a broken heart thanks to Bingley. He began thinking about whether he had any friends that would appreciate her sweet manner. He was close to Bingley, but the man was not his only friend. Surely there would be someone. Maybe one of his neighbors? That way, they could avoid separating Elizabeth from her sister.

"William, when we get back to London after everything gets settled here, we must have Elizabeth and her family over. Or maybe, would you be interested in going shopping with myself and Mrs. Ansley? I would love to meet your sister, Miss Bennet. You are so lucky to have sisters. I have always wanted sisters." Georgiana put her hand over her mouth as if it embarrassed her that she had blurted everything out.

As Elizabeth spoke, she reached out and took hold of Georgiana's hand, which was resting in her lap. "I would love to go shopping with you and I am sure Jane would too. I am certain we can convince William," Elizabeth glanced at him with a smirk, "to arrange a dinner or some such gathering if we work at it together. After all, if he gets his way, I will live there soon enough."

"It is not something you will have to exert much effort to convince me. In fact, it is one of the top things on my list, after getting your father's permission to court you officially."

"I better write a note for you to take with you. My father may toy with you otherwise. He has most likely ignored the letters I have sent him. He is horrible about correspondence. If he is too difficult, I believe you could always threaten to tell my mother that you wanted to court me. He would comply simply to keep the peace."

"I like the way you think, Elizabeth." And he did. He appreciated her mind and everything else about her.

Chapter Twenty-One

Six Months Later

ELIZABETH LOOKED OUT THE carriage window, the colors of fall outside a sight to behold, but she was ready to reach their destination and explore. She sighed. Though she had always wished to travel, and she would not have traded one day of the trip, she felt like it was time to put down some roots.

Elizabeth remembered back to when she had gone back to London after Lady Catherine's funeral. It was strange to feel such a strong sense of missing Darcy, especially since she had not been apart from him for long. Despite the pain, the deep ache reassured her it had not all been some odd dream. Her love was actual, real and true. She had only been at Rosings for a short time, yet her emotions had undergone a transformation from mutual dislike to deepening affection. The shift in her feelings had been so fast that it had almost not felt real after she had left Rosings.

Seeing her aunt and uncle and their four little ones brought a smile to her face. It had been a welcome relief to experience normalcy after all the drama at Rosings. It was even better to see Jane. That night she had confessed all. She had been slightly nervous to let Jane know about Mr. Bingley and what had developed with William. Jane had only given her a knowing look, as if she had suspected something of all her earlier protests. As for Bingley, she had simply given her a grim smile and said it was better to know now as opposed to after things had progressed any further.

William had to stay at Rosings for some time after the funeral to get everything sorted, but then, as soon as he could, he went to Longbourn. Having received her father's permission, William followed her to London. He fulfilled his promise and wooed her openly in front of everyone, with no hesitation. Taking her to the theater and to the orchestra, with Jane and the Gardiners in attendance. He came calling to her uncle's home on the unfashionable side of town and took her to Gunther's for ices. Her favorite thing was going to the museum with Darcy and looking at the exhibits. They had some very interesting debates about what they saw. Lady Catherine had been correct—he did bite his lip to keep from smiling. She watched very closely when they debated now.

Their time in London was not all entertainment, though. They had both been called to testify at the trial. Despite the distance, she could hear Mrs. Stevenson's piercing screams as she was dragged away after being found guilty of murder. They carried her sentence out the next day. Elizabeth still felt odd knowing that they had hung her. She mostly tried not to think about it.

As Elizabeth thought about the trial, her mind wandered to Anne. Seeing Anne before they headed back to Pemberley had taken time, but it had been nice. They had also seen Theodore, which was always enjoyable. It still felt odd to her to call him that even in her mind, but he insisted she was family now and he was no longer a colonel. William had convinced Theodore to leave the Regulars and take up residence at Rosings. He managed the day-to-day things and received the profits that came from it. It would allow him to marry as he chose and not search for an heiress that suited him. They had gotten a governess for Anne, which worked much better than having a companion ever did. She kept her engaged and learning things, and Anne was happier for it. They had brought Anne a puppy back with them from William's property in Scotland—an adorable little black thing with the softest fur and a darling expression. Anne had been so happy to have another dog. She named her Ink.

Elizabeth had even spoken with Charlotte while at Rosings. They had both cried, their emotions raw as they spoke for what felt like an eternity. She was glad that Mr. Collins would no longer be an impediment to her long-standing friendship. At least on the surface, Mr. Collins's behavior appeared to have changed for the better. He knew that if he spoke out against her, there would be repercussions. Theodore visited him regularly to discuss matters, which seemed to keep him in check.

They did not stop at Longbourn as her mother would have preferred. Elizabeth refused to let her mother try to parade her around the town as if Elizabeth's marriage was her accomplishment. By the time Elizabeth married William, she had grown weary of her mother's endless crowing about their engagement. Her mother's repeated remarks on her daughter's marriage ended up creating a divide between her mother and the other ladies in town. Another deep sigh escaped her lips as she realized she couldn't put off writing to her any longer.

"Are you tiring of being in the carriage, my love?" William's soft voice in her ear warmed her heart and sent shivers down her spine. She snuggled closer to him and felt a sense of contentment.

"I am only eager to arrive. We did not stay at Pemberley long before we left on our wedding trip to Scotland, and I want to get home and settled."

Looking out the window to check the scenery, he responded, "We will get to Pemberley soon enough. I think we will arrive shortly after dark. Are you so eager to be back?"

"We were in Scotland for two months and between two weeks in the carriage and two weeks at Rosings, it has been three months. I want to see Georgiana and Jane. Besides, I have things I want to accomplish." Elizabeth nuzzled William's neck the way that she had learned would get the response she wanted.

He turned towards her, cupped her face in his hands, and kissed her deeply on the lips before tenderly kissing her forehead. "What is it that you are wanting to do at Pemberley?"

"I would like to redecorate some rooms, if you do not mind."

"No, I do not mind. There have not been updates on most of it since my mother passed. What rooms were you wanting to work on?" William asked, a smile on his face as he looked into her eyes.

"I thought I would start with the nursery." Elizabeth held her breath, waiting for her news to dawn on him.

"Nursery! Are you? I mean, really?" He was so overwhelmed with joy that he swooped down and kissed her passionately, losing himself in the moment. His flummoxed response did not disappoint Elizabeth in the least.

***

THE MORE DARCY REFLECTED on his life, the more he realized how incredibly fortunate he was. Six months ago, he had been on the brink of a devastating downfall. He had been so close to ruining things with Elizabeth. His pride had almost cost him the love of a truly wonderful woman. He did not like to think of what could have happened if he had proposed the way he had originally meant to.

As he looked down at Elizabeth, he could feel her steady breaths against his chest, and he was reassured. All things considered, everything had turned out incredible. They were finally on their way back to Pemberley, not that he regretted one moment of their extended honeymoon.

Though he would never say that he was glad his aunt had been murdered, he was glad that he could work with Elizabeth to bring her murderer to justice. He had the chance to improve their relationship by getting to know her on a deeper level and presenting his best self. A light that had been sorely lacking. It was astonishing to him just how poorly he had represented himself until that moment.

After his aunt's funeral, he had to stay behind at Rosings while Elizabeth had gone on to London to be with her family. The absence of her presence was almost unbearable. Seeing her constantly and then not at all was not good for his constitution. He became easily distracted until Theodore pulled him aside and told him to get his act together or he would never make it to London and Elizabeth. Eventually, everything was in order, including Theodore's resignation, and he was able to get on his way.

Dealing with her father had been a problem. Apparently, the only thing he knew about Darcy was that he had insulted his daughter. His position in society did not help his suit. Mr. Bennet eschewed society as Darcy knew it, preferring instead to submerge himself in literature and idle contemplation. Darcy had observed the man's study and found nothing he could truly like or admire. Although he coveted several books, he found nothing else to respect there. What bothered him the most was the stack of old correspondence that was entirely neglected. He knew that stack contained more than one letter from his daughter that he had not cared enough to read or respond to. What if she had needed help? Elizabeth had been suspected of murder and yet her father could not be bothered to read her letters. There was no excuse for such negligence.

Darcy had secured the man's permission to court and wed his daughter, but he couldn't shake the feeling that they would never see eye to eye. His lackadaisical perspective on the world was in sharp contrast to Darcy's emphasis on responsibility. He departed Longbourn with haste, making his way to London to reunite with Elizabeth.

Getting to know the Gardiners had been a surprise. An elegant couple, they socialized with an eclectic cross section of society. The first dinner he had attended at their house had been eye opening. Gathering with a writer, a well-known orator, a member of Parliament, and an inventor working with electricity was something he never would have considered. Despite his initial doubts, it turned out to be the most enjoyable gathering he had attended during his time in London. He had learned where Elizabeth had gotten so many of the qualities that he appreciated.

The warmth and hospitality of Elizabeth's family made the time he spent with them truly enjoyable. He cherished the memory of taking Elizabeth, Jane, and Georgiana to Hatchards and seeing the pure delight on her face. He had never thought to see someone else who was so enraptured by books as he was. The only thing better had been seeing Elizabeth blush when he told the proprietor to add her to his account.

The trial had been an unpleasant and melancholy affair, leaving a cloud of sadness over all involved. The outcome was exactly what he had anticipated, yet he still felt the weight of its impact. At least they were spared a lengthy wait for Mrs. Stevenson's death, as it was swiftly carried out.

Though Darcy was in mourning for his aunt, a month had not gone by before they became engaged. They waited until he was out of mourning to get married. It had felt like forever and not only because he had wished to be married so badly. Mrs. Elizabeth's 'achievement' had Mrs. Bennet brimming with enthusiasm, and she eagerly paraded her daughter around to anyone who would listen. Darcy was not at all fond of the way she went about it. While acknowledging her daughter's lack of beauty compared to Jane, she also expressed doubts about his choice of an unsuitable bride. The woman seemed to have a talent for insulting both Elizabeth and himself every chance she got. He was delighted to find a way to avoid passing through Longbourn on his journey back to Pemberley. Elizabeth had felt no different.

He started when he noticed Elizabeth sigh and shift slightly against him. They had been in the carriage an extended period of time, and he hoped it was not too much for her. "Are you tiring of being in the carriage, my love?"

"I am only eager to arrive. We did not stay at Pemberley long before we left on our wedding trip to Scotland, and I want to get home and settled," Elizabeth spoke while cuddling closer to him.

As he gazed out of the carriage window, he recognized the familiar outline of the trees and felt a sense of comfort. "We will get to Pemberley soon enough. I think we will arrive shortly after dark. Are you so eager to be back?"

"We were in Scotland for two months and between two weeks in the carriage and two weeks at Rosings, it has been three months. I want to see Georgiana and Jane. Besides, I have things I want to accomplish."

As Elizabeth traced her nose along his jaw, she felt his body shudder in response. His hands cradled her face as he leaned in to kiss her deeply, but he quickly stopped himself, remembering they were in a carriage and would arrive at Pemberley soon. Tenderly kissing her forehead, the question he had been meaning to ask finally came to him. "What is it that you are wanting to do at Pemberley?"

"I would like to redecorate some rooms, if you do not mind."

"No, I do not mind. There have not been updates on most of it since my mother passed. What rooms were you wanting to work on?" William's eyes were fixed on hers as he asked, a smile playing on his lips. He had never thought of her as someone who would enjoy decorating. He braced himself for a bit of humor.

"I thought I would start with the nursery."

That was not at all what he expected. "Nursery! Are you? I mean really?" Darcy felt as if words were impossible and would only fail him, so he acted instead. Darcy leaned in to kiss her, feeling her lips part slightly as she let out a soft sigh. He kissed his wife with a passionate intensity, showing her how much he loved her. He expressed his gratitude for everything she had done for him and for simply being herself.

Just moments ago, he had been happy with his life, but Elizabeth was bringing him an even greater sense of joy. He realized in that moment that she would always bring him more happiness. He felt a surge of anticipation, knowing that something truly wonderful was on the horizon.

Author's Note

WHAT EXACTLY WAS THAT red bead?

I knew when I started this novel that I wanted Catherine to drop dead in the first chapter. I knew I wanted it to be poison. For some reason, I couldn't shake the thought of her being poisoned on Wednesday and dying on Friday. I just loved the idea that the act of murder was not on the same day that she died, thus my title *Murdered on a Wednesday*.

I began to research, trying to find something that could kill Lady Catherine and match the symptoms I was going for. Nothing was quite right until I came across a fairly recent article about poisonous jewelry. Now, wasn't that a cool thought? Enter rosary pea jewelry. Rosary peas are also called Jequirity beans in some places, although the scientific name of the plant is Abrus precatorius. The plant produces shiny, scarlet-red seeds with a black spot. It is native to Africa, Asia, Australia, and the Pacific region. The whole plant is highly poisonous, especially the seeds.

In tropical areas, native peoples have long used the seeds for ornamental purposes, such as to make bracelets, jewelry, and children's toys due to their striking and beautiful appearance. An article I found spoke of the dangers of jewelry being brought in from overseas and the risk of accidental ingestion causing poisoning. Apparently, the importation of jewelry from overseas is not a new issue. Most adults won't try to eat their costume jewelry, but a child might chew on a bracelet or possibly a pet. The poison from these seeds is one of the deadliest in the world. Apparently, even today, there is no cure for the highly effective poison.

My research revealed that you can still buy these seeds for crafts. I noted that most sites had the disclaimer 'toxic if swallowed, keep away from children and pets'. So buyer beware, even pricking your finger while trying to string the peas has been rumored to be lethal. I could find no scientific journals that proved the rumor, but still. Apparently, as long as the pea is intact and unopened, it is safe to handle, but once it is open in some way, be it pierced with a needle, crushed or chewed, it is deadly if it gets in your system.

People throughout history have viewed rosary pea jewelry as protective. This fact made me consider the possibility of someone buying them in a tropical region to sell alongside medicinal potions elsewhere. Yes, it may be far out there, but this is my imagination we are talking about. So, Lady Catherine's table was always full of exotic tinctures, evidence of her love for buying unique items from other countries with her money. She bought the bracelet for Anne, never knowing the risks.

Here is a link to the article that caught my attention if you are interested in checking it out.

https://www.dailymail.co.uk/news/article-2078362/Thousands-deadly-seed-bracelets-recalled-Eden-Project-gift-shop-reveals-beans-twice-fatal-RICIN.html

***

WHAT WAS IN ALL of those bottles?

I figured that Lady Catherine was an old-fashioned woman and might rely on medicine from the Georgian era, so that is where I began my research. Would you believe that most of what I read about medicine of that time mentioned three principal ingredients: alcohol, opium and mercury. Yes, I know what you are thinking—how did that help anyone? I am uncertain if any of it was beneficial in any way. Remember, this was also the time that bloodletting and purging were thought of as best practices for most of what ailed you.

There were a lot of folk remedies that involved distilling plants with alcohol or spirits or boiling them down. Syrup of violets appeared to be popular as well, especially for throat irritation and coughs. Not all medicine of the time was terrible, but I was startled by some of the things I discovered. A quick search online for Laudanum, Paregoric, or Calomel may reveal some shocking information.

Lady Catherine's table was filled with medicine tinctures, and it was highly probable that most of them contained alcohol, opium, or some form of plant extract. The other thing I can guarantee was on that table was mercury, which appeared to be very popular for all kinds of ailments from the 16th century onward. In my imagination, the medicine that the poison was put in was some mixture of alcohol and opium, which was used for sleeplessness and was quite addictive.

https://www.historytoday.com/archive/feature/quack-medicine-georgian-england

https://penandpension.com/2016/11/09/the-georgian-and-rege
ncy-home-medicine-chest/

https://www.sciencefriday.com/articles/the-murderous-medical-
practice-of-the-18th-century/

https://wellcomecollection.org/articles/WckzzigAACe3DJPD

***

WHAT WAS WRONG WITH Anne?

I had never originally intended for Anne to be any different from
she was in cannon. However, that changed when I was doing research
about medical practices from 1813 and before. I reasoned that if
Anne was sickly, she would have been receiving many of those
medicines from childhood. That is when I zeroed in on mercury and
its popularity for children's medicines. It was in all sorts of things,
including teething medicine.

So long story short, Anne has symptoms of mercury poisoning or
Erethism. People suffering from mercury poisoning may experience
things like temporary confusion, nervousness, and staring spells.
One very interesting symptom I noticed was excessive shyness.
Things get more real when they have long-term exposure. People
used to use mercury in making things like hats. Ever heard of the
Mad Hatter? Or what about Mad Hatter Syndrome? I found what I
learned quite fascinating. I definitely got lost in that rabbit hole for
quite a while.

Individuals who have prolonged and low-level exposure to it
may display fatigue, frustration, memory loss, and sadness. Mercury

exposure in children can cause cognitive impairment, developmental delays, and fertility problems. In my book, I imagine that poor Anne would have been exposed to mercury continually in the form of medicine. Regency era society would not have accepted her due to her cognitive impairment and other symptoms that made her different.

***

COULD ANNE HAVE BEEN put in an asylum?

Yes, yes she could. Have you ever heard of Bedlam? Bethlem Royal Hospital was also known as Bedlam. People could pay to go observe the people who were there like we pay to go to the zoo today. At the time that *Pride and Prejudice* took place, patients were chained to walls and conditions were deplorable.

How did you make it into an asylum at the time? A male relative had to say you were insane. You could do it without the need for a doctor's confirmation or a physical examination. I found a list of reasons given for being committed that was mind blowing.

Hysteria, laziness, fever and jealousy, suppressed menstruation, time of life, grief, bad company, asthma, religious enthusiasm, parents were cousins, novel reading (we are all doomed), syphilis, medicine to prevent conception, over taxing of mental powers, uterine derangement, bad habits, and the list goes on and on. So basically, whatever they wanted to say to put you in there.

https://www.historyextra.com/period/victorian/bethlem-royal-hospital-history-why-called-bedlam-lunatic-asylum/

***

My hope is that you found my book enjoyable, and you appreciated the creative process behind it. Thank you for reading.

Acknowledgements

Before you go, I would like to express my gratitude for reading Murdered on a Wednesday. It's been a joy to create this work of love, but without readers, it would be an exercise in futility. If you enjoyed reading this book, please consider leaving an honest review on your favorite site. It does not have to be very long, but I would really appreciate the feedback.

Cooming Soon

The act of writing has completely consumed me, and I cannot stop. I am currently immersed in writing another full-length Pride and Prejudice Variation, which is set to be published in May 2024. Coming Soon: Mary's Daring Demand.

Elizabeth's mother, Fanny, is the subject of my short story, Fanny's Strength. It tells the tale of how she found the strength to raise five amazing daughters and find her own happily ever after. By subscribing to my newsletter through the link below, you'll receive a free copy, as well as exclusive updates on my upcoming releases and other exciting content.

https://dl.bookfunnel.com/66ax5bftkb

About the Author

My journey with words started out as a painful one. The letters on the page seemed to taunt me, and I spent countless hours with my mother trying to decipher their meaning. Our reading journey started with Little House on the Prairie and continued with other books, mostly in the historical fiction genre. Slowly but surely, I started reading independently, advancing from historical fiction to fantasy and science fiction.

The stories I found in the books I read held me captive, and I often lost track of time. The realization of the true power of the written word inspired me to pursue writing. Unfortunately, I had to put it on the back burner in order to deal with pesky things like paying for food and housing. Then a dare from my sister brought back memories of my passion for writing in high school. It was a passion that I was determined to rekindle.

When I got back into writing, I turned to my latest reading addiction for inspiration, Pride and Prejudice Variations. My mind was fixated on the regency era and the romance of Elizabeth and Darcy, making it hard to write anything else. So I went with it and here we are.

I graduated from college and promptly realized that a degree in American Sign Language was not as helpful as one would hope.

Moving from working as a sign language interpreter to home health and hospice care and mental health services, I have had a diverse career.

www.ingramcontent.com/pod-product-compliance
Lightning Source LLC
Chambersburg PA
CBHW061230310726
48971CB00007B/2001